THE
DEAD PARADE

Survival is not an Option

"James Roy Daley's literary style is achingly accessible and a grand pleasure to read."

—Weston Ochse, Bram Stoker Award-winning
author of *Scarecrow Gods*

"James Roy Daley's writing is simple, with an undercurrent of depth and despair that continues to haunt me."

—DF Lewis, winner of the British Fantasy Society's
Karl Edward Wagner Award

THE
DEAD PARADE

Survival is not an Option

A Novel by
JAMES ROY DALEY

SWARM PRESS

www.SwarmPress.com

THE
DEAD PARADE
Survival is not an Option

A **SWARM PRESS** book
published by arrangement with the author

ISBN10: 1-934861-10-3
ISBN13: 978-1-934861-10-3
Library of Congress Control Number: 2008932540

Swarm Press is an imprint of Permuted Press (permutedpress.com).

Cover art by Nicolas Caesar (www.scary-art.com/nicolascaesar.htm).
Copy edited by Leah Clarke.

AUTHOR'S NOTE:
This is a work of fiction. Martinsville is a fictional place, a borrowed reality designed from the bits and pieces of the world I know. The people within this tale are fictional. If you run across a character that is reminiscent of a friend, neighbor, relative, or (gasp) you, rest assured—this is a work of invention, a forgery of the real, an imitation of truth. Storytelling is a about lying. *The Dead Parade* is about storytelling.

This novel is dedicated to my Mom and Dad. Thank you for always being there for me.

I love you both very much.

I suggest you stop reading now. In a few pages all hell breaks loose.

FOREWORD

For an art like storytelling, very often it can only evolve by rebelling violently against what has come before. This doesn't necessarily mean attacking the tried-and-true conventions of the past, but it does mean defying them. James Roy Daley stands defiant alongside other rising talents in horror fiction, and you're about to bear witness to it.

I read *The Dead Parade* in a single sitting. And I told its author that there were a lot of words that could be used to describe it: relentless, merciless, a thrill ride. (I also told him I wouldn't use clichés in the foreword, but it's far too late now.)

The point I'm getting at by listing off those adjectives, which have been beaten and ground into the dirt by reviewers worldwide, is this – Daley's writing defies them, too. You think you know relentless? Turn the page, and come along on a bloody road trip with vengeance personified. Merciless? You ain't seen nothin' until you've hit the back cover. And as for the often-used thrill ride... there are thrills to be found, but *The Dead Parade* is more than that. Its lightning pace is matched only by the choking despair that permeates every chapter. This is no ride. It's an infection.

A damn good one.

—David Dunwoody
Author of *Empire*

PROLOGUE

Joseph gripped the wheel and Penny screamed. Headlights, larger than most, blinded both of them. Joseph tried to say something, anything, but his mouth opened and the words stayed in his throat. It didn't matter; there was nothing to say and no one would have heard. Penny's voice had become a high-pitched siren that dominated all potential discussion.

In the backseat of the car was little Mathew. A moment ago he was juggling between singing and drinking. Sing—slurp. Sing—slurp. Then came the grim sound of his mother's bellow. This caused his concentration to falter and his juice box to slip from his fingers. The box slid along his t-shirt and bounced over the strap that held him. The straw designed to pierce the box hung from Mathew's lips, dripping purple sap.

He wondered if there was a monster in the front seat. If so, maybe it was eating his mother. Monsters can do that, he considered. Every kid worth two cents plus three cents knows that.

Being too small see over the front seat, the headlights did not blind Mathew. His eyes, round and bulging, remained sheltered as they shifted between his mother and father. He did not comprehend the problem, but he knew something was wrong. Mommy never sounded like this before.

Joseph cranked the wheel a little too late. The truck would not be avoided; impact was imminent.

Mathew's hands moved towards his ears and knocked the straw away. He inhaled deeply, preparing his throat for a cry that would never come.

They collided with a CRUNCH and the world became a blur.

Mathew's body lunged forward and his seatbelt locked; it strangled him like it hated him.

On Joseph's side of the car the steering wheel folded into a strange and misshapen zero, and on Penny's side, the intense and dominating scream came to an abrupt and horrific halt. The windshield shattered as both parents went through. The pavement would be stained red for weeks.

Then came darkness.

And for what seemed like a long time—Mathew was lost in nothing.

PART ONE:
JOHNNY'S GIFT

1

Anne handed James a tissue. He took it and thanked her. A sniff and a sigh later he stood up and walked across the clinical room telling himself that he wouldn't cry. He wouldn't. Not for a second longer, dammit. He was thirty-three years old, not thirteen, and this was no way for a thirty-three year old man to act. Not here. Not now. Not in front of his mother.

The bullshit self-declaration seemed to work and his sniveling briefly subsided. But even as James pulled his act together he could feel another wave of grief coming. The gloomy hand of misery was peeking its fingers around the corners of his mind, squashing his half-hearted vow like a steamroller over a sandcastle. The circumstances were dreadful: Joseph and Penny were dead. Mathew was hanging by a thread.

He began to cry again.

***

A minute came and went. James took a deep breath, listening to the sounds of the hospital as he glanced at his mother.

Anne looked traumatized and pale. Her depressing and confounded stature was tragic. Just seeing a person this way made James feel miserable. He thought his heart would break.

She lost her first-born son, he thought. Wow.

Anne said, "There, there," giving James motherly comfort the way she always had—with queer, half-thought sentences that didn't mean much. *There, there. Lordie, lordie. If it isn't one thing it's another.* Anne had a million of them.

"I'm okay," James said.

"Of course you are," Anne replied, and before she could say anything more, James and Anne were interrupted by a phone call.

James pulled his cell from his pocket. "Hello."

"Hi James. It's me, Johnny."

"Oh hi, Johnny."

"I need you to come over here. It's an emergency."

"I'm sorry but I can't. I have an emergency of my own. A big one."

"If you don't come to my place I'll kill myself. I swear it." Johnny hung up, and when James called back—Johnny didn't answer.

2

Anne sat in the corner of the room, beneath a television that was attached to a bracket that was bolted to the concrete wall, far away from the IV, the perfect sheets of the hospital bed, and a curtain that divided the room in half. Seeing the expression that James made at the end of the call, she knew something was up. She said, "You okay?"

"Yeah," James responded broodingly.

"Are you going somewhere?"

"Maybe."

In Anne's left hand, she held a tattered copy of the Bible. A rosary strangled the fingers on her right. Her knuckles were colorless. Her gray hair was pulled into a bun showcasing ears without jewelry. Her eyes looked tired and swollen.

It seemed to James—as his mother rocked back and forth in her chair, knocking her heals together fretfully—that she was being the strong one this morning. Mother had finished her crying. Oh yes. She let it out in one big bawl. Now her emotions were under control, fully managed and completely organized. James figured she'd stay that way 'til the day was done.

***

Anne prayed, initiating a silence that lasted ten minutes. Finishing her twenty-first Hail Mary, her swollen-knuckle fingers shifted from one rosary bead to the next. "You're going to take care of him, James," she said, after finishing a prayer. "I can't. I'm too old. I can't raise another. Not now. Not again."

James nodded his head and closed his eyes. His hands became fists.

"He needs someone young," she continued, "and Lord knows he needs to be with someone that loves him, with family. You know the boy needs a father. It's as clear as the walls around us. It's as clear as the sky above. He needs you, James. It's time to step up and do what's right. It's time to act like a man and do what you were born to do. It's time for you to raise that boy."

James felt his nerves giving. "Let's talk about it later."

"There's nothing more to talk about."

James sighed. "Sure Mom. Whatever you say. But let's talk later, okay?"

Anne closed her eyes and lowered her head.

Unrolling his fists, James eyed the boy in the hospital bed solemnly—the boy with the bruises on his face, two broken legs, a crushed hand, five broken ribs, a bruised spine, a dead mother, a dead father and all of his front teeth smashed from his mouth; his six-year-old nephew—Mathew—the only person expected to survive the accident.

He kissed his mother and said good-bye.

He would never see her again.

3

James stepped into the hallway. Like a single-minded herd his family and friends approached with fake-smile faces and slumped shoulders. They hugged him, shook his hand and offered condolences. They said things like, "It isn't fair." James countered with, "Thanks for coming." Soon the condolences turned to questions and questions turned to inquiry. James found himself wishing he had stayed in the room. Oh well. Out of the frying pan and all that jazz.

Once the questioning settled, James walked past the nurse's station, an open concept waiting room and a row of vending machines. He considered buying some chocolate, decided against it and approached an elevator with his eyes sweeping the patterned floor. He hit a button. Before long he was in-and-out of the elevator and standing on the main floor. Then he was outside. Then he was inside his car, driving across the hospital parking lot and away from it all.

He checked his watch: 11 am.

The day was warm, the sun was shining and the wind blew with considerable strength. James remembered the weatherman mentioning a storm. Somehow it didn't fit; there wasn't a cloud in the sky.

It was time to visit Johnny.

***

James knocked two times, waited a few seconds and was about to knock again when the front door swung open.

Standing in the doorway, Johnny looked at James with a blank stare and little emotion; he didn't look good. His sunken red eyes seemed to be glossed-over from a lack of sleep. His hair was matted, crusted to the side of his head in a greased, savage frenzy. His skin was pale and his clothing was dirty. His teeth were grimy and stained. He had cuts around his eyes that seemed to create a design of some kind.

James wondered if the wounds were self-inflicted.

Johnny's image gave James a discomfited feeling, making him feel like an unwanted guest. But James wasn't unwanted, was he? With his mind shifting gears, James re-evaluated his visit.

What's going on? He wondered. Is Johnny upset?

After a confused bout of reflection, James came to a conclusion: he sized things up incorrectly. After all, Johnny invited him over—and it couldn't be time to go already. He hadn't even said hello.

"Johnny," James whispered, sounding apologetic. "You okay?"

Johnny exhaled; his eyes became puffed slits. He leaned against a wall, listening to something. But what was it?

Soon enough James was listening too. He listened to the sounds of the house, the street behind him and the birds in the sky. But there was nothing to hear—nothing unusual that is, just small-town silence.

"Johnny?"

Five full seconds passed before Johnny's eyelids opened wide enough to let the late-morning sunshine in. He rubbed his face, cleared his throat and said, "James, you came."

James fabricated half a smile.

"Of course I came buddy," he said, wondering if beneath his white shirt and his black tie he looked as ghastly as Johnny. It was possible. He had a rough morning. "Are you okay? You look a little..."

The wind blew stronger, causing the trees to sway, the grass to rustle and the door to swing open. Once the door was open it squeaked and rattled inside its rusty hinges.

"I'm tired." Johnny said unresponsively, letting the door sway.

"I was going to say that. Have you been sleeping?"

Ignoring the question, Johnny said, "I'm hungry, did you bring food?"

James felt his nerves give. He laughed uncomfortably and sounded like a fool. "No," he said. "I don't have food. But I'm thinking... I might be hungry too. I could eat. You want to order a pizza, or go somewhere—a restaurant maybe? What do you think? Wanna do lunch?"

"Pizza," Johnny said, unleashing a miserable grin.

"Yeah?"

Johnny pulled away from the wall and rolled his head in a half-circle. He looked over his shoulder and down the well-lit corridor. He eyed the crooks and curves in the floorboards, the dust-puppies that crept from corner to corner when nobody was looking. He stretched his back and tightened his stomach. It seemed as though something cold had crawled across his skin, and into his ear—whispering, warning him to behave. Then his face transformed, becoming a hideous scowl. "We shouldn't go out," he said. "It doesn't like to go out."

Like a zombie, he walked an unbalanced line inside the house; he left the door blowing in the wind. And all the while his eyes crept along the walls—the wall on his right, the wall on his left, the hardwood beneath his feet...

Grudgingly, James stepped inside.

With the doorknob in hand he looked across the vacant, small-town street. He glanced at the swaying trees, the blowing leaves and the empty driveways. He heard a dog barking and the faint sound of a beeping horn. And feeling like a condemned man he shrugged his shoulders, disregarded the yapping animal and the beeping horn, and closed the rattling door.

4

James expected Johnny's house to be a disaster, but it wasn't. It was perfect, too perfect. The tables were gone. The plants were gone. The bookcase and all of his books were missing too. The TV was still there along with a couch, which sat next to an antique chair that had large holes in the fabric. Aside from some dirty dishes, that was about it.

"Hey Johnny. You changed the room around, did you? Got rid of a few things?"

Johnny fell into the old chair. The chair moaned and dust puffed out of it. Its wooden legs screeched against the hardwood.

"Pizza?" Johnny said. "Did you bring a pizza? You did, right?"

The statement was absurd, of course. And at first, James thought Johnny was kidding.

"No man, I didn't bring food." There was a moment of silence. James swallowed uneasily. "But I'll phone. You want pizza, huh?"

James reached into his pocket and pulled out his cell phone. He scanned the address book, closing his eyes when his dead brother's phone number rolled across the screen. Then he found the number: Tony's Big-Topping Pizzeria—the best pizza in town.

He glanced into the backyard through the large garden window. The backyard was loaded with Johnny's furnishings: dressers and beds, tables and chairs, bookshelves and clothing—plus boxes and boxes and boxes. James, confused, shook his head. He wondered what had happened and why.

Did Johnny snap?

Without wanting an answer, he walked down the hallway. If he was going to order food he needed Johnny's address. He opened the front door. Against the brick wall was the house number: 1342. He dialed the number and phone began ringing. Once, twice…

"Hello, Tony's Pizza."

"I'd like to order a pizza for delivery."

"Address?"

"1342 Tecumseh Street."

"Name?"

"James McGee."

"And you'd like to order?"

James stepped into the living room and realized that Johnny had frayed newspaper clippings attached to a wall. He approached the clippings and ran his eyes across the headlines. One headline read: TWO MORE FOUND DEAD. Another: MURDER IN HIGH PARK. A third was: 4 BODIES, 24 HOURS.

After reading the headlines he glanced at Johnny.

Something was horribly wrong. He knew those stories—those headlines on the wall. Everyone did. The string of deaths was puzzling the police. Evidence suggested that the killer might be some kind of animal. But they didn't know for sure.

Maybe it was Johnny.

5

James stepped away from the wall, lost in thought. He approached his friend, noticing that the room was cold. Really cold. And Johnny was curled up on the chair with his legs pulled high, hiding his face beneath his arms. Eyes peeked above kneecaps.

"It's here." Johnny whispered with a raspy voice. "Oh my God it's here again. It's in the room with us. Why won't it leave me alone?"

James stopped dead in his tracks. Then he heard a distant voice, "Excuse me? Sir? You'd like to order? Yes? No?"

"Uh…"

"Sir?"

James focused. Somehow he had forgotten that he was in the middle of a phone call.

"Oh yeah," he said. "I'd like to order a large pepperoni pizza. Thin crust, extra cheese… and I'll pay cash. But I've got to go, there's an emergency. I'm at 1342 Tecumseh. See you soon."

He hung up, hoping he had given enough information. Then he slid his phone into his pocket and said, "What is it Johnny?"

"It's here."

"What's here?"

James took a step towards the couch.

Johnny pulled away from James and crushed his body into the chair. His fingers curled and his toes squeezed together. His stomach, which felt empty and rotten, clenched.

"Oh God. Don't move," he said, with his lips pulled into a bizarre snarl.

James looked over his shoulder. Again—there was nothing to see. "Johnny?"

James made his way to the couch and sat down. He had forgotten all about the drama that surrounded his family now. His focus was on Johnny, who seemed one small step away from madness.

"John." He said with a flat but kind tone. "We should talk, man. We should talk."

Johnny looked up; his eyes were beyond wild. Drool had formed in the corners of his lips, which were cracked and dirty and a perfect fit with his unhinged smile.

"What the fuck, Johnny?" James said.

James wondered where the old Johnny was—the Johnny that liked soulful house music, extreme boxing and getting drunk with his friends; the Johnny who had a big smile and a hearty laugh; the Johnny who went to college to be a chef and was excited about cooking; the Johnny he knew; the Johnny he loved; the Johnny he came to visit.

"What's going on, bro? You're scaring me; you're freaking me out."

"I wish we had more time," Johnny said. "'Cause I sure am hungry. That pizza would hit the spot right now. Don't you think? If only we had more time."

"The pizza will be here in thirty minutes," James tried to reason. "But who cares? Johnny, what's going on? You're being a weirdo today. Why's your stuff outside? And what's with the clippings on the wall? You don't know something about the murders, do you? Dear God man, tell me you're not involved!"

"Do you have it with you?"

James shook his head. "What... the pizza?"

"Yeah."

James felt the sharp prick of annoyance. It was a mild irritation, but it seemed like something that could get out of hand quickly. Like a gift from the anger fairy, a thought blasted his thinking: slap Johnny across the face, wake the son-of-a-bitch up and snap him from his daze.

James resisted the urge. The physical approach didn't seem appropriate—at least, not yet. "No man, I don't have a pizza. But it's coming."

Johnny nodded and reached his hand into the crease of the chair. He pushed down, hunting inside. "That's too bad," he said, shifting in his seat.

He jerked something free.

"What is it Johnny?" James asked, but then he knew.

It was a gun.

6

The wave of danger hit James in the chest like it was a material thing. His head began spinning. He became dizzy. Everything seemed surreal.

"Oh God Johnny, what are you doing?"

"Shhh. It's okay," Johnny said. "It's the only way."

As Johnny raised the weapon, James thought about running—but then what? He'd take a bullet in the back? No thanks. James didn't need a slug tearing a hole into his ribcage, his heart or his lung. What he needed was a paid vacation and a couple of weeks lounging around on a tropical beach that was loaded with beautiful, intelligent women. Or better yet, a plan—a good plan—a plan that didn't have him screaming in pain and dying a coward's death with a bullet in his spine.

Johnny put the barrel beneath his jaw. His finger tightened and the trigger moved slightly. Apparently James wasn't in danger; Johnny was about to kill himself.

"Oh shit," James said without hesitation. "Don't do it. Don't even think it!"

Johnny cackled twice and sneered. "I'll tell you what Suzy told me, if you'd like."

"Suzy?" James said, puzzled. He noticed that the room was getting colder. "Suzy Rae?"

Suzy Rae was a mutual friend. She was a nice girl, kind, considerate; she knew how to make people feel welcome. She was born in Haiti and still had the accent in her voice. Her dark curly hair seemed to draw attention to her strong jaw line and full lips. She had a pretty face that made guys look twice. James knew her; he liked her quite a bit.

"Yeah, Suzy Rae."

"Okay, whatever. Just don't do anything stupid."

"Stupid?"

"Yeah. Be cool man. Be cool."

Johnny lowered the gun two inches and his smile widened. "This was Suzy's gun," he said. "And now she's dead."

7

"What did you say?"

Johnny laughed. "Sue shot herself a couple of weeks ago. I went to visit and found her curled up in the basement. She had her arms stretched out and a shotgun pointed at her chest. I'm not sure if she'd be able to pull the trigger—the way she was sitting—but she was trying. That's the important thing, I suppose. It's the trying that counts. She was acting crazier than shit too, like a loon; so I talked her into giving me the gun and I brought her upstairs. The next thing I knew the dumb cunt had a handgun. I thought she was going to kill me." Johnny waved the gun carelessly. "She didn't. She did herself in. Well, after that I guess you could say that I was dazed. Dazed and confused, if you catch my drift. And the blood was drainin' from her head like something from a movie. It was squirting, if you want me to be honest with you. Squirting in the air. And I grabbed the gun. I don't know what I was thinking exactly, but I took it and ran as fast as my legs would carry me."

James couldn't believe his ears. Sure as dirt, Johnny had gone insane. Maybe running wasn't such a bad idea, James thought. He was quick and athletic. He could probably be out the door before Johnny realized what was happening.

"I know you think I killed her," Johnny said, reading James with his eyes. "But I didn't kill anyone… I should have but I didn't."

James felt his patience running thin. "Johnny, I don't understand."

"You don't have to. It's just that… I tell you what." Johnny made an expression that seemed thoughtful, heroic and scared shitless, all at the same time. "You can kill me. I won't stop you."

Up until that moment, James thought he had heard it all. Turned out that he hadn't. "I don't want to kill you." James said cautiously. "We're friends, remember? You're one of my closest buddies. You're my boy. And you're just fucking around, right? Aren't you?"

Johnny shrugged. "Sorry man. I'm sorry it's you. But if I don't pass it on it'll be with me forever. I don't want that. God, can you imagine? It hurts just thinking about it."

"This isn't happening."

Johnny smiled. "Oh yes it is. Just remember to pass it on, 'kay? And don't get it mad. You don't want it mad. Know what I'm saying? It'll get the best of you. Trust me. It'll get even. I know. I got it mad a few times and… just don't do it. That means don't tell anyone."

Johnny put the gun to his temple. He pulled the trigger, just a little. His eyes scanned the floor. "Is this okay?"

"What're you talking about Johnny?" James said, and he noticed the strangest thing. His breath hung frozen in the ice-cold air. The room was officially freezing.

"I'm talking about a Bokor Incantation," Johnny said. "And it's not my fault."

"What the hell is that?"

Johnny shook his head. "Too late."

"Can't we work this out?"

"I am working this out James. See you on the other side."

"But—"

"But nothing. See you soon. Try not to dream."

On the floor, a shadow moved.

Johnny opened his mouth and dragged the gun along his face. He slid the barrel past his lips and rested it on his front teeth. Then he closed his eyes and pulled the trigger.

8

There was no pain.

But Mathew was screaming for Uncle James.

James was sitting inside the Demon's lair, completely oblivious. He didn't know he was in danger. Not real danger. But Mathew did. He could see it—see the demon hiding in the shadows. See the demon with the black skin, the long fingers and the glistening eyes—the demon that had lived a thousand lifetimes and slain a hundred thousand men.

Mathew could see this, and Mathew was screaming. But to the outside world, the child looked the same. He was lying on the hospital bed, silent and unmoving. To the outside world he was a boy—like all boys. No different. Only his injuries and experiences distinguished him from the rest. Nobody knew he was a unique child with an unrecognized gift, a special talent. Nobody knew his biological chemistry was uncommon. Not Anne. Not the doctors. Nobody.

Mathew could see things, things that are not often seen.

It was a gift.

Given time—two or three years, perhaps—Mathew would develop a large tumor in his brain. The tumor would be diagnosed as cancerous. The doctors would say the cause of the tumor would be unknown, but likely genetic. They would tell his family that Mathew had a rough road ahead. And a short while later, after the medical community punished his body with cell destroying chemotherapy, they would say he had less than a month to live. And they would be correct. But the tumor that eventually kills its host comes with a flipside that is rarely seen. In a way, it is the gift of sight, and the accident-induced trauma had exposed it.

Mathew's eyes were opening now. He was seeing things, seeing into the lives of the people he loved. He didn't like what he was seeing.

And inside his tiny, broken body—Mathew was screaming.

9

Click. The chamber was empty.

"WAIT!" James begged with his stomach doing back-flips. "FOR GOD'S SAKE, STOP WHAT YOU'RE DOING!"

Johnny pulled the gun from his mouth and eyed the weapon suspiciously.

"Let me talk a minute," James said. "Please!"

Keeping his fingers ready, Johnny lowered his hand. "It won't do any good. There's nothing you can say."

"Fine. But give me a chance will you? Can we talk a little before you blow your friggin' head off?"

Johnny exposed his dirty teeth. "Alright," he said. "I'll give you five minutes."

"Five minutes?"

"Yeah."

James thought about his nephew Mathew lying on the hospital bed with a thick circle of bandages around his mouth and both of his legs in casts—suspended in the air, looking like something from a Discovery Channel emergency program.

"My brother Joe died last night," he said. "So did his wife Penny. Mathew is in the hospital. He might not make it. Things haven't been good."

"Really?"

"Yeah. Car accident."

The insanity drained from Johnny's eyes a little. "Are you serious?"

"Unfortunately, I am. It happened on the highway around eleven-thirty. We got the call early this morning. My mom is at the hospital now, with Mathew. You remember Mathew, right? Joe's five-year-old... blonde hair, built like a baby lumberjack."

"I remember." Johnny said. His eyes lost their ultra focused lunacy. His shoulders, which had been raised, came down and his voice softened a notch. "Honest? You're telling me the truth?"

"Honest."

"Damn. I'm sorry to hear that."

"Thanks."

"No really. I'm sorry."

The two men looked at each other, each feeling ashamed of the moment.

"Do you mind if we talk about it?" James asked, wondering if the sympathy angle would hold.

"Go ahead."

James cleared his throat. "But what am I supposed to do here, have a heart-to-heart with you then watch you blow your head off? Jesus man. We both have problems, but I was thinking we could help each other, make things right."

Johnny shrugged. "I don't know what to say James. I'm backed into a corner here. This is my way out."

"Don't say that."

"It's true."

"No man, it's not. Is that gun loaded?"

Johnny shuffled the gun from one hand to the other. "Yeah, it is. The next time I pull the trigger it'll be the money shot."

"You're being stupid."

"Okay. If you say so."

"And why the hell is it so cold in here? I'm freezing."

"Is this really the way you want to spend the last minutes of my life? Talking about the fuckin' temperature?"

"But Johnny… it's August."

"So?"

James shook his head. The small talk wasn't working, however, Johnny was more coherent now. Much more. He wasn't mumbling, rolling his eyes or talking crazy. That had to be worth something.

"My mother's pretty upset," James said. "In fact, she's a bloody mess."

"That's understandable."

"She says I'll have to adopt Mathew. Between you and me, I don't know if I can do it. I don't know if I can be a father. I mean… I love the little guy, but I'm not ready. Mathew is such a handful and I can be… well, you know me."

Johnny didn't respond so James kept talking.

"You know me," he repeated. "I'm scattered at the best of times. Always have been—always will be. I'm the guy that walks to the store to buy milk and comes home empty handed."

With an expression, Johnny agreed.

"But you know what?" James said, considering a new approach. He figured he could dilute Johnny's issues with his own. Maybe it would work, maybe not. It was worth a try. "Once upon a time, I wasn't such an idiot and my head was on tight. And at that time, I wanted children. I wanted to be a father. But then something happened, something bad. I was sixteen, maybe seventeen. And there was this guy. Harold was his name. I guess Harold would have been eighteen or nineteen, maybe twenty." James smiled unexpectedly. "Harold had these big, awful sideburns that ran down his neck. When he wasn't around, we made fun of him a great deal. Muttonchops, we called him. Of course, he didn't know that. We didn't think Harold would appreciate being called 'Mutton-chop Harold'. But that's who he was to us. Mutton-chop Harold, the youngest father we knew."

Johnny nodded.

"Harold wasn't ready. He wasn't prepared inside his mind, you know? And his girlfriend at the time—who was a few years younger than Mutton-chop—she wasn't much of a thinker, and she didn't care about him. Didn't care what he thought or what he wanted. You see… this girl wanted a baby, end of story. And if the kid grew up inside a broken home with fighting parents and nothing in the cupboard, well… so be it."

"You know what we call girls like that, don't you?" Johnny said.

"No, what?"

"White-trash bitches."

James smiled insincerely. "Well, I don't know if the girl was a white-trash bitch or not, but she lied all the time and always played the victim. She also smoked a pack a day through the pregnancy. At least, that's what Harold said. If that's white-trash, so be it."

"I hear ya."

James noticed that his knees were shaking. He made an effort to keep them still. He made an effort to keep calm. He made an effort to keep talking. "The smoking drove Harold nuts," he said, nervously. "He complained, but what could he do? You know the law. The mother's right even when she's not. Even if she's an self-righteous idiot with a grade eight education."

"That's a bullshit law," Johnny said.

"It's a bullshit world. Anyways, trying to be a dad while dealing with this bitch was upsetting. I mean, from what Harold said, she got pregnant on purpose two weeks after they started dating. You clearly don't give a shit if you pull that move."

"Some people aren't very bright," Johnny agreed. "They don't think about the lives they fuck up."

As soon as he finished speaking he thought about shooting James. Shooting him right in the Goddamn face. He wanted to do it, almost needed to do it. The gun felt warm inside his fingers. The thought of killing his friend made him smile from ear to ear.

"Yeah," James said. Then he smiled because Johnny was smiling.

Maybe it was time to pull the gun from Johnny's hand.

10

"They broke up a couple months after the baby was born," James said. "It was a boy, I think. Can't remember the name. Whatever. Doesn't matter. Point is… Harold couldn't take the bitch any longer and they broke up. Then came the babysitting. He'd have the kid a day or two and she'd have the kid a day or two. This went back and forth a while without any screw-ups. Then one day Harold makes a mistake. It was February and he was going—wherever—it doesn't really matter and I don't honestly know. For arguments sake let's say he was going to the mall. So Harold gets the kid ready, he bundles the little feller up in his snow-pants and whatnot and he takes him to the car. And the baby is strapped inside one of those baby seats… sleeping or whatever. Knowing Harold, the baby-seat is probably two sizes too small with three pounds of dried puke on it. Anyways, Harold sits the baby on the ground. He unlocks the car, opens the door and gets inside. Then he drives away and leaves the baby sitting at the side of the road."

"Oh no."

"Oh yeah. And it gets worse. Harold's not thinking about the baby, see? 'Cause deep down he's not ready for the baby... he was never ready for the baby. So now the little feller is sitting outside and it's February. And it's as cold as tits on a seal out there and Harold's gone to the mall. After a while he realizes what he's done and holy shit does he feel bad. Real bad. So he comes racing home as fast as he can... but the guy lives downtown, you know? And when he gets home the cops are everywhere. The baby's dead—got run over by a truck."

"Oh shit."

"Oh shit is right. And when the smoke finally clears, Harold gets two years. Needless to say, the girl hates him and her family hates him, in fact—both families hate him. And worst of all, he hates himself. So guess what? After he's released from jail the first thing he does is get drunk. Then he jumps off a fucking bridge. He kills himself."

"Oh man, that's hard," Johnny said.

"Tell me about it." James looked at the gun. It was inches away, hanging loosely in Johnny's hand—and Johnny seemed lost in thought. If James wanted the gun bad enough he could take it. He could reach right out and grab it. But James wasn't grabbing anything. He was so worried he was trembling. Talking. Keep talking, he told himself. Talking seems best. "After the funeral I realized something. I'm not ready to be a dad. I decided—I'd never be a dad. And now this happens and my mom expects me to take care of Mathew. She expects me to be a father. And I'm not ready, Johnny. I'm scared shitless. I'm scared I'll make a mistake—a big mistake. I'm scared I'll fuck up, like Harold did. I'm telling you... I'm not ready for this. It scares me half to death."

The two men sat in silence.

Looking at the gun, James ran both hands along his arms. He was cold. The house was freezing.

"You know what?" Johnny said, suddenly smirking.

"No, what?"

"Your five minutes are up."

Johnny didn't shoot James. Instead, he slid the gun into his own mouth and tried his luck again. This time, the blast was deafening.

11

Anne sat with Mathew. Then a nurse named Patricia (who had a face like a mule if Anne ever did see one) entered the room asking Anne if she would like something to eat.

"A tea would be nice," Anne said, offering a smile. "If it wouldn't be too much trouble, that is."

Patricia took a quick glance at Mathew's chart, which was attached to a board at the front of the bed. She checked the IV, tilted her head and returned the smile. "No trouble at all, Mrs. McGee." She spoke with that low-level cheer all nurses seem to be naturally equipped with. She sounded happy, but not *too* happy. She sounded like she cared but probably didn't. "Is there a tea you'd like best, any particular flavor?"

Anne considered her options, while running a finger along her rosary beads. "Earl Gray?"

Patricia nodded. "I drink that myself, first thing in the morning. Can't start my day without it. You like milk? Sugar?"

"Milk please. I don't take sugar."

"That's the way I take it too, with a shot of milk. You and I are peas in a pod Mrs. McGee. Oh yes we are. We're two of a kind. Is there anything else?"

Anne smiled kindly. She noticed, for the first time since she had arrived, how medical everything smelled. She wondered if the woman had brought the medicinal smell in with her somehow. She wondered if something had been spilled in the hallway. The aroma was way beyond strong; it was almost science fiction. "No dear. The tea will be just fine."

Pat glanced at Mathew one last time with eyes that had seen it all. "One tea, coming up. I'll be back in a few minutes. Maybe I'll bring cookies. Sometimes I like to have a lemon cookie with my tea."

Again, Anne smiled. "Thank you," she said thinking, *forget the cookies; I won't eat them.*

With her shoes skimming the floor Pat made for the door. Then she hesitated. "Oh by the way. I met your son James earlier. He seems very nice."

"Yes," Anne said. "He is. He's as nice as they come."

"Well dressed too." Patricia smiled, seeming to be lost in thought.

Anne wondered if the nurse had developed a bit of a crush. It was possible. Lots of women found James attractive; he'd had girls chasing him since he was eight years old.

"Well," Anne said. "I suppose he is well dressed."

Patricia laughed lightly and showed her dimples. They made her look younger, and almost made her pretty. "I'll see you in a moment Mrs. McGee. I won't be long."

"That's fine. Take your time."

Patricia left the room and Anne stood up. She placed her rosary on the chair and opened the window. She stood beside the bed and took Mathew's small fingers in her hand. His skin felt cold and thin. Shallow breathing came from his open lips in slow moving gasps. The bandages around his head needed to be changed once more—his blood and sweat had soaked through.

Anne wondered if Mathew would ever laugh again, or smile again, or be a happy little boy again. She expected that he would, trusting that when this terrible tragedy had passed him by, he'd be able to pick up the pieces of his life and continue on without too much sorrow. She knew it would be hard. No child should lose both mother and father in a single stroke. No child should endure such pain.

She squeezed Mathew's hand and the boy opened his eyes unexpectedly. His fingers wrapped around hers.

"Run James," he said with a dry voice. Then he fell silent and his eyes closed.

Anne stood above the child, voiceless and distressed. She watched his shallow breathing and waited for him to speak again. But Mathew did not speak. He didn't budge. He laid unmoving, laboring shallow breaths as if nothing had happened.

PART TWO:
RUNNING WITH THE DEVIL

12

After the gun went off Johnny's head fell back. His eyes faced the ceiling. A cloud of smoke puffed through the bubbling hole in the back of his skull, and rose up through his nose and mouth. His body slouched; his knees knocked together. Then Johnny's balance shifted and his shoulders fell forward. His hand slid down his chest and the gun slipped from his fingers. As the gun slapped the floor Johnny's head slumped and fell to one side. A stream of blood, teeth and charred tongue ran over his gums and down his chin. His legs slid apart and his body leaned forwards. When he fell, his body hit the floor with a wet, grim thud.

Then a shadow shifted and the hardwood creaked.

James held his breath.

The shadow was the size of a small tombstone and shaped like some type of animal, a raccoon maybe. James wondered how this was possible. He wondered if was imagining things, if his eyes were playing tricks. Was stress causing him to hallucinate?

He saw it again, and this time there was no denying it. There was a shadow on the floor and it was moving. But how could this be? James was alone in the ice-cold room, with Johnny—who lay dead and bleeding on the floor.

13

James got up from the couch and walked towards the door slowly. The shadow followed so he walked faster. Tiny footsteps could be heard beneath the sound of his own. Part of him wanted to run. Another part wanted to wave his hands in the air the way a child does when a wasp gets close. Things felt that way now—like a wasp was buzzing, or ten wasps, or an entire hive had come together in battle. And Johnny's words, which had sounded crazy less than five minutes ago, began haunting him.

Sorry man, Johnny had said. *I'm sorry it's you. But if I don't pass it on, it'll be with me forever.*

What the hell did that mean? Did Johnny pass something on to him; something worse than angry wasps, something cold and invisible, something so bad that Johnny put the business end of a gun inside his mouth and pulled the trigger?

James walked faster still. He grabbed the doorknob, twisted his wrist and pushed. The door swung open. Wind grabbed it and slammed it against the wall. Brass plated house numbers rattled against the brick.

James was running now, he realized—running down the steps and across the driveway. He threw open the car door and leapt inside. After ramming a hand into his pocket, he fumbled with his keys, shifted through them and slammed a key into the ignition. The car started and James backed out of the driveway at a racers pace. Air blew through both open windows. The radio spewed commercials. Changing gears, he tore down Tecumseh Street like...

A madman, James thought. Jesus... now I'm the crazy one.

As he followed a bend in the road he turned the radio off. The temperature inside the car dropped five notches and something became crystal clear:

He was not alone.

14

James slapped a hand against the passenger seat like a schoolgirl. He wanted to squish it, kill it; destroy it—whatever *it* was. But there was nothing to get rid of. How could there be? He was alone—alone with the ice-cold air and the empty seat and the eerie moving shadow. Fucking hell.

Maybe he wasn't alone! He pounded a fist against the cushion and shouting obscenities.

The outline was there, racing in circles and evading his assault.

He pounded his fist again.

James swerved the car left and right. The book inside his mind turned a page and a new bolt of fear hit. He stopped shouting and stopped hammering the seat. His frantic behavior all but vanished and the hairs on the back of his neck stood straight enough to be in the army.

The car was colder now; he had made *it* angry.

"*And whatever you do James,*" Johnny had said. "*Don't get it mad. You don't want it mad. It'll get the best of you. Trust me. It'll get even. I know. I got it mad a few times.*"

The creature hissed.

Oh shit.

In the corner of his eye he saw a tiny alien; it was foreign in every conceivable way.

Then it was gone.

James wanted to believe that his eyes were playing tricks on him—but they weren't. His eyesight was top notch; he could read a street sign from two blocks away.

So what did he see?

James wasn't sure, but whatever it was—its skin was black and its eyes were huge. James knew that much. Past that, he had no idea what the creature looked like. It came and went too quickly. And it didn't matter. Not really. The important thing was this: he made the demon angry and now he'd pay for it.

He hit the brake. It didn't respond.

In fact, the car moved faster and faster.

15

Mathew floated with balloons inside the endless scenery of his mind. He knew things now. He knew that once Johnny died things would become bad for Uncle James.

And Johnny died.

And things changed.

But time was funny inside Mathew's mind. Time had become askew. He wasn't part of the system now; he wasn't part of the game. He was in a coma and he wandered the compositions of linear time at his own pace, in his own way. He didn't know how to control this time flux; minutes could be days; hours could be lifetimes; years could be seconds.

Mathew followed a green balloon inside Johnny's house. He saw Johnny sitting in a chair and James beside him. He saw the beast grow dull and the shadows lighten. Then a sudden movement came and a red cloud exploded in the air above Johnny's head. He watched Johnny's head move back and forth like a pendulum. He saw Johnny grin.

Then the balloon turned red, popped, and James was gone.

Mathew was confused. He didn't see James leave the room. He didn't see him run for the door, or disappear, or fade away. In one moment James was there—and in the next moment the reality of the situation had been altered. It seemed possible that James had never been there at all. The room had darkened and the edges of Mathew's perception felt crusted with a metallic tinge. Like the fabric—the very molecules of the room and everything that was within it—had become alive. And was moving. Slowly. Twisting and turning, changing Mathew's visuals while keeping everything miraculously unaltered.

He heard the walls creaking around him. He heard voices in the distance that sounded like crying. And there was an odor. He couldn't put his finger on it but it reminded him of soda in the can.

Motion stood still.

Mathew saw another balloon, a red one. As he reached for it time began rolling again. He watched events happen through the eyes of James. He watched Johnny kill himself. And although time was rolling along now, rolling faster with each implicit second, this was the hang-time between life and death, between here and there, between this world and the next.

Johnny had a never-ending river of blood pouring from his chin. And while the blood bubbled he lifted his head and smiled through a mouthful of jagged teeth fragments.

He said, "Mathew," his voice sounded unrefined and deep. "He's with us now, child. James is with us. Soon enough, you'll be with us too."

16

James drove past crosswalks and driveways and a house that his parents considered buying when he was a boy. He soared past small homes with large yards and trees that were older than the town. He drove under a bridge and passed a STOP sign. He entered a subdivision that was just being developed. Some of the houses were still empty. Unsure of the situation, he looked over his shoulder and into the backseat. That was empty too.

The fake leather steering wheel slid through his fingers and James snapped his head around faster than his eyes widened. The car accelerated, the engine revved. The seat shook beneath him. The radio turned on and off.

If he didn't know better, he'd swear the car was haunted.

James slammed his foot on the brake pedal again and again; it was no use. The pedal went up and down but the car wouldn't respond. He put a hand on his face and rubbed his eyes as long moments of dread rolled through his mind. There was an intersection with a stoplight getting larger by the second. The light was green. James closed his eyes and held on tight, wondering if he was about to die. The car ripped along and a few seconds later the intersection was behind him. But it wasn't over, not by a long shot. There was another intersection coming and without a doubt, another one after that. He drove in a straight line and a squirrel ran in front of the car, did a little dance and went back the way it came. He zipped past a kid that was tossing a plastic football in the air while leaning against a corner mailbox. Up ahead a green light was changing to yellow.

A bee squashed against the window. It was big; might have been a queen.

The speedometer read: 79 MPH.

The light changed again: RED.

I'm jumping out of the car, he thought. Oh mother of mohair and shit on a stick—help me! I'm jumping out! I'm jumping out of the car!

He grabbed the door handle and pulled hard on the lever. He strained his fingers but the handle didn't budge. There was no escape.

"FUCK!"

The crossroads drew closer.

James pulled the handle again. The corner was less than 100 feet away now and he was going to drive right through it. There was no question; physics demanded it.

On his left, James spotted a surprised mother pushing a pink stroller along the sidewalk. She had been reading Vogue magazine, which had a well-dressed, under-fed, teenager on the cover. Their eyes met and her jaw dropped. The woman waved both hands wildly as the carriage came to a rolling stop. The magazine flapped and fluttered around her head with pages blowing in the wind. It looked like a bird was attacking.

James began screaming. His wasn't a high-pitched siren, not like his sister-in-law's had been. His was a machinegun blast, a burst of screams packed tighter than a roll of quarters.

The shadow leapt from the seat and landed between his legs. Long, unseen fingers wrapped around his ankles and although James didn't know it, the beast opened its mouth preparing its attack.

17

Cars, trees, lights, and signs—the essence of the small town intersection—flew past James in one swift blur. He had gotten lucky. Then his luck ended. Tiny, razor-sharp teeth ripped a piece from his leg. Blood soaked through his dress-pants and ran a line to his shoe.

James held back his shriek; his face pinched into a ball and tears rolled down his cheeks. He pulled his wounded leg together and lifted his feet high.

The creature shifted its weight, repositioned and primed itself for another assault.

Keep your eyes on the road, James thought, with his fingers choking the steering wheel. Keep your eyes on that fucking road.

But James wasn't in control of the car—and his eyes weren't on the road. He was looking at the blood pooling beneath his legs, the living shadow at his feet, the steering column, his lap, his shoes, and the floor. He was looking at everything except the road. Then the car forged a new path. It drifted off the road and up a curb. It ran over a man: Doctor Anson. He had just come home from work.

Anson slammed against the ground and wheels rolled over his chest and kept on going. A second later the car hit a tricycle; the tricycle went flying. Then the car connected with a young and slender elm tree, cutting it in half. Branches dusted the hood and smashed the window before spinning through the air. They bounced off the curb and rolled onto the street in broken fragments. Leaves scattered. Splinters flew.

James was in a state of panic now. His hands were in front of his face and his eyes were shut tight. He whispered, "I just killed a man. Oh shit... I killed him for sure."

The car kept going.

James maneuvered his way back onto the road for several blocks before he lost control again. Then the car ripped through bushes, driveways, flowerbeds and lawns. It hit a fence and white pickets exploded. A barking dog gave chase. A young boy ran. A man yelled.

And again, the creature opened its gapping maw.

James looked down, feeling new pressure around his legs. "WHAT THE FUCK ARE YOU…"

The invisible intruder bit down again, tearing another hole in his leg. Fresh pain sent a shock through his system. His feet jerked, and blood squirted across the floor. With his teeth clenched, James kicked hard, accomplishing nothing. And in the top corner of his eye he saw something. Something big.

He looked up and gaped like a fish.

James understood that it was only a matter of time before the car ride would end—only a matter of time. Time was up.

The car was about to hit a house.

And a moment later—it did.

18

Anne stepped away from Mathew and picked up the phone, which was sitting on a table beside the bed. She dialed nine and waited. The line clicked over and she dialed James's cell phone number. The phone rang but no one answered.

Dialed again—still no answer.

She hung up the phone and walked across the room. She was thinking about James now. She was worried and confused.

Why did Mathew speak? Why did he say, 'Run, James'?

This seemed to be a mystery without an answer, without logic or reason—unless James was in serious trouble. But even if James was in trouble, how could Mathew know this? The answer was simple enough—he couldn't know. It wasn't possible. Besides, what dilemma could her son be in?

She picked up the phone a second time and dialed again. Same result. James must have his phone turned off, she thought. And he's probably at his girlfriend's place.

Debra.

Anne cringed. She didn't want to call Debra. She hated that two-faced, lying slut.

19

Just around the time Anne was phoning James, Debra—the two-faced lying slut—opened her eyes. She had just finished a nasty dream about a zombie, which was a first. Debra rarely dreamt, and had never known the joys of an unsettling nightmare. She wondered where the nightmare had originated. She never watched zombie movies or read scary books. She considered all forms of horror entertainment stupid and adolescent.

But the corpse within her dream wasn't stupid. It was... Johnny?

The nightmare faded away. She put a hand to her face and rolled on her side. Her eyes opened and closed, opened and closed. Her breathing calmed.

At the side of her bed was a table, and on it was a small stack of fashion magazines. Behind the magazines was a love letter, written by James. It was in plain view and had been read by all of Debra's friends. Keeping the letter exposed was important to Debra. It kept James wrapped around her finger. Just looking at it brought a smile to her face.

Boys could be so dumb; so easy.

Next to the letter was a retro style alarm clock. It was stylish and expensive, a Christmas gift from her mother. Debra didn't like the clock or her mother, but the clock sustained impeccably accurate time. And the time was 11:35am.

Her mouth was dry. The taste of last night's alcohol coated the grime of her teeth. She sat up and thought, what happened? Then it came to her and a whore's grin crept upon her face.

Oh yeah, girls-night.

Girls-night was a pussy-pass for Debra and her tight-lipped friends. It was the perfect slut move, the one night she could keep her boyfriend away, the one night she could justify being angry if he called or dropped by. Girls-night afforded Debra the freedom to do what she wanted—with anyone, with everyone.

There were always plenty of boys at girls-night.

Although her mind was fuzzy, Debra remembered most of the evening. She remembered having dinner at a restaurant, drinking a few pints of beer and then changing her drink to vodka and OJ. She remembered going to a bar, doing shots, flirting with men, and women, flashing her tits a couple times and sitting on some guy's lap. She remembered telling her friends not to say anything, like always. And her friends laughed, like always. She remembered one of her girlfriends kissing a hip-hop thug, which pissed everyone off. The guy was a loser that wouldn't fuck off, which threw a downbeat twist into the party. She remembered going back to a friend's house, making out, getting felt-up and scoring a phone number. Then the night gets blurry.

If Debra had been asked why she acted this way she would say, "I was drunk." Being drunk was the only excuse Debra needed. Besides, as long as James was kept in the dark it was no big deal. No big deal at all.

In fact, Debra got drunk all the time.

It was no big deal at all.

20

James lifted his head and opened his eyes.

The doors were open. The back tires were spinning and the front tires were flat. A sea of bricks sat across the crumpled hood. The windshield had a spider-web design embedded in the glass. The smell of gasoline was strong and a small fire was aflame beneath the hood.

James coughed. "What the—?"

A few seconds slipped by before he started thinking the car would explode. The thought seemed logical, perhaps likely.

A few feet back, a brick fell from the hole in the wall followed by another. He could see dust rising and settling, turning and falling. Beyond that, he could see that the bricks, framework, drywall and furniture were slammed together in a splintered mess. Beneath the car more rumbling and settling occurred. It seemed that everything was finding its place.

He lifted his foot from the pedal; the back tires stopped spinning.

Memories came: his family, the gun, Johnny's suicide, the creature inside the car, the vicious attack on his legs—it was a lot to swallow. He wasn't sure what to think.

Suddenly, the fire beneath the car doubled in size. If the car were going to explode, it would do so soon. He needed to escape. Running—that was the important thing now. But James couldn't move; he couldn't run. Something was holding him down. After a moment of panic, he looked at his chest.

The seatbelt was on.

James muttered something negative. He didn't remember putting a seatbelt on, but then again, everything happened so fast. He probably clicked the belt without thinking. And he always wore his seatbelt—just incase.

James unbuckled. The belt slithered across his waist.

Blood dripped from his nose.

Then he heard a voice inside his head. Run James, the voice said. And, for some reason, he thought of Mathew.

He put a hand on the door and pulled himself from the vehicle. He dragged his feet through a heavy pile of broken brick. Hot pain burned both shins. He coughed twice and noticed that his lungs hurt. Then he rubbed a hand across his face and small stream of red smudged across his cheek; the wound was minor, but throbbed once he noticed it.

On the other side of the room a middle-aged woman wearing a scarlet flowered dress emerged with two young boys. She had dark skin, dark hair and wore a pair of thin-rimmed glasses.

"Dios mió," she said, panic-stricken.

James shook his head. Aside from 'hola' and 'gracias,' he didn't know Spanish. Only English.

"¡Mira lo que has hecho, has destruido mi casa!"

"I don't know what you're telling me."

"Estas loco? Mira a tu alrededor, todo está arruinado!"

"I don't understand," James said. But then he did understand; it was so obvious.

He was inside the woman's house, inside her living room. The car had destroyed her home and the woman was frantic. Of course she was. Who wouldn't be?

The oldest boy rubbed his eyes and held his body against his mother's waist. His fingers grappled the fabric of her dress. He had a dirty face, watering eyes and chocolate ice cream stains on his shirt. Snot ran down his nose.

The youngest boy pointed at the bricks and screamed, "Mama! Mama! Miro! Hay un monstruo! Veámonos de aquí!"

James wondered if he had killed someone, a child perhaps. He hoped not. The last thing he wanted to do was kill somebody.

The air turn cold and he realized what the child was saying. Children are more perceptive than adults. And they could see it—see the black skinned demon with eyes like sunken pits of coal. See the beast that was responsible for this nightmare.

And they were afraid.

They were right to be afraid.

21

James edged towards the family. He saw a mangled tricycle at his feet and the urge hit: he needed out of the house. He needed to get away from the smoke, the car, the family and everything around him. He needed an open space. He needed to find a place where he didn't feel trapped, a place he hadn't destroyed. It was time to run, time to hide, time to go.

The youngest boy was standing in a hallway. That had to lead somewhere—a window. A door.

As James approached the Spanish woman, she grabbed his tie and pulled. Then she yelled something and shook the tie angrily.

"Stop that!" James barked. "I don't know what you're saying!" He slapped the woman's hand and pushed her aside. He stepped into the hallway saying, "I don't have time for this!"

What was the family doing before the car arrived, he wondered. Watching television? Eating ice cream? Playing video games?

Damn. This wasn't fair and he knew it.

James took a deep breath and coughed.

Then he thought about Debra. He loved her so much, maybe too much. He thought she was beautiful; he thought she was fun and wished they were together. He believed—the way all foolish lovers do—that without her he couldn't go on. He needed Debra to hold him, love him and comfort him. He needed the woman he had fallen in love with now, in his time of need, to make things better.

I wish I were lying next to you, he thought. I love you and I need you more than you'll ever know. You complete me.

He heard a child scream.

Then the car exploded.

22

Debra's hangover came in throbbing waves of sickness. She mumbled, "My brain is killing me." Then she wondered if she was alone. Looking over her shoulder, she found the other half of the bed empty.

Praise Allah for small miracles.

After a minor struggle with her anally pleated sheets, she got out of bed and ran her fingers through her steel-wool hair. She pushed her drooping chest out and made dirty-girl faces in the mirror. This usually invoked a smile but today her heart wasn't in it. The veins in her pale breasts seemed more noticeable this morning; Debra looked and felt like shit.

There was a low-cut shirt on the floor. She pulled it over her skin and made her way to the kitchen. She drank a glass of water and popped a couple Tylenols.

More memories came:

She took a cab home with friends. Her friends came inside. They listened to music, had a couple drinks and hooked up with their dealer. (The dealer was a guy named Gary she had nailed more times than she cared to remember.) They cranked a few lines of ketamine and Gary invited some friends over.

And then... ?

Debra turned the kettle on and stepped into the living room, expecting a sleeping body on the couch. The couch was empty but the coffee table was a different story. It was loaded with beer cans, wine glasses, tumblers, ashtrays, cigarette butts, remnants of powder and assorted rubbish that included everything from eyeliner pencils and lipstick, to an eight-inch ribbed dildo.

"Huh." She said, rubbing her eyes with her fingers. The aftermath of girls-night was always interesting.

The kettle screeched and Debra turned it off. She made tea, sat on the couch and pushed her feet into the heart of the mess. With the push of a button she turned on the television. Her fingers tapped the controller. Tap, tap, tap. She lifted a pencil from the table, put into her mouth and nibbled on the end. She flipped channels until she found Dr. Phil talking to a girl that had run away from home to become a prostitute. The girl was saying she loved getting attention and hated her parents. Dr. Phil was saying she needed to get her act together.

She could relate with the girl.

Tap, tap, tap. After twenty minutes, Debra finished her tea, turned off the TV and returned to bed.

Two minutes later the phone rang.

"Hello?"

"Hi Debra. This is Anne."

23

After the explosion James was on his hands and knees, disoriented. His white dress shirt dangled below him, black with dirt and ash. His tie hung low and was resting in a pile of rubble. His hair was ashen with powder and his eyes were thick with dirt. The car was on fire and the heat was unquestionable—six hundred degrees and rising. Black smoke filled the air like smog over Los Angeles.

James endured a long bout of coughing and pulled himself to his knees. Sound had become a constant ring, like a chiming bell that wouldn't fade. And there was something inside that sound, a noise of some type hidden beneath the ringing.

He coughed again, tasting filth and blood. But what about that sound, he wondered. Was a phone ringing? Was it the fire? Was it a siren?

The fire was loud, but no, that wasn't it. This sound cut though the fire. It was a high-pitched noise, different than everything else; it was an unrefined echo. It sounded like screaming.

No—

It *was* screaming.

The family was burning.

James had been standing inside the hallway when the explosion occurred and the walls had protected him. But the family had been standing at the doorway and now they were paying for it. Now they were ablaze.

A dancing inferno of arms and legs could be seen—a head swaying, feet kicking, hands grabbing at nothing. It was the woman. She was alive and burning, burning and screaming.

And the boys—where were they?

The youngest boy was lying face up on the floor. His legs were in flames and a huge chunk of metal impaled his chest. Along the side of his nose the gray matter from his brain oozed, producing a small mound near his upper lip. The other boy was missing entirely. James wondered if he had escaped but he knew it was unlikely. He was probably lying on the floor, buried in the rubble.

I need to get out of here, James reminded himself. The temperature was increasing and the flames were expanding. Plus the smoke was getting thicker, blacker. Deadlier.

He pulled himself to his feet.

The burning woman fell against the wall twitching and screeching. Her mouth opened and closed as she hit the floor. Fingers curled and legs contracted. Her dress opened, exposing the bubbling skin beneath the flames on her chest.

James turned away. The image was madness, but the grilled, barbequed stench was worse. It made him feel nauseous and revolted at the same time. There's nothing I can do for the woman, he thought. And he was right. He was in no position to help—not while the blaze was eating the walls and broiling him alive. He was right about another thing too: he needed to get out of the house.

Avoiding the flames, James placed his hands on the shredded drywall, which was plagued with many holes. Some of the holes were big enough to crawl through. Others were like bullet holes.

I'm in a hallway, James thought. Follow the walls… find my way out.

James stumbled away from the room. The smoke thinned and the heat dissipated. He staggered past a pile of rubble, a box filled with plastic toys and a small table with a rotary phone on it. He walked past a family portrait, a stack of newspapers and a closet. He found a doorway that led to the kitchen and heard a child crying.

That sounds like a baby, he thought. Someone is in here.

He dismissed the cry (But why? That's not like me…) and kept moving.

On the other side of the room was a pile of shoes, a long rack of coats and jackets, and a doorway that led outside.

"Safe at last," James whispered. But he was wrong. Dead wrong.

The day had just begun.

24

As James made his way into the front yard a man in his late forties with grey hair and brilliant green eyes came running. The man ran gracelessly, like it had been awhile since he moved with any urgency. His feet dragged against the pavement. His arms flopped around like they were made of rubber.

"Are you alright?" Green-eyes said. He put a hand on his chest and swallowed a huge breath; he was panting and wheezing.

James nodded.

Green-eyes continued battling for air. "That family," he said. "The family with the five children, oh dear Lord, they're not in there are they? Are they? Please tell me they're not inside the house!"

James turned away; he thought about the baby. But he had nothing for this man—nothing to give, nothing to say. He considered running down the street.

"The children!" Green-eyes barked angrily. He knocked his heals against the ground and swallowed his gum. "Who do you think you are? Don't you care? Can't you see the house is—"

"I don't know!" James interrupted rudely. "I don't know what to tell you mister, I'm sorry!"

"But my God son... what happened? This isn't right! What were you thinking? What did you do... drive into the house at full speed? Were you alone? Are you on drugs? Talk to me son, talk to me!"

James looked away from Green-eyes, having grown tired of his bickering and questioning. He lowered his head and noticed that his shoes, which had been purchased three days earlier, had smoke drifting from the toes. They looked almost comical: it was the amazing adventures of Smokey the Shoe and his sidekick, Puff.

Still ignoring the man, James suffered another bout of coughing—six in a row. When he finished his throat felt raw and his eyes burned. He glanced into the heart of the fire. The car was blazing. It looked like someone had thrown a giant fireball through the front door of the house.

Green-eyes moaned. He was completely distraught.

Finally James said, "Go into the backyard. Go inside the house, break the windows if you must, but get inside. If anyone's alive they're 'round back. The front of the house is finished. Trust me, there's nothing you can do around front."

Green-eyes had his feet glued to the ground. He didn't understand the command. He didn't understand that he was the one that needed to look inside the inferno. The lives of the children were resting on him now.

"But the fire…"

"Go!" James demanded. "Go now dammit! Before it's too late! Shit man… look for survivors, people are dying, children are dying. Get them out of there!"

"But—"

"But nothing! I can't do it! I'm wounded!"

James coughed again. This time he faked it, demonstrating that he was in no condition to play hero.

Green-eyes rubbed a hand across his face and scurried around in a broken loop. "Oh damn!" he said, putting a finger against his temple. "Oh shit! Oh shit! You really want me to go back there? Oh man!"

Reluctantly the man ran up the driveway and disappeared into the backyard. As he did this, the first of several fire trucks came down the street with sirens blaring. It wouldn't be long until the police arrived.

James lowered his head and assembled his thoughts.

This is a sticky moment, he thought. How do I explain this one?

25

Shuffling her fat, pastel-white body across the road in an overly frayed nightdress was a woman named Tina Comfrey. "What happened?" She asked. "A fire?"

James nodded.

"That looks like a car in there. You the driver or somethin'?"

"Yeah."

"Whatcha do?"

James didn't want to talk because—what could he say? There was a gremlin gnawing at my leg and I lost control of the car, sorry for the inconvenience? And if not that, what? What lie could he sell? His car was on fire forty-five feet from where he was standing.

"I don't know what happened," James mumbled. "Guess I lost control."

"Should pay more attention," Tina said with an ugly smirk. Then her attitude changed. "This is total bullshit you know. Total bullshit. Drivers like you I always say. You're the reason my insurance bill is bad. Guys like you driving around the town like maniacs. You shouldn't have a license in the first place. If people like you weren't allowed to drive it'd be one safe country. Mark my words. It would be safe. Fucking asshole drivers are making things tough for the working class, every fuckin' time. You fuck-knucklers should be lined up and shot. You should have your eyes pulled from your head"

"You don't understand."

"Bullshit. You're a crappy driver... probably the worst driver around. How many accidents have you been in? Be honest now... three? Four? Five? You're a fuck-knuckler and you shouldn't have a license. The proof is in the puddin' honey. The proof is right there, burning down my friggin' neighborhood."

Tina pulled a tissue from her tattered handbag and foolishly, James thought it was for him. It wasn't. Tina blew her nose, licked her lips sloppily and eyeballed the excrement. Then she tucked the rag into the folds of her purse and waited for James to say something. When he kept quiet she called him a fuck-knuckler again and spat on the ground near his feet.

James forced another batch of coughs free and looked for Green-eyes. There was no sign of him.

The fire seemed bigger.

And—

The demon was coming. James couldn't see it but he could feel it. Oh yes. The air had become as cold as winter.

It was time to get moving.

26

James limped down the street holding a hand against his forehead. As he glanced over his shoulder Tina hollered, "Hey asshole, whatcha doin'? Where ya goin'?"

She waddled after him. Her huge naked feet slapped the pavement and her nightgown flapped in the wind, but she couldn't bridge the ever-increasing gap that James was creating so she spun her husk in a circle yelling, "That's the driver! Stop 'em! Somebody stop 'em!"

Tina had become judge, jury, and would soon be executioner, if possible. James considered telling her to shut-up but it was too late, way too late. Several people were already upset, and soon they would gather in greater numbers—men, women, and children—pointing and shouting, alive with judgment and accusations.

With nothing to be gained by sticking around and arguing, James kept moving. He felt like a character from the Twilight Zone—the business-man singled out as a fresh meal, the housewife unlucky enough to win the lottery. It wasn't a great feeling.

Tina raised her hand in testimony, and with her index finger angled outwards she pointed straight at James. "He's responsible!" she yelled. "I know it! That's the guy! That fuck-knuckler is responsible for everything!"

James stopped and looked back, but only for a second. He eyed Tina. He eyed the crowd. The unruly mob seemed to be growing. There were twelve of them now, a perfect dozen. Plus another twenty were on their way. They looked like protesters, angry and upset with the situation. And they were protesters, although most of them had not yet realized it.

A lanky black man was dialing a number on his cell phone and two teenagers were looking at the fire, then at Tina, then at James. They seemed ready to fight. A woman had her arms crossed. A fat tattooed man rubbed his giant knuckles into an open fist. A boy wearing a t-shirt that said HUMAN KIND held a long stick. A dog barked and leapt from person to person. It was the same dog that James had almost run down. In the area behind the crowd a fire engine parked in front of the house. Firemen were unraveling hoses and scrambling about like troops.

And Tina stood in the heart of it all, yelling and pointing and steering the mob with her poisonous tongue.

James was beaten. He limped on, but where was he going?

I'm running away from here, he thought. Away from Tecumseh Street, the fire, and the swarm of people that wanted to see a good man hang.

But am I really a good man?

Up ahead, two police cars raced towards the scene.

James crossed the boulevard in front of them and limped over a well-kept lawn. He moved up a driveway, zipping past a tall wooden gate, which separated the backyard from the driveway. He shut the gate loudly. With his hands on his knees he breathed deeply and stole a moment. The August sun was baking him.

After James calmed himself he sized up the backyard. The yard was big and pleasant. A swimming pool sat between two rows of Easter Red Cedar trees, which were thirty-five feet high. Each row of thick evergreens was likely hiding a fence.

It would be tough to escape though those, James figured. Impossible, even.

On the other side of the swimming pool long, healthy grass was a day away from needing a cut. It was infiltrated by several flowerbeds, fountains, benches and statues. The statues appeared to be Italian in design. At the very back of the property line, which was a considerable distance away, a mid-sized fence divided the posh garden from a schoolyard. James understood why the fence was exposed. It allowed a nice view and made things less claustrophobic.

With school being out for another few weeks the schoolyard was quiet. Only scattered people could be seen: three twelve-year-old girls were grouped together—two blondes and a redhead. A skipping rope dangled from the redhead's hand; the blondes were bickering about make-up. Behind the trio, a small boy raced in circles on his bicycle. He sang tunelessly and couldn't have been more than five. There was an old man with a grey hat, which was pushed to the very back of his head. He sat on a bench reading the paper. His glasses hung off his large, age-freckled nose almost magically.

And that was it.

Okay, James thought. The schoolyard it is.

27

A man with dark hair and a strong upper body opened a sliding door at the back of the house. He held a margarita in a fancy glass and wore nothing more than a red-and-white striped bathing suit—if you didn't take into account the cherry patterned towel that was draped over his left shoulder. When he stepped onto the patio and noticed that he wasn't alone, his eyes sprung open. A healthy blend of irritation and embarrassment washed his face clean.

"May I help you?" The man said as he pulled his baby finger away from his tumbler in a feminine manner.

"I'm sorry." James replied. "But this thing is chasing me."

"Pfft. Of course it is." The unimpressed man rolled his eyes. It was clear that he didn't believe a word James was saying.

Then suddenly—as if scripted—cold air flooded the yard. Margarita-man staggered and his eyes watered. His mouth popped open and his towel fell from his shoulder. He screamed—not in pain, but in shock. The cocktail slipped from his fingers and the glass fell. It shattered on the stone patio, liquid sprayed, a slice of lime rolled, a straw went flying and ice-cubes bounced in the air.

The man—Stan was his name—stumbled against the side of the house and slid to the ground. His back scraped against the unforgiving brick, grinding a handful of skin free in a loosely curled ball. He toppled onto his side and reached for his legs. Then the skin around his knee wiggled and stretched. Blood sprayed into the air. As his meat was being ripped from his body and hurled across the deck, pain engulfed him.

The demon began crushing his throat.

Stan's eyes bulged and his feet kicked. He said something but the words were hard to make out. It sounded like 'save me,' or perhaps 'kill me.'

James covered his gasp with a hand. He didn't want more bloodshed. He wanted everything to stop, but what could he do? What would he do? A man was dying here, and he couldn't let that happen. Not after losing Joseph, and Penny, and Johnny, and the woman in the house, and her two children (or was it three?), and Sue, and the man he had run over with the car.

Oh God—

Did I run someone over?

Once he counted the probable death-toll, terror seized him.

How much time had passed since Johnny pulled the trigger? Fifteen minutes? Twenty? Jesus, thirty-five minutes ago James was ordering a pizza. How had things gotten so bad, so fast?

Everything was wrong today. Humanity, life, and the nature of things had all changed in the blink of an eye. What breed of world was this? Is anything possible? Is anything safe?

James staggered much like Stan had. He had no beliefs now, none he would truly stand behind and defend enthusiastically.

Logic and reason had fallen.

28

"Anne?"

"Yes. It's me." Anne took a deep breath. She felt like a phony talking to Debra with a pleasant tone—she hated this girl. Her son deserved so much better, if only he could see it. But, like most men, James was easily swayed by the charms of a smiling whore. And Anne didn't want to fight with this whore. Not again. She didn't want to spark new problems or fuel the old ones. She didn't have the energy. She didn't have the need.

"Do you know where James is?" Anne said flatly. "Is he with you?"

"No."

"Have you talked with him today?"

"No, why… is everything alright? Did something happen?"

Anne hesitated. A mother knows the difference between a rose and a thorn and Debra was no rose. She was probably lying. James was probably standing right beside her with his thumb up his ass, oblivious. "If he's there put him on the phone. This is important."

"He's not here. Why? What happened Anne? Is James hurt?"

With a deep breath, Anne began speaking. "There was an accident," she said, but then she stopped herself. She didn't want to cough up any details. Debra had a way of turning information into weaponry. Her tongue was a sword. Her thoughts were a verdict. "You haven't talked to James at all?"

"No. I'm just waking up."

"Oh."

"Anne, are you telling me that James was in an accident? Is that what you're saying? If it is, I'd like to know. I'd like to know if he's okay."

Anne tuned Debra out and watched Mathew's shallow breathing. The boy looked more research exploration than child, being held by tubes, cords, bandages and machines. He looked like something from Modern Science magazine.

"Oh, I don't know Deb. I'm at the hospital now, and I'm busy. I don't have time for details."

"The hospital!"

"Yes." Anne rubbed a hand across her face and discovered that she had been crying. She said, "Tell James to call."

"But I haven't seen him!"

"I'm sure you will," Anne said. She hung up the phone and closed her eyes, whispering, "You always do."

29

The demon showed itself. It was a foot-and-a-half tall; it had dark ears and long strangely twisted teeth. Its huge black eyes took one-third of its skull. Its thin fingers had far too many knuckles. Its arms looked like broken sticks, capable of moving swiftly. Turning its head, the demon's eyes widened. Its mouth opened. Then it snapped its mouth shut and disappeared.

Stan—the man who had wanted nothing more then a quick dip in the pool and an afternoon cocktail—screamed again. Something like a gulp was heard and Stan's larynx—along with half his thyroid gland—was pulled across the patio. His eyes rolled back and locked into place. His arms and legs trembled. His hands opened for the last time.

As far as James could tell the death toll had just reached nine (or ten…).

James ran past the pool, the Easter Red Cedar trees, the flowerbeds and the fountains. He ran to the back of the yard where the fence stood tall. He threw himself upon it and the metal cage shook back and forth, accidentally clipping his face. His fingers found openings and he pushed upwards. His shoes didn't quite fit the holes in the fence, but it didn't seem to matter. His tongue skimmed across his teeth; he could almost taste the iron-copper flavor of Stan's throat on his lips.

Or maybe it was the fence. His mouth was bleeding again.

James looked over his shoulder; there was nothing new to see. Nothing—but then Stan's wife Emily appeared at the door. She had an oversized t-shirt from Disneyland covering the top half of her green bathing suit. She wore lime colored flip-flops on her well-manicured feet. She looked at her husband, the corpse. His blood had grown into a thick puddle. Her eyes expanded, her face turned pale and her shoulders slumped. A lock of hair fell across her face. She stepped through the doorway and saw James crawling over her fence.

James wanted to explain. He wasn't a killer. He wasn't a sick, murderous fiend. It wasn't his fault. He would never kill anyone—ever. Honest.

Emily started to cry.

James crawled to the top of the fence. Cold, hard, barbs ripped his clothes and skewered his skin. Little dots of blood began forming on his shirt. He didn't care about the pain. He cared about escaping.

He tossed himself over the wire and landed hard. His knees gave and his legs crashed into his chest, knocking the wind out of his lungs. His arms spun in circles and he landed flat on his ass. Then he was standing. He limped across the yard, past the trees, the sandbox and the swings. He limped towards the school and noticed that the gymnasium doors were wide open. He wondered why, but didn't really care. Maybe they were airing the place out. Maybe they were moving new lockers inside, or getting rid of the old ones.

But if that was the case, why was the parking lot loaded with cars?

Without much thought he ran inside the school and he found himself standing in the middle of a girls' basketball game.

A whistle blew. From the stands, three hundred and eleven pairs of confused eyes turned towards him. A strange, uncomfortable silence came. Then the people started yelling. The competitors began complaining. The referee blew the whistle twice more and approached James with quick steps and a sour frown. When he spoke, James didn't hear the colorful words, only the angry roar of the audience.

James raised his hands in defense and opened his mouth. But again— what could he say? How could he possibly explain?

"Whadaya think your doin', huh?" a ballplayer said with a huff, looking down at James from six two.

"I'm sorry." James replied.

"Then get off the square!"

James began walking, thinking that the girl was perfect for Springer. She was sixteen, big and likely dumb as a stump.

"Okay," he said. "I'm going."

Fans began booing and people threw things—nothing big, just cups and stuff. It's the thought that counts.

Before long he was across the gym. He passed through double doors and made his way down a hall. He could see another hall and decided to turn left. But then came the shrieks and the screams.

He stopped cold and turned around.

The gymnasium doors blasted open and people poured into the hallway. Before long the hallway was loaded with spectators and ballplayers alike. Some people pushed in one direction, some in another. A woman tripped and was quickly trampled. Another got shoved into a water fountain.

Smart people hustled outside. Some wanted to see what was happening. These were the gawkers, the rubber-neckers, the idiots that created traffic jams every time someone had a flat. These were the local halfwits that could host a mob mentality in the blink of an eye. These were the people who watched seven hours of television a night and had a mouthful to say about everything; it was only a matter of time before they demanded answers.

54

What then? James wondered. Will they blame me for the horrors inside the gym?

The answer, of course, was yes. They'd blame him for everything they could. And if the mob had its way, he'd go home in a body bag.

A pair of teenage eyes caught his.

James had been recognized.

30

A girl with short pigtails ran past. James followed her into a crowd of hostile men, frantic ladies and crying children. He made his way outside and discovered car doors opening, engines starting and people driving.

He ran into the parking lot.

A young woman jumped into a car and slammed the door. She drove over a curb and onto the street. Other cars followed. A Chevy truck sped past a group of people and became locked together with a Sunbird in a congested huddle near the exit. A small accident occurred at the nearest intersection. Angry drivers jumped from their cars and shouted obscenities; the street became instantly impassable.

A few feet from the intersection two men began shoving. One punched the other. The other punched back. They began fighting. Another joined the battle before two brawlers—cloaked in the shroud of peacekeeping—stepped in, making matters worse.

A street-war was quickly brewing.

Then came screaming—not shouting, but screaming. People turned their heads. Mouths opened and eyes widened. A scattered few began crying. Some began praying.

A boy lying on his back battled something nobody could see. He was sixteen, maybe seventeen. His arms were swinging and his feet were kicking. He had blood on his face and terror washing across his features like water. One of his arms suddenly locked in place, high above his head. His face turned pale and for a moment things seemed surreal.

Then his arm snapped, people gasped. The arm snapped again.

Suddenly the crowd was moving away from the boy like a frightened herd. No one wanted to lend a hand; very few considered the notion an option.

James heard his cell phone ringing; he ignored it.

Then a man with a tattoo on his neck shook James with a strong hand. "You can come with me if you want," he said.

James nodded. "Sounds good."

The man sat down behind the wheel of a classic 1978, two-door Mustang. Without hesitation James tossed himself into the passenger's seat and they were off.

The man cranked the wheel and his arms flexed. The muscles on his tattooed neck bulged and the car spun ninety degrees. The car bounced over a curb; he drove through a soccer field. Tires shredded the lawn.

"My name is Nash," the driver said. He looked like a wrestler.

"I'm James."

"What happened back there man?" Nash said. "What the fuck is going on? I saw that woman getting killed in the gym... you saw that right? Oh man, that was so fucked up. I think her head twisted in a circle. Did you see that? How is that possible?"

James coughed and looked the man in the eye. "I don't know," he said. "Just keep driving. Don't stop."

They drove in silence for five seconds before Nash slammed on the brake. The lawn beneath the two back wheels tore apart.

"What are you doing?" James asked.

"You're that guy!"

"What guy?"

"The guy that ran into the gym! You're the one that made this happen!"

"No I'm not!"

"Yes you are! Look at you! You're him! This is YOUR fault!"

"No!"

"YOU'RE HIM!"

"No!"

"Yes!"

"Let me explain!"

"Fuck that," Nash shouted, pushing James with his large hand. "Get out! Get out of my car man! I don't want you here!"

"You've got to be kidding me!"

"Get out!"

"Wait a minute," James said. He could hear his phone ringing again.

"No! Either you get out or I'll drag you out."

"Just listen to—"

"NOW!"

"I'M NOT GETTING OUT OF THIS FUCKING CAR!"

Just as James screamed the window on the driver's side exploded. Glass flew like tiny diamonds.

Nash shielded his face and said, "What the fuck?"

The car leapt a half-foot and stalled. Then the invisible demon grabbed Nash by the hair and pulled him through the broken window; the shattered glass treated him poorly.

31

Anne called James one last time. There was no answer.

Calling him was pointless. He was probably sleeping or watching TV. Or maybe he turned his phone off because he needed time to think. Or maybe he was with the whore. She had no way of knowing and it didn't really matter.

She looked at Mathew, lying quietly on the bed. Had he really mumbled the words, 'Run, James?'

Yes, Anne decided—he had.

But did the words mean anything?

After a long while Anne decided no, of course not. The words didn't mean a thing. The boy was dreaming. That's all.

Mumbling 'Run, James' didn't mean anything she told herself.

And for the next while, she forced herself to believe it.

32

James ran across the schoolyard, leaving the man and his Mustang behind. The girls with the skipping rope watched him run. Heading straight for them, he wondered about the boy on the bicycle and the old man with the grey hat. Where had they gone? Were they at the school now? Is pandemonium a magnet for the flesh?

The redhead shouted, "What's happening?"

James dismissed the redhead and her friends and he ran past them. Then he realized that these girls would be the next people to die and he didn't want to have *that* hanging over his head. He had enough hanging there already.

James stopped running and turned around.

The girls stood together, watching the tattooed man being dragged— kicking and screaming—through the car's broken window. James wondered how the little creature managed to break the window and pull a grown man though it. But this question—like many others—would have to wait. Now wasn't the time for philosophy; it was time for action.

James screamed at the girls, "Get out of here, now!"

The redhead's mouth dropped open, and the taller of the two blondes began running towards the school. It seemed that running was exactly what she wanted to do. Her strides were long and powerful. She ran as fast as her little legs would manage, faster than James ever could. The other two girls hesitated for a moment before following.

"Thank God," James whispered, watching them move. And when he heard his cell phone ringing again, he decided to answer it.

33

"Hello?"

"Hey lover," Debra said, faking a sexy voice. "It's me."

"Shit babe," James said. "I can't talk now."

Debra's manner hardened abruptly. "Why? What's the matter? Are you at the hospital? Are you hurt? You're mother said you were in trouble."

James began limping through the schoolyard. He couldn't run; he wasn't even sure how he did it before. Adrenaline, he guessed. But his legs felt like they had been through a meat grinder, which was getting hard to ignore.

Needing an escape route, he explored his options: he could jump the fence again and return to Tecumseh Street, but he didn't want to be near the fire. He also didn't want to go near the school. That could only bring more bloodshed. So what was left?

James looked around. The girls were gone now and the tattooed man had stopped fighting. It's following me again, he thought. "Shit."

"What? What is it?"

"Debra, listen. I love you lots but I can't talk right now. I've got to get going."

"Where?"

"I can't explain. I've got to go."

"Come on James... tell me what's happening."

He walked faster. His eyes shifted left and right. Blood ran down his face and leg. "I don't have time for this, okay? Give me a break will ya?"

"Just tell me."

James huffed. "I can't."

"Why not?"

"Fuckin' hell. I love you, okay? I love you lots. But I can't talk on this fucking phone right now!"

Debra was infuriated. "Sure. Whatever. Don't tell me. See if I care... I don't. I don't care about us at all."

James hated it when Debra got her bitch on. It made him frustrated and annoyed. He said, "I don't know what to say Debra. People are being killed here; you get it? I love you but I can't talk right now so please stop being a pain in the fucking ass."

James killed the connection and slid the phone into his pocket, grinding his teeth as he did it. On top of everything else he was bitter now. He was bitter and aggravated by his domestic dispute. Sometimes that chick made him crazy.

He limped past a row of freshly cut shrubbery and over a small bridge. He followed a shaded path that led onto a street: Baldwin Street.

As he lugged his shoes along the sidewalk, a police car raced by him. He stopped walking; there was a decision to be made: if he walked straight he would move towards Johnny's house. If he turned right he would be heading towards home. If he turned left he'd move towards Debra's condo, the hospital, and the police station.

But did he want the police involved?

Getting help seemed right, but being held for questioning seemed wrong. And he'd have lots of explaining to do. What would happen then, he wondered—when the demon arrived at the police station?

"I'll die," he whispered. "And so will a lot of other people."

With a deep breath James turned right.

He decided to go home.

34

He managed to travel a half block on his wounded legs, before spotting a bicycle leaning against someone's front porch. It was a woman's bike with a purple basket on the front (which looked completely idiotic, in his book). The bike was just his size. He approached it optimistically before his heart sank like a stone.

The bicycle's frame was locked to a railing that was attached to the house.

James blew a breath of frustrated air and kicked the tire, knowing he couldn't steal the bike. Then he noticed a second bicycle lying on someone's lawn. With a great deal of haste James made his way towards it. Sure enough, the bike was unlocked. He grabbed the frame in his hands and lifted it to its wheels. The bicycle was a five speed. His threw his leg over the seat and dropped his foot on the pedal. With a push he was off, speeding down the road.

Theft was easy—nobody even noticed.

He hoped.

As James made his way home he could hear the sirens blaring. He wondered which disaster he was listening to. Perhaps it was a combination of both—the Tecumseh Street fire and the Dolan Street High School evacuation crisis. He found himself wondering how many police officers, ambulance drivers, and firemen had their hands full. All of them, he supposed—every last one of them.

Martinsville was not a big town.

35

A swarm of police cars surrounded his house.

Oh my God, James thought. *They've come for me… but how? Why?*

It was obvious. His car was embedded in someone's house, and the car had a license plate, and the license plate defined the owner, and the owner was…

"Shit!"

James squeezed the hand brakes and spun the bike around. Going home was not an option, at least not yet. So where could he go?

His first thought was Debra's condo. That's where he had spent most nights anyhow, but… no. He didn't want to go there. Actually he *did* want to, but that was beside the point.

He pedaled a little slower.

Where am I going?

In front of him was Cortez Street. He turned onto it pedaled hard as he could. The bike wobbled from side to side as it gained speed. Driveways, lawns, houses, and trees zipped by. Then he leaned back and let the bicycle coast. He could hear the hum of the tires rolling over the pavement.

Where am I going, he wondered again. What do I need? What do I want?

One thing James needed was a restroom. The pressure inside him was mounting. But what else did he need—a weapon?

Johnny's gun?

The idea of retrieving Johnny's gun was intriguing. But returning to Johnny's house didn't seem like much fun. *But,* he thought, *if I kill the demon everything could return to normal.* James shook his head. Normal. Yeah right. Nothing would be normal after this. He peddled again; he coasted again. When everything was said and done, James had some explaining to do. He had police to deal with and apologies to make. Not that saying 'I'm sorry' was an appropriate solution for causing a string of deaths. It wasn't. But still, what alternatives were there?

He rode another block and came to his conclusion: he would return to Johnny's house. Getting the gun was a good idea, he decided. Defending himself was a good idea. Having a destination was a good idea.

A plan had been set. He turned left on the next street.

36

A police cruiser approached from behind. Had James looked over his shoulder to see it, he would have panicked. His nerves were wound tighter then a drum core snare and the odds of him doing something incriminating were greater than he would like to admit. Luckily for James, he steered the bike to the side of the road and let the cruiser pass by. When it did, the sirens didn't spring to life. They stayed quiet. A moment later the car turned a corner and was gone.

I dodged a bullet, James thought. And he was right.

His description had been sent over the wire fifteen minutes earlier: James McGee. White male, 30's, 5' 10", medium build, short brown hair, white dress shirt, black dress pants, black dress shoes, black tie—last seen fleeing 276 Tecumseh Street on foot, which is located at the corner of Tecumseh and Spalding. Suspect may or may not be covered in dirt and ash, and may or may not be showing signs of injury. It is not believed that the subject is armed, but he is considered dangerous. Approach with caution.

The description was meticulous. And yes, he had dodged a bullet. Had the two officers in the police cruiser not been bickering as they passed by, odds were, they would have noticed and arrested him.

James stood up on the bicycle and he pressed hard on the pedals. His feet throbbed. The ground rushed beneath him. The wind pushed against his face and chest. He zipped around a corner, pushing hard as he leaned over the handlebars. A bug hit his knuckles as he went over the roll on a hill; he felt his stomach lift into his chest. He had always liked that feeling. It reminded him of being on a rollercoaster. He kept pedaling and his legs began to burn. He rolled over a sewer; the handlebars rattled and his feet threatened to slip from the pedals. He moved past a STOP sign that someone had vandalized. Now it said: STOP - EATING MEAT. Sitting on the curb not ten feet from the sign, three boys—all of them between five and seven years old—were wasting the day away. The boys stopped talking and watched James go. He offered them a smile. In return, a boy with spiky hair tossed a rock at him.

James turned corners twice more and peddled for three more minutes. Then he found himself on Tecumseh Street looking at police cars, an ambulance, and what he figured to be a car belonging to the coroner.

James stopped cold.

It was Johnny's house. The authorities had the place enclosed, but why?

Suddenly, James remembered the gunshot. Somebody must have heard the gun go off and called the police. Or maybe it was the pizza. He ordered pizza and gave the operator his name and address. Did he leave Johnny's door open? Did the pizza guy step inside?

Did reasons even matter?

James was the prime suspect in a string of deaths. Nothing else was relevant. Maybe it was time to come clean.

James put a hand over his face and rode away from the scene. He turned a corner and disappeared from view. Then he felt his muscles tighten. The stress was getting to him.

No, he thought. *Coming clean is a bad idea. The demon—*

James slowed down and looked over his shoulder. The demon was gone.

Holy shit, he thought. *I did it!*

With animated eyes James pedaled hard. For the first time all day he was smiling; he felt like he was in charge again. The sensation sparked an idea designed to put him in an offensive position. It wasn't a good idea. In fact, the idea was absolutely terrible.

He was going to Suzy's house to get the shotgun.

***

And in the hospital room Mathew whispered, "No."

But nobody heard a thing.

PART THREE:
BECOMING THE BEAST

37

James knocked two times, waited a few seconds, and was about to knock again when he experienced déjà vu. He felt like he had done this before, and he had—at Johnny's house. But this time things were different. For one, James didn't look fresh; he looked haggard and beaten, like he had strolled through a war zone on the way over. And James didn't feel the way he had this morning: numb. He felt energized, almost exhilarated.

As he waited, he noticed that Sue's lawn needed to be cut and her shrubs needed to be groomed. He wondered if the backyard was loaded with junk. It probably was. Instead of knocking a third time James opened the door and stepped inside.

"Hello?"

The house seemed to be deserted; he could hear the flies buzzing and smell the rotting meat. As he walked through the door he eyed the floor and the walls the same way Johnny had earlier. But there was nothing here this time—he hoped. And the house wasn't cold; the August sun had turned the place into an oven.

He walked through a near-empty living room and entered the kitchen. He found the refrigerator door wide open. On the counter he could see a stack of dirty dishes next to a basket of bananas, which had melted into rot and decay. On the floor several bags of garbage had been stacked into a pile. A dead cat lay facing the corner. It stank. Everything stank. Dishes on the dinner table sat beneath a stack of unopened mail. Flies crawled on top of everything.

He closed the refrigerator door, which was a big mistake. The flies became airborne and circled the room annoyingly. There must have been a thousand of them.

James walked down a hall and entered a bedroom. The room was completely empty.

Then he entered a bathroom and relieved himself. After washing his hands and face he checked another bedroom. The room had wall-to-wall furniture, reminiscent of Johnny's backyard. He wondered why, and then it came to him—Johnny didn't want to give the creature a place to hide. And neither did Sue.

The assumption was logical, but wrong.

Shaking his head, James entered another bedroom.

He found Sue, dead, as he knew she would be. The bullet had entered the temple on her right side and circled endlessly, never finding its way out. He wondered how it felt to have a bullet doing donuts inside your head as blood squirted into the air; he wondered how long she had managed to keep on living.

James rubbed his eyes. Of course, Sue's handgun was missing; Johnny had taken it. And the shotgun was nowhere in sight.

But James knew where to look; he had known all along.

It was time to check the basement.

38

James slid a hand along a dirty wall and found a light switch. After a single bulb came to life, he walked down an old wooden staircase, eying the ridged shadows that cut the rooms into sections. Even with the lights on the basement was dark. It was also damp, and gloomy. The walls were an off yellow color. The ceiling was oppressively low and a long metal heating duct weaved its way along it in the center of the room. As James followed the duct his stomach began to turn. The basement smelled like cheese that had gone bad.

At the far side of the room was a door.

James approached it covering his mouth.

He clicked another switch and the glow of sixty watts washed the room. He saw a workbench and some tools, a desk and a bookshelf, a small beer fridge and something that ran shivers up his spine and made him stand very still: three bodies were lying next to each other on the floor, each of them covered in a white sheet.

James couldn't pull his eyes away. The sheets were game-show mystery boxes, the answers to all his questions.

He lifted the first sheet and found Sue's sixty-year-old father.

The man had not been shot, but attacked. Half his face was missing. His skin color had changed from a warm coffee tan to a hard, moldy black. His single eye was swollen and closed. His lips had been torn off; his mouth resembled a large wormhole of broken teeth, tattered gums, and a thick web that housed a sack of spiders.

James imagined the body sitting up and grinning as tiny white arachnids scurried from inside its throat. He imagined the corpse gurgling, "It's not over. It'll never be over. Not for you James, not for you."

Feeling a moment of dizziness, James put the sheet over the corpse and placed a hand on a wall. A spider ran across his fingers.

He noticed a packet of shotgun shells sitting next to a pile of books. There were books on Voodoo, Bokor and Vodoun, two on Haiti witchcraft, one on Nkisi and several loose articles in a language he didn't recognize. He also spotted several seashells, cornhusks, an animal horn, and a large hoof, which was turned upside down and stuffed with black soil.

James turned away. His eyes narrowed slightly.

The spider was crawling up his arm now; he knocked it to the floor.

He looked at the bodies again and felt disgusted. He imagined the swollen eyes of the dead opening. He imagined the bodies standing one at a time, like something from a vampire movie—with arms reaching and faces white.

But the faces under those sheets aren't white, James reminded himself. They're black and moldy. They're covered with bugs.

A mouse scurried from one corner to another.

He followed the mouse with his eyes and noticed Suzy's shotgun sitting on top of a wooden box, just beyond the bodies. The box itself was large, two by three feet. He hadn't noticed it originally; the white sheets had overshadowed everything.

On the side of the box eccentric letters formed archaic words. They seemed antediluvian, like a bastardized version of Egyptian script. Below the mysterious markings in small faded letters were four words written in English: CONGO, BASIN, MINKISI and BAKISI. The words were burned into the wood. He didn't know what the words meant, but Congo—that was a river, wasn't it?

He reached across the desk, picked up a pencil and wrote the words on the back of an envelope. Then he stuffed the paper into his pocket, grabbed the shotgun and the shells and made for the exit.

39

James stood near the front door. He leaned the shotgun against a wall, placed the shells on the floor, pulled his phone from his pocket and dialed Debra's number.

The phone rang once.

"Hello?"

"Debra, it's me."

"Oh."

"Don't be mad."

"Why not? You called me a bitch. You remember that don't you?"

"No. As a matter of fact, I don't."

"Well, you did."

James shrugged. "Debra, listen to me. This is important, 'kay? My brother is dead and Penny is dead. Johnny's dead. And Sue's dead too… in fact, her entire family is dead."

"What?"

"Honest. I'm not kidding. I'd never make jokes like this. I couldn't talk earlier 'cause everything was going crazy."

"Joseph and Penny are dead? How?"

"Car accident."

"And Johnny?"

"He shot himself."

"Oh my God, why?"

"I don't know. Actually I do know, but I can't explain it now."

"Why not?"

"I just can't, it's a huge story that I don't really understand. I'll tell you everything I know later."

"Well… where the hell are you? Can you tell me that much?"

"I'm at Sue's house. I might stay here a while."

"Which Sue are you talking about? You don't mean—?"

"Suzy, the cute black chick. The one that throws those parties… you know who I'm talking about, right? We were at her place for—"

"The Christmas party! She has that little Siamese cat."

James nodded, thinking, *not anymore she doesn't.* "Yeah. That's her."

"Oh shit. She's dead?"

"Yeah."

"What happened? Did Sue kill herself too?"

"I think so."

Debra expelled a large mouthful of air. She was speechless. A moment ago she wanted to yell at James but now her thoughts were spinning. She still felt angry but she couldn't yell. Not now. She wanted more information.

"Oh man," she said. "This is bad."

James opened his mouth but said nothing. He wanted to explain—the car, the fire, the incident at the school, the disturbing things he had seen in the basement. But as soon as he tried to put his day into words, he broke down. Suddenly his chest was heaving and his bottom lip was trembling. His fingers strangled the phone.

"Oh my God, I don't know what happened," he said. Then he cried a few seconds, and in-between breaths he spat out, "My brother is dead and I don't know what to do!" After that, tears ran down his face and dropped to the floor like rain.

Thirty odd seconds passed before Debra said, "Shit baby, you're scaring me. Are you okay?" Her voice was calm and soothing.

"No, I'm not okay! Everything is so fucked up!"

"Have you called the police? They can figure this stuff out for you. If people are dead it's a police matter."

"I can't call them."

"Why?"

"They'll think that I did it!"

"That's ridiculous."

"No it's not!" James barked. Then he slammed an open hand against the wall. A photograph of Sue's grandparents rattled, threatening to fall.

Debra let him have his moment. When he was finished she said, "Why would the police think you're involved?" There was an uncomfortable silence followed by a moment of uncertainty. "Are you involved? Why are you at Sue's house?"

"Something is chasing me."

"What's chasing you? You're not making any sense."

"I don't know what it is... no... wait!" James wiped the tears from his eyes; he reached into his pocket and retrieved the paper that he had scribbled on. "I need you to check something for me."

"James, listen to me. I've got to ask you something."

"What?"

"Did you do something wrong? Tell me the truth, okay? I want to help you but I need to know what the situation is."

"No. I didn't do anything wrong."

"Honest?"

"Yes."

There was a pause in the conversation. "Okay then, I'm calling the police. It's for the best."

40

"No!" James barked.

"Why not?"

"Because the police will think I'm responsible! And..."

"And?"

The words got caught in his throat. He wondered if he should tell her. He wondered if he should explain.

"Who cares what the police think?" Debra said. "You didn't do anything wrong, remember? Just tell them what happened and sooner or later they'll believe you."

"You don't understand."

"Then explain, what don't I understand? What are you not telling me?"

James couldn't go on. He wanted to scream. He wanted to punch someone. He wanted to kill himself. "Fuck, Debra!" He screamed abruptly. "Don't call the police! I mean it!"

"You don't have to yell."

"But you're not listening to me!"

"Well come to my place so we can talk about it, alright?" Her words were soft like butter, like she cared a great deal.

James shook his head and hung it low. "Oh God, I don't know. You have no idea what you're asking."

"I'm asking you to come to my place. Is that so bad?"

"I don't know…"

"If you don't come over, sooner or later I'm calling the police. You know that, right? I'll have no choice."

"Debra, don't."

"What else can I do?"

"If you call the cops we're finished."

"Yeah right," Debra said, completely unthreatened.

"I mean it."

She wondered if he did. He probably was being truthful, but that didn't mean anything. She could always bring him around again. All she had to do was caress him physically and give him the affection he rarely received. He would come around, he always did. James was an easy instrument to play.

"Then come to my place and talk to me," she said. "I'll make lunch for the two of us. We can cuddle up on the couch and have a drink and find our way through this together, okay? Don't force me to do something we'll both regret, James. I want to help; you know that don't you? Please let me help you."

"Stay away from the bloody phone, is that so fucking hard?"

"You told me that people are dying. This is a police matter. You know it and I know it."

"Okay," James huffed. "Fine. I'll come over. But don't get mad when something bad happens."

"'Something bad' is not going to happen."

"You don't know that."

"Are you coming over?"

"I don't know."

"Are you coming, yes or no?"

James expelled a deep, displeased breath. "Okay, I'll come."

"That's all that matters."

"Alright, whatever. Whatever you want. We'll do it your way... we always do it your way."

"That's not true," Debra said, knowing that it was true. They always did things her way. She often wondered why he allowed it. She wondered why all her boyfriends allowed it. "Don't say that."

James felt conquered. "I'm sorry," he said. "I'm just stressed out and I've had a bad day, a very bad day. God. I can't even believe this is happening, and I need a favor. I need you to do something for me."

"Okay babe. Whatever you want."

"Is your internet working?"

Debra raised an eyebrow in distrust.

She wondered if someone had posted photos of girls-night online; she wondered what photographs had been taken. Had James seen something incriminating? Did someone write a party review on a message board? Had someone told him something? She hoped not. Sooner or later he'd find out the truth about her, sure. It was inevitable; it's hard to keep people fooled forever. And it was a full-time job. But she didn't want the relationship over. Not yet. Not today. She didn't want the relationship to be over until she had another man lined up. And she hadn't soured James completely. He was still good for a while; he could still buy her things and take her places. Plus, her condo needed to be painted and her bathroom could use a renovation. She wasn't finished with him yet. And he didn't make the rules, she did.

Cautiously, Debra said, "I think my internet's working. Why?"

"I need you to check something."

"Oh, okay. What is it?"

James unfolded the paper that was in his hand. He said, "Congo Basin Minkisi Bakisi."

41

James rode his bicycle with a loaded shotgun and a box of shells sitting across his lap. It was an awkward journey, but in time he learned to pedal comfortably and balance his belongings like an acrobat. He didn't rush; he didn't feel the need. Keeping aware, that's what was important now. Seeing things clearly was job number one.

A car turned a corner and trouble arrived, showing its face in the form of a woman: Tina Comfrey. He had met her earlier: she was the large woman in the overly frayed nightdress, the one that called James a bastard.

Passing James inside a Honda Civic, Tina shouted, "Stop the car!"

Without inquiring, the man behind the wheel did what he was told; he parked the car a short distance in front of James. He looked very bookish.

James predicted trouble and decided to face it head on. He stopped peddling and slammed on the brakes.

Tina stepped out of the car.

Her outfit had changed. It now consisted of Nike shoes, faded grey track-pants and an oversized t-shirt with the words NEW YORK CITY printed in glittery letters on the front. A fashion queen she was not.

"That's him." Tina said to the world. "That's the guy the cops are af-ter. I should know. I'm the star witness and I watched the bastard run away. This son-of-a-bitch should hang. Mark my words, he killed five people."

James was stunned; he didn't know what to do. Should he run? Should he hide? Should he try to explain himself? As he struggled for answers Tina said, "Hand me your cell phone Elmer. I'm callin' the cops on this asshole."

Everything became crystal clear: James was at war, and this was a war he could win. The aggravation that had been chewing a hole in his mind eased. He said, "You're calling the cops on me?"

"Of course I am. The cops are looking for you and I found you. You're a murdering prick. It's my duty."

"I'm not a killer," James challenged.

"Yes you are, and you're going to jail. That's what happens when you kill people and run away like a coward. You go to jail."

"That's not what happened."

"Yes it is. I should know. I saw it with my own two eyes. Mark my words, asshole, you murdered five people, and like it or not, you're going to pay for it."

James grinned. "You positive?"

Elmer handed Tina his phone nervously. He could feel the tension mounting, but he couldn't see what James had sitting on his lap. Neither of them could.

"Yeah," Tina said, hesitantly. "I'm positive… you're a killer all right, and I'm phoning the cops. What do you think of that?"

James dropped the bike and the ammunition together. The bike did that thing that bicycles do: it bounced and settled and the front wheel went spinning. The box of ammo broke open and shells spilled across the pavement. One shell rolled into the sewer. James raised the shotgun to his shoulder and walked towards the car, pointing the barrels straight at Tina's face. From less than twenty feet and closing the odds of missing his target were almost non-existent.

Suddenly Tina realized who was in charge here, and it wasn't her. She gasped at her new revelation and held the phone in front of her, proffering it to James unconditionally. It was a peace offering.

The man inside the car didn't move.

James saw the phone and the nervous look in Tina's big round eyes. He didn't care; he enjoyed watching her squirm. He bridged the gap between them until he was close enough to press the gun against her head, and then he forced her to step back.

"What are you doing?" Tina said. "You can't be serious! You can't shoot me! Tell me you're not serious!"

James grinned. "I'm a murdering prick, remember? It's what I do."

"No, no you don't, I made a mistake… that's all!"

"Oh, now you've made a mistake. Five seconds ago you didn't care what my story was and now you've found compassion? Now you're ready to talk about it? Is that it?"

"Yes! That's it, that's it!"

"No it isn't."

"Yes it is!"

"Fuck you."

Somewhere in the distance a dog barked.

Tina's eyes opened wider than before. She gained a deeper understanding of her predicament. "Oh God," she said. "Don't kill me! Please don't kill me!"

"But I've already murdered five people, remember? What's one or two more?"

"It was an accident, right? That's what you're sayin', isn't it?"

"No." James said, sarcastically. "You were right the first time. I'm a dangerous killer that needs to be locked away. You should call the cops. It's your duty—it doesn't matter what my day has been like. It doesn't matter what I've been through. As long as you do your duty, right? Is that the way it is? You don't care about me or my situation at all, do you? No, you don't. You don't care if my brother is dead, so why shouldn't I pull the trigger? You're not my friend. You don't care about me."

Tina began panicking. "What the hell? What do want from me? You drove a car into somebody's house! It's my responsibility to call the cops! People died! This is a job for the police! Everybody knows that!"

"Then why are you involved? Huh? Can you tell me that?"

Feeling almost embarrassed, Tina quietly said, "I'm the star witness. You know... I saw it happen. I was there first."

For a split second James felt bad. This was the biggest, most important chuck of worthless crap this woman had ever seen. And now, her good times had turned bad.

He considered letting her off the hook.

But then—

"No," James whispered. "No fucking way." He looked at Elmer. "If you drive away I'll blow her fat fucking head clean off her cow-shaped body. You understand me?"

"Yes," Elmer said with a smile.

"You sure?"

"Oh yes. You're the boss."

"Then wipe that stupid grin off your face."

The man in the car changed his expression and James looked Tina in the eye. "Move away from the car and hand me the phone."

Tina did what she was told.

"Well done. Now go get the shotgun shells for me... all of them. And you... stupid driver, make some room. I'm getting in the car."

42

James sat in the back seat on the passenger's side with his knees crammed against the seat. His feet hung down, not quite touching the floor. The nose of the shotgun sat comfortably on the headrest, snuggled against the back of Tina's head.

"Turn left on Baldwin Street," he said, and the driver followed the order. "What's your name?"

Tina turned her head and began to open her mouth.

"I'm not talking to you!" James said. "I know your name; it's 'Stupid Bitch Fatso Slut'. So shut your fucking pie-hole."

With the statement stinging her ears, Tina started to cry.

It wasn't long before James wanted to apologize, but he couldn't. If James showed compassion, weakness, or understanding, Tina would have James for dinner. He knew it. There were no equals in Tina's life. There were only those she dominated, those that dominated her, and a huge pool of unknowns that fit into one slot or the other.

"You," James said. "Driver. What's your name?"

"Elmer."

"Is that what your friends call you?"

"Yes."

"Okay. Listen up Elmer. Up ahead is a big condo. I want you to take me there. If you live around here you know the place I'm talking about. You also know busy that area can get. That little coffee shop has turned the street upside down. Some days it's like Manhattan. Point is… I want you to circle the block. Look for cops. Any questions?"

"No."

"Can you do this without forcing me to blow your wife's head off?"

"I think so."

"Great. The condo, you see it?"

"Yes."

"Okay. Good. Give me your wallet."

"Come again?"

"Your wallet, give it to me."

"Why?"

"Because I want it, that's why."

Debra's condo drifted past them. Elmer reached into his back pocket, pulled his wallet free and handed it to James. James took the wallet, opened it and quickly looked inside. Elmer had a little more than eight hundred dollars and a couple pieces of identification. Surprised by the cash, James slid the wallet into his front pocket. *Payday or rent day*, he thought. *It had to be one or the other.*

"I suppose you want my purse?" Tina said, unimpressed.

James shook his head. "Nope."

Tina shrugged, somewhat insulted.

James kept his eyes fixed on Elmer.

Elmer, James decided, was something of a mystery. He only spoke when spoken to and his tone never wavered. His age was hard to define. He might have been as young as thirty, or as old as fifty. His shoulders were neither broad nor wide. His face was slim. A clean looking moustache sat low on his lip. His dark hair had begun to recede, or maybe it had always sat high on his forehead, giving him a timeless look that worked very well with his demeanor.

"What do you do, Elmer?"

"I work."

"Where do you work?"

As if embarrassed, Elmer nodded his head twice and said, "At a coffee shop. Not this one here; I work just off highway nine."

"Coopers?"

"Yep."

"You the manager or something?"

"I'm the night manager."

"Shouldn't you be sleeping?"

"I've got a couple days off."

"I see. Is that where you met Fatso?"

Elmer drove the car around a corner and said, "More or less."

"Let me guess. She hung out there night after night, slurping coffee and eating donuts."

Elmer briefly closed his eyes. "Something like that, yes."

"She probably still comes by, is that right?"

"No. Not like she did before."

"Oh? Why's that?"

"She has bingo three nights a week and we have two children."

Tina shot Elmer a funny glance.

"Is that right?" James asked.

"Yes."

"And you're trying to feed a family of four, plus pay her coffee and bingo habit on a single salary?"

"Yes."

"Do you think that's fair?"

Elmer paused. "No. I guess not."

"Then why do it?"

"Because I have to, I suppose."

"Why?"

"For the children."

"Do you really think you're doing them a favor, keeping them locked in poverty and yourself locked in misery?"

"What else can I do? If I did anything else she would take the children away from me."

James nodded. "Yeah, this self-righteous bitch probably would. She'd probably go out of her way to make your life a living hell too. But you know what? You'd get your life back. And it wouldn't be long before your children loved you for it."

"Do you really believe that?"

James shrugged. No, he almost certainly didn't believe it. The children would likely be bitter and resentful, poisoned by every negative comment and emotion they were subjected to. And as the days went on, and she quietly and secretly pushed Elmer away from the family, they would probably blame him, forgetting about his love, his efforts, and what lay within his heart. They would become a tool of their mother's selfishness and never learn the truth about the situation.

"Do I turn here?" Elmer asked.

"Yes."

Elmer turned the corner and they drove a half block in silence. Then James asked, "Do you love her?"

"Yes," Elmer said without hesitation.

"No," James said with a soiled tone. "Don't feed me bullshit 'cause Fatso wants to hear it. Tell me the truth now. If you're lying, I'll pull the trigger. Don't think I won't."

"Okay."

"Do you love her?"

James watched Elmer's expression change. He looked like he was thinking. Finally, after a moment of thoughtful silence Elmer weaved the car around another corner and said, "I used to love her. But now... this is the way my life turned out."

"What made things change? Did she change?"

"No, I did. She hasn't changed a bit."

"Really?" James glanced out the widow. The streets looked good; he didn't see any police. "And how did you change?"

Again, Elmer was lost in thought. Then he said, "When we got together I was very lonely, and very unhappy. I was glad to have found someone. But now I think I'd be happier with this relationship behind me. I don't wish that her and I had never met... I'm glad we got together. It's just that... I wish I didn't have Danny and Beth to think about all the time. I've taken all I can from our relationship, and now it seems like I'm tied to it forever."

Tina was as cold as stone.

James said, "Danny and Beth?"

"My son and daughter. I love them so much. I don't want to leave them, and I don't want them sitting in the middle of a custody battle. There's no easy answer."

"How old are they?"

"Beth is six. Danny is eight."

"Where are they now?"

"They're gone to summer camp for the week."

"When will they be back?"

"Thursday."

Elmer drove past an old lady standing on the curb and around another corner. James was surprised to see Debra's building before them so soon.

"Stop here," he said. "We're going inside."

43

They sat in the car waiting for the people on the sidewalk to thin out. While waiting, James said, "Okay Elmer, this is the plan. I'm going to give you a set of keys." He reached into his pocket and pulled them out. "Here, take them."

Elmer opened his hand.

For the first time since James entered the car, Elmer's eyes met his. They locked. Both men were trying to read each other. With a smirk, James dropped the ball of unorganized keys in Elmer's hand, which Elmer immediately embraced.

"See the biggest key?"

Elmer looked into the ball. "Yes."

"The one that's twice the size of the others?"

Elmer shuffled through the set and held the appropriate key from the bundle. "This one?"

"Yeah. That's the one. That key opens the building's front door. I want you to get out, leave the car door open. , I want you to walk across the sidewalk to the front of the building. I want you to open the door with the big key. Once the door is open I want you to hold it and wait for us. Don't try anything funny or I'll shoot the stupid bitch in the head. Understand?"

"Yes."

"Now listen, Elmer. Maybe you're thinking that a shotgun shell in your wife's brain is exactly what your relationship needs, is it?"

"No. Of course not."

"Are you sure?"

"Yes. I would never think that."

"You better not, because if you do something foolish—Fatso won't be the only one dead. Oh no. I'll come hunting, and before you know it little Danny and Beth will be dead too. Their smiling faces will be splashed against the nearest wall and you'll be the one to blame. Not me. You. Get what I'm saying?"

"Yes."

"I have your wallet and I know where you live. And I'll murder them both without hesitation, first the boy, then the girl—one after another. I'll do it slow, and I'll make sure you're alive to know it."

"I'll kill you if you do."

James grinned. "I doubt it."

Tina squealed something incoherent. This prompted James to push the double barrel against her head with more force then he intended. Her neck snapped forward; it looked like it hurt.

"OUCH!"

"Shut up!" James said with an evil grin, really driving the boundaries of this 'character' he was developing.

As the bookish man and the slob woman waited for more instructions, James admired his own untapped acting skills, which were not bad for a beginner. If he were exploiting them on stage his friends would say he had a future. At least, that's what he was thinking.

The tough-guy image of Clint Eastwood came to mind, almost making James giggle. And that's who he was now, inside his own traumatized head: Clint fucking Eastwood.

In character James said, "I'm ready to kill you right now bitch, so shut your fucking mouth or I'll shut it for good!"

Tina whimpered.

Then James laughed. In a way, he felt amazing. He was living the adventures of the classic anti-hero. And everyone loves the anti-hero. If this were a movie the public would be all over it.

It could happen, James thought.

And even if it couldn't happen, James was beaming now. He failed to see that his thoughts weren't logical. They were his defense; he couldn't handle the situation. He had no game plan, only the odd play or two. And sooner or later (probably sooner) things would catch up with him.

Elmer watched James spinning his mental wheels and wondered if he had snapped. This notion didn't sit well with Elmer; it made him nervous. It made him think.

"So, Elmer," James said, rubbing his face. "Are you ready for this?"

Elmer said, "I think so." His tone was grave.

"You think so? You better know so brother. Are you ready for this shit or not?"

"Yes. I'm ready."

"Good." James turned his eyes on Tina. "Hey slut, you still with us?"

Whining, Tina said, "Yeah?"

"Good. You're going to stay right where you are until I tell you to move. Then you're going to open the door, slowly, without drawing attention. You're going to step outside. You're going to walk to the building in a calm and cool manner. Let me repeat that… a calm and cool manner. You're going to wait for me inside. Nothing else. If you decide to start yelling, or if you decide to run, or do anything you shouldn't be doing, I'm going to shoot you. And guess what? I'm not going to shoot you in the head. I'm going pump two shells into your back, halfway up your spine. Then I'll blow one of your hands off at the wrist and mail the fingers to your mother. Maybe you'll live, or maybe you'll die. But either way you'll spend the rest of you life with a broken back and a missing limb, wishing you had done exactly what I said. Do you understand what I'm telling you?"

"Yes."

"Do you have any questions?"

Expelling a giant mouthful of air, Tina asked, "Why are you doing this?"

Elmer closed his eyes and leaned back, thinking that James would pull the trigger. He didn't. Instead he made a sound like 'pfft' and said, "No you stupid cunt. Any questions regarding what I've told you?"

"No."

"Good. Elmer, open the door."

Without looking at Tina or James, Elmer opened the door.

"Now go."

Elmer stepped out of the car and began walking. He walked fast and thought about nothing. When he reached the building he slid the key into the keyhole and applied the appropriate amount of pressure. The lock turned. The door opened. Then with a nod of his head Elmer held the door, just like he had been told.

"Good." James said, turning his eyes towards Tina. "Okay slut. Don't fuck up. And remember, I'd love to blow a hole the size of my fist through your back, so don't do anything stupid."

Funny thing, he wasn't kidding.

44

Tina opened the car door and stepped outside. The street was clean and the stores were not quite busy. A few scattered people walked by, laughing and smiling, paying no attention to anything but themselves.

"Do you want me to close the door?" Tina asked, pushing the boundaries of acceptable behavior.

James pulled himself from the car and held the gun close to his leg. He recognized what Tina was doing. She was challenging his authority and it made him angry—very angry. He wanted to teach her a lesson. He wanted her head to explode like a popped water balloon and her blood to spray across the street. He wanted everyone she loved to see it and he wanted to laugh as it happened.

But that wasn't like him. That was sick.

After the malicious moment passed, James felt something churn inside of him. What was it? Fear? Hate? Guilt?

No, it wasn't guilt, but it was something like guilt. It was responsibility. And this responsible feeling, James feared, was something he'd experience again and again as the day moved on.

Getting the shotgun is a mistake, he thought. "Close the door, and don't look back. Keep moving."

Tina slammed the door and walked.

James felt another moment of bloodlust as he followed Tina with shifty eyes. He kept the gun low. Within seconds they were inside the building. James lifted his chin, informing Elmer to start walking.

Elmer walked quickly. The lobby was neat and clean. Small, metallic mailboxes cut the foyer in half. A stack of flyers and phone books sat near a bulletin board. And there was nobody around, only James and his hostages.

When they reached the elevator James said, "Push the button."

Tina reached for it and James rammed the shotgun into her back. "I'm not talking to you, bitch. I'm talking to him."

Tina, grim and humorless, moaned in defeat. Her arm fell heavy against her t-shirt and bounced off her gut. Elmer pressed his index finger against the white circular switch. From somewhere above, the elevator started moving. While the trio waited for the doors to open, James couldn't help feeling like he had regained some control over his life, even if things had taken an unexpected turn.

Then the door opened.

Ironically, a blonde woman in her early thirties was standing inside the elevator—challenging the very control James thought he had regained. She was tall, voluptuous and strikingly beautiful. A light colored blouse hugged the ample curves of her body. She wore a short brown skirt and tall chocolate boots. Her scent reminded James of cherries.

Inside the woman's hand a thin, black leash led to an energetic puppy. The puppy James recognized as a pug. James loved dogs, especially pugs. Seeing the dog made James want to reach down and make stupid noises that were guaranteed to get the animal excited. But instead of petting the pug and making friends with the woman, he played the only card that he had.

"Don't move," he said. "I'm not kidding."

The woman stepped back and looked at the gun that was pressed against Tina's back; her mouth dropped wide open.

The elevator doors began to shut.

"No!" James barked, pushing Tina forward.

Tina did what she had to; she moved through the doorway and pressed herself into the corner.

The elevator doors reopened.

James said, "Everybody in."

Elmer made his way into the six by seven cubical and turned around. The woman with the dog mumbled something, but before she could put her thoughts into words James interrupted her.

"I'm sorry," he said. "But you're coming with us." He put his foot against the elevator door to stop it from moving; he kept the shotgun angled appropriately. "Everybody turn around and face the wall. Elmer, move to the far side."

Elmer and Tina responded without hesitation, making it easy for James to enter. But the woman didn't move; she held her ground.

"Please mister," she said. "Please let me go. I didn't do anything wrong. This has nothing to do with me."

James said, "I know that, but I can't let you go. You've seen enough movies to understand… of course you have. But I'll tell you what… don't do anything foolish and I promise I won't hurt you."

"You promise?"

"Yes."

"Do you keep your promises?"

"Yes I do. The good ones, and the bad ones." James glanced at Tina. He wanted to shoot her, more now than before.

"What's your name?" The woman said.

James smiled. He didn't expect a question that was so direct, so revealing and dangerous. Because she was beautiful the question turned him on.

"James," he said. "My name is James McGee."

"My name is Mia Powell. And I won't do anything foolish. Just promise me…"

"I won't hurt you unless you earn it Mia. I give you my word, okay?"

"Okay."

"Now give me your phone."

"What?"

"A girl like you has an expensive cell phone in her purse and a lot of friends worth calling. I need to take the phone away from you. You can have it back when this is over."

"But I don't…"

"Either give me your phone, or hand me your purse. The choice is yours."

Mia thought it over. She reached into her purse and pulled out the phone. Grinding her teeth lightly, she handed it over. Then she faced the wall, feeling sick and defeated.

The puppy looked up at James with confused excitement. It licked its snout, wagged its tail and sat down impatiently.

James smiled at the dog, stepped inside the elevator and pressed the number five. The doors closed behind him. His thoughts shifted to Debra. *What will she think when I arrive with three hostages and a puppy?*

The very thought made his stomach flip.

Debra was a worrywart. Her condo was usually clean and organized. She was fond of simple situations that offered clear and apparent solutions. She enjoyed looking cute and feeling attractive, which wasn't easy. She wasn't a pretty girl but she dressed like she was. She acted like a princess. Stressful situations made her nervous and when she was nervous she became agitated and somewhat hostile.

James closed his eyes and took a deep breath, lost in his thoughts.

Debra was an ugly, hostile princess that was easily agitated and somewhat hostile.

Damn.

Walking into her condo with three hostages, a shotgun and a dog was going to do more than ruffle a few feathers. She was going to lose her fucking mind.

45

The elevator rumbled up the shaft and stopped on a dime. The doors opened.

James stepped halfway through the opening, pointed the gun at Tina's head and said, "Okay, one at a time. Mia, you first."

Mia turned around.

"Walk out slowly. Go to the railing. Stay there. Don't make me shoot the fat woman in the head."

"Can I ask you something?" Mia asked.

"Sure. Make it quick."

"Why are you doing this?"

"You wouldn't understand."

"Try me."

"I haven't the time."

"Come on, there's got to be a reason. Give me something. Anything."

"Something was chasing me. One thing led to another and here I am." The elevator door tried to close and James stopped it.

"What was chasing you?"

"I don't know. Now get the fuck out of the elevator and shut up, you're pissing me off."

Mia nodded and walked to the railing, which was seven or eight feet away from the elevator. Next to the railing was an open concept stairwell that led to the front foyer. It was ornamented with plants and windows. If Mia stood at the edge of the stairs and yelled loud enough half the building would hear. And if she decided to be brave and run down the stairs, it would take three seconds to be out of firing range, assuming James didn't follow and she left the dog behind.

Mia considered her options.

"Okay Elmer," James said. "You're next. Remember Danny and Beth now. You don't want anything to happen to them, so don't fuck around."

Elmer lowered his head and joined Mia at the railing. Being unfamiliar with the complex, he looked down the stairs, chewing over different scenarios in his mind. None made him feel comfortable, only anxious.

"Okay, Chubby. You're up."

Tina turned around. Both barrels were an inch from her face. She pushed the shotgun aside and said, "Why me, huh? Why are you always picking on me?"

James forced the gun back into first position. "Shut up."

Tina stepped into it, letting the steel touch her face. "No, really. How come I'm the last one out of the car, and the last one out of the elevator? How come the gun is always pointed at me? Why not Elmer? Or that girl you're drooling over? They're here too you know!"

"I said stop it!"

"No! You stop it. Stop harassing me. Go bother Tits for a while, would you? Maybe you'll get a blowjob out of it. Maybe you'll get laid. She probably likes that sort of thing but I don't, and I don't like being harassed."

"Shut the fuck up!"

"No! You shut the fuck up. You're always picking on me! It's not fair! In the car you had the gun against my head the whole time, and it hurt, and Elmer was driving. Not me. Why didn't you put the gun against Elmer's head, huh? He's got a good-sized melon, so why me? And you keep calling me names… you're not being fair you know. This is bullshit!"

Tina's voice grew louder; it seemed that she was calling his bluff.

James became nervous. He didn't know what to do and worst of all, Tina was right. He'd been riding her pretty hard; it wasn't anything personal, he told himself. He just didn't trust her. Tina was unstable; therefore she was the biggest threat. James was trying to control the situation. That's all. He was just trying to keep everyone in line.

"Now listen…" James began, as the elevator tried to close again.

"No! You listen. You started this. I was watching TV and minding my own business when you drove into my neighbor's house, remember? You remember that? This is your fault, not mine. I came outside to see what was going on. Is that such a crime? Is that so bad? No! It isn't! It's the same thing that you would do—the same thing everybody would do! This is such bullshit! Complete fucking bullshit! And get that fuckin' gun out of my face!"

Tina pushed the double barrel away a second time.

James tightened his trigger finger, shuffled back a few inches and regained his position. His heart was really pumping now; he felt nervous all over. With a tremble in his voice he said, "Get out of the elevator Fatty! Now!"

"No! And stop calling me names; I don't like it. My name is Tina, Tina Comfrey, not Fatty. And you're the fuck-knuckler, not me. You're the one that created this mess!"

The elevator doors tried to close a third time and James rammed his elbow against the door's rubber casing. Behind him, Mia and Elmer stirred.

James glanced over his shoulder. "Get out and shut up."

"No!"

"Get out. Now!"

"This is bullshit!"

"Out!"

"What are you going to do? Shoot me? I don't think so. I don't think you've got the stones."

"I said out and I damn well mean it!"

All at once (as if Tina had rehearsed this moment inside her mind) she started yelling, "NO! IF YOU'RE GOING TO SHOOT ME, SHOOT ME! IF YOU'RE GOING TO KILL ME, KILL ME! DO IT! DO IT NOW!"

"Get out of the—!"

"NO! I DON'T WANT TO GET OUT OF THE ELEVATOR! YOU'RE NOT BEING FAIR! YOU KEEP PICKING ON ME! I DIDN'T DO ANYTHING WRONG! I'M ONE OF THE GOOOOOD GUYS!"

"Get out—!"

"NO! I DON'T WANT TO!"

"Don't make me—!"

"FUCK YOU!"

Suddenly, Elmer's face tightened into a ball and he stepped forwards, screaming, "SHUT THE FUCK UP TINA YOU STUPID UGLY BITCH! YOU'RE PISSING ME OFF AND YOU'LL GET US ALL KILLED!"

James turned his head quickly, pinching a glimpse of Elmer.

Tina threw her hands in the air, shaking them like a football fanatic celebrating a touchdown at the Super Bowl. She screamed, "THIS IS TOTAL BULLSHIT! I DIDN'T DO ANYTHING WRONG! IT WAS YOU, NOT ME!"

And James tightened his trigger finger without noticing it. He was sweating now and felt hot all over. He knew Tina was stupid but my God, he didn't expect her to be so stupid. She was being absolutely fervent. This was off the hook.

Under duress, James stepped back a little further; he kept his foot in the elevator doorway. He looked at Elmer for support, but Elmer couldn't help him; he couldn't control Tina. Not when she was like this.

And Elmer was very close, too close. If he wanted to make a move the odds were in his favor now.

The elevator doors tried to close again.

James was terrified now. He had lost control of the situation and something bad was about to happen. He could feel it. Even the dog could feel it—and it barked. Once. Then twice. Then the dog was barking.

Mia shuffled her feet in an attempt to calm the animal down. She said, "Quiet, Bully!" But it didn't work.

Bully didn't care what Mia wanted and Bully didn't want to be quiet. The dog was acting on instincts now, and trouble was brewing.

The dog barked, Mia tried to stop it, sSweat began beading on Elmer's long forehead.

James squeezed the trigger a little more than he intended and Tina screamed, "NO! IT'S NOT FAIR! IT'S NOT FAIR! YOU'RE NOT BEING FAAAAAIR! THIS IS BULLFUCKINGSHIT!"

James felt dizzy. Each moment was louder then the moment before it. He heard the ringing of a thousand telephones in his ears. He heard a child screaming.

He whimpered under his breath, and said, "Oh shit."

And finally, when he could take no more yelling, no more barking or fighting or ringing or screaming, no more chaos, no more turmoil or commotion, he closed his eyes and did something bad, something he didn't want to do, something he didn't think he would ever do—something exceedingly violent.

And part of him loved it.

46

Mathew let go of a green balloon and fell though the sky forever; he feared that all was lost. But when the forever had finished, his falling turned to drifting, and drifted became floating, and floating led to walking.

He walked through empty spaces and blank landscapes. He walked through sunless days and moonless nights. He walked across plains of nothing and barren wastelands. He walked a thousand years. He walked for hours. He didn't walk at all. Time was askew; it meant nothing.

And all the while, his thoughts were beset by the demon with the black glistening skin and large soulless eyes.

It had infected his Uncle James; he knew this now. But James didn't. James—who was on the brink of a terrible mistake he could never undo, a mistake that would lead him to madness—had no idea that he was infected. But he was. He was filled with shades of the demon's rage, the demon's thoughts—the demon's curse. It coursed through his veins like hatred. It poisoned his mind like vengeance.

Mathew had to stop it.

He walked across farmlands with no crops and roads with no traffic. He walked through forests with no life and swam across oceans with no waves. He walked though winters without frost and summers without heat. He crossed rolling hills and empty cities and desolate towns.

He then came to a place of great walls, a room in the center of a world filled with nothing. The walls were higher than any he could have imagined. They were higher than his eyes could see. They were higher than the sky. They were higher than time.

There was a phone.

There were thousands of them.

Mathew was inside a giant room of phones, a sea of phones, a world of phones, and all of them were ringing. He lifted one and screamed into it, knowing it was too late.

But maybe it wasn't.

Maybe James would hear.

Maybe James would understand the ringing.

47

With arms waving madly, Tina prepared her lungs for another outburst of yelling. Her eyes were closed now, squeezed together like a pair of fists—not that it mattered much. A blanket of red was all she could see. The shapes and angles of reality had faded, leaving Tina alone with her fury, her wrath, and the pounding of her over-sized heart. This was her time to shine, her moment of truth, the climax of her dreary and uninspired life.

With grinding teeth and flexing strength, James stepped into the center of the elevator. He shifted the shotgun inside his hands. He tightened his fingers and raised the gun like a baseball bat. He arched his back and swung.

Both barrels of the weapon scraped along the elevator wall, digging a groove into the steel. Iron hit flesh. Tina's head slammed back. A river of pain rushed through her nervous system, causing both of her eyes to pop open and both of her hands to jerk away from her body. A thousand tiny droplets sprayed into the air like a red mist. Her jaw split wide enough to allow fragments of shattered teeth to roll through it. Blood splashed against the wall in an upward line.

Mia and Elmer gasped.

James grunted—thinking again that the shotgun was a mistake.

Tina fell to the ground like a sack of wet laundry, making a two hundred and sixty-five pound PLUNK on the floor. The elevator bounced beneath her. A second slipped by, and then she screamed a chain of screams. Her voice was no longer hoisted in spoiled brat rebellion, but lifted in pure, incontestable agony. And with each horrific scream a gush of bloody gore ran down her face, and through her jaw, and over her fingers, and across her hands, and along her arms. Her rebellious nature had been cuffed. She looked like she was drowning.

Elmer decided to run. He took a couple quick steps towards the door that led into the 5th floor hallway. He grabbed the doorknob and pulled. The door opened an inch and slipped from his fingers. A second later the door clicked shut. As Elmer fumbled for the knob a sad, faint groan escaped his lips.

The elevator doors began closing.

James spun around, pushed the doors apart and stepped out of the elevator. He re-adjusted the shotgun and pointed it at Elmer. Then at Mia—she had not budged an inch.

Both Elmer and Mia froze.

James screamed, "Don't move!" Spit sprayed from his lips.

Mia said, "I didn't."

Suddenly the door that Elmer had been toying with flew open and a man emerged. He wore black pants, black boots, and a black and grey dress shirt. He had a little potbelly and long sideburns. His dark hair was slicked back in a crooner's fashion. He looked like Johnny Cash.

Unfortunately his abrupt entrance was unanticipated.

It made James flinch.

And pull the trigger.

48

From inside an ocean of telephones, Mathew looked up. The massive walls that were higher than the sky began crumbling. Huge chunks of brick—the size of football fields—started to fall.

The phones stopped ringing.

And Mathew ran.

He ran through the sea of telephones. He ran through desolate towns, empty cities and rolling hills. He swam oceans with no waves. He traveled forests without life. He ran though summers with no heat and winters with no frost. He ran through roads with no traffic and farmlands with no crops. He ran over baron wastelands and across plains of nothing. He ran through moonless nights and sunless days. He ran over blank landscapes and empty spaces. He ran a thousand years. He ran for hours. He didn't run at all.

Time was askew. Time meant nothing.

All was lost.

49

The shell ripped a good-sized hole in Cash's front and a massive opening in his back. Parts of his stomach and spine slammed against the freshly painted brick, which seemed to explode. He stumbled against the wall with a squeal and a gust of red mist spewed free.

Mia screamed and Bully barked non-stop.

Elmer reached for the door, which had just begun to close.

And James turned towards Tina. His thoughts were blackened and glistening with ancient evil. He pumped the chamber and pulled the trigger again.

Somewhere inside his mind he could hear the word 'wait' being said over and over again. . WAITWAITWAIT-WAITWAITWAIT… But it was too late. Another explosion happened inside his hands, accompanied by a second deafening blast.

The shell caught Tina just below the chin. The top half of her neck was destroyed and her head fell back; it hung by a loose thread of skin.

Then James spun around shouting, "Stop!"

But Mia and Elmer were not listening; they were escaping. They ran through the doorway and down the hall. The dog followed.

James didn't.

He watched in horror as headless Tina fell onto her side like an over-turned keg. Blood and bone fragments poured from the stump of her neck and along her shoulder, creating a pond on the elevator floor. Her legs twitched. Blood dripped from the ceiling. Her fingers curled as if the loss of body fluids had dehydrated them.

Then Johnny Cash's legs finally buckled and he slid along the wall to the floor. He was done breathing, done holding his position.

James stood between the bodies like an executioner.

Somewhere in his mind the word 'wait' had vanished; it was replaced with four new words: What-have-I-done? What-have- I-done? What-have-I-done?

But the answer was simple. The answer was double murder.

50

James didn't mean to pull the trigger and kill the man that looked like Johnny Cash. And although nobody would ever believe him, he didn't mean to kill Tina either. In fact, it wasn't even him—it was his character. It was Clint Eastwood.

It was...

No. These were lies.

He had killed two people within two seconds (and liked it). He had taken hostages (and liked it). He had made threats (and liked it). He had talked tough and acted tougher (and liked it).

James was no longer an innocent victim trapped in an uncompromising position. He was a criminal. He was armed and dangerous. He had a smoking gun in his hand and dead bodies at his feet. His victim's blood speckled his face.

How apparent can a situation be?

And how the hell did this happen, James wondered. *And why?*

Answers, the new killer feared, were just around the corner of his mind. He figured he knew why he did the things he did, and how he arrived in this predicament. But he didn't know he was infected. He didn't know that the demon's thirst was coursing through his veins.

After being pushed, I pushed back, he thought. *Simple as that. And now there's a decision to be made.*

Was it time to break down, or time to be strong?

It was decided.

He would be strong; the price tag was half his sanity.

***

The elevator doors closed and gears started rumbling. Tina's corpse was changing floors.

James opened the door that led to the hallway and was surprised to find Elmer running towards him. When Elmer lifted his head he saw James grinning like a maniac. Without pause he stopped running and turned away.

"STOP!" James shouted.

Elmer stopped.

James walked like a gangster, with long easy strides. "Where's the girl?"

"I don't know."

"What do you mean 'you don't know'? She was with you."

"Yes, but we got separated."

"How?"

"I don't know, apartment doors were opening and closing. She ran inside one of the apartments, I guess. I would have too but no one would take me. People thought I was dangerous and they slammed the door on me."

"Which door did Mia enter?"

"Where's Tina? Did you shoot her? Did you kill her? Oh God, you did—didn't you? You killed my Tina!"

"Which door?"

"I don't know!" Elmer moaned. "I was over there at the time!"

Elmer pointed down the hallway with a steady hand. When James looked, several inquisitive people closed their apartment doors in fear.

"Fuck," James said. He rubbed a blood-speckled arm against his face. "Give me the keys."

"Where's my wife? Is she dead? She is isn't she?"

"Give me the fucking keys!"

"What?"

"The keys. Give me my fucking keys. You still have them."

"Oh." Elmer reached into a pocket and pulled the keys out; he held them up.

"Thank you." James said, taking the keys and stuffing them away. After a brief silence James said, "You can go."

"What?"

"Fuck man, do I have to repeat everything? Go on. Get out of here. Run, you stupid fucker, run. You're free to go."

Elmer turned and walked down the hallway.

James lifted the shotgun and aimed it at Elmer's head. But he didn't pull the trigger. He wasn't that far gone yet.

But he soon would be.

51

As James stood at Debra's door, the hallway seemed different. The walls looked darker, and felt closer. The ceiling appeared to be falling and he could hear the bugs scurrying behind the walls, he could smell the town's decay; he could taste the blood of his victims.

And of course, he liked it.

But that was wrong.

James turned the knob. The door was locked. He pulled the keys from his pocket, riffled through them and opened the door.

Debra stood near the balcony with a cell phone in her hand. She was getting ready to dial. She wore a low-cut blouse, tight jeans and big black boots. Her makeup was impeccable.

"Hi babe," James said, grasping at the ordinary, grasping at his sanity. "I'm here."

There was a moment of silent confusion.

"What's happening?" Debra asked.

Then she noticed the gun, the blood, and the look of bewildered terror that had set up camp on James' ashen face. She noticed that his tie had small holes in it and hung loose around his neck. She noticed that his untucked, mottled shirt was open at the throat, with buttons missing at the top. Dirt and ash stained his fingers, hands, and clothing. His shoes looked like they had been on fire. His hair was matted with blood and filth. Debra noticed it all.

"My God," she said. "What happened?"

James considered walking onto the balcony and throwing himself over the rail. "Oh man…"

"James… what did you do?"

James moved towards her, cautiously. He wondered if Debra was a good person. It occurred to him that she probably wasn't. He thought about killing her. He placed the shotgun on the table and sat on the couch with his head down and his shoulders slumped. Then he said, "I shot somebody."

"But why James… why?"

James took a deep, uncomfortable breath. He glanced at the balcony and grinned. "Debra, I'm in trouble."

Debra placed the phone on a table. "You shot somebody? What the hell are you talking about? Why would you do that?"

"I don't know."

"Why did you come here?"

James looked her in the eye. "You told me to come here."

"Yeah, but not like this. Not with a shotgun in your hand. Look at you. You look like hell. What happened?"

"I was in a car accident."

"So you shot somebody? Why'd you shoot somebody?"

"I don't know… it wasn't like that."

"I've called the police you know, just now. They're on there way here."

"Oh God," James said. He put both hands over his eyes and began to cry. "I told you not to call…"

"Well I'm not the first person to call the police so don't get like that. The lady on the phone told me that the police had already been dispatched. Everyone in the entire apartment has called the cops by now. Was that you shooting a gun out there? It was, wasn't it? Wasn't it?"

"I told you there'd be trouble." James said. He began shaking all over. His eyes were wild and distant. "Oh man, I've got to get out of here."

Debra walked across the room, looking at the floor as if a solution had been typed across the hardwood. "Fuck, James!" She screamed, feeling tears of fire surface beneath her lids. "I fucking hate you right now!"

"I'm sorry!"

"Bullshit!"

"No, not 'bullshit'! I'm sorry, I really am!"

"Did you say you were in a car accident? Did people get hurt?"

"People died. I told you that."

"So you decided to kill someone, because of a car accident? Why are you here? What the fuck do you think you're doing?"

James got off the couch and walked towards the refrigerator. He opened the door and drank juice from the spout (Debra hated it when he did that). He dropped the empty carton on the counter (Debra hated it when he did that too) next to an ashtray and a couple of empties. He wiped his mouth and entered the bathroom. After splashing water on his face he stepped out of the room and pulled his phone from his pocket. He turned it off and slipped it away. The last thing he needed was a call from his mother.

Right now he hated his mother, that bitch needed to die.

"I've got to get out of here," James said. He ran his fingers through his hair. "If you love me, you'll come with."

"Are you out of your mind? No fucking way. I'm not coming with you. I want no part of this. I can't become a fugitive, you idiot. I just can't."

James nodded in frustration. Again, he thought about killing her. "Okay. But I've got to go."

"That's not fair to say, you know. 'If I love you, I'll go with you.' It's not fair at all."

"Okay. Fine. I don't have time to fight about it."

"You shouldn't say things like that."

"Debra, not now. Please."

James took the shotgun from the table, noticing the evidence of girls-night. He swooped in and gave Debra a quick, awkward kiss on the cheek and ran a hand along her back. He needed affection so badly it hurt.

Debra pulled away—disgusted by his touch, his filth and the things he'd been saying.

James cleared his throat. "How was last night?" He asked.

Debra forced a half-smile. "It was fun, you know, nothing special."

James nodded and made his way to the exit shaking his head in despair. As he stepped into the hallway, Debra realized he was hurting in a way she never had, and she felt herself softening.

"James?"

"What?"

"I love you."

"Yeah?"

"Yeah. Of course I do."

James felt his eyes flutter. It was exactly what he needed to hear. "I love you too."

"Be careful, okay?"

"Yeah, okay."

"You should turn yourself in. You know that, right?"

"Maybe."

"No, not 'maybe'. Definitely. You should turn yourself in and bring an end to this."

"Okay. If you say so."

"Will you?"

"I can't. At least, not yet."

Debra nodded. "Listen… if you want to get out of here before the cops get you, take the stairs to the basement and cut through the parking garage. It's the only way you'll get out of here now."

"The stairs, huh?"

"The stairs to the basement. Nasa Street will be much better than Baldwin Street. Promise me?"

"Alright. I promise."

"Be careful."

"I will," James said. Then he closed the door, disregarded her words, and headed for the elevator.

52

James walked quickly with his gun held low. Many residents watched him through peepholes. One man watched through an open door, and another stood in the hallway, leaning against the wall like his body had turned to stone. If James looked at the man directly he would have seen color drain from the man's face. But James didn't look. He passed without a glimpse and opened the door that led to the elevators.

Two middle-aged men and a young woman stood around Cash's corpse. The woman was crying and her body trembled. The men talked with stern, despondent emotion. When they saw James the conversation ended.

James said, "Get the hell out of here or die." And they were gone. He pressed his finger on the elevator button and waited patiently, not looking at the man he had murdered until his morbid curiosity got the best of him.

The pool of blood that circled Cash's body was enormous.

The empty elevator arrived. James stepped inside and pressed the LOBBY button. The doors closed. When they opened again twenty-one people were standing before him, trying to understand why there was a woman with no head inside the building. Some looked excited, some looked disgusted and others seemed downright horrified.

James raised the gun and moved it from left to right, putting everyone in the room in danger.

An old woman who was standing close to James shrieked. Then she fumbled into the arms of a young man. The young man pushed her away and made for the door. Somebody yelled. Somebody shoved somebody else. People started cursing and scrambling and soon enough an exodus was underway. Ten seconds later James was alone, or so he thought.

The other elevator was out of service and the doors were locked open.

Inside the elevator James found Elmer on his knees, holding Tina's headless body in his arms. He had blood up to his elbows and a strange look on his face. If anything, he looked like he was yearning.

53

Elmer's features grew cold. "You bastard," he said, letting Tina drop. "How could you do this to my wife?"

"You never loved her." James replied, knowing his excuse was pathetic at best.

"Yes I did—and even if I didn't that's not the point. She was another human being for God's sake. What kind of monster are you? Where's your heart?"

"Give me the keys."

"You killed my wife!"

"The keys, now!"

"I already gave you the friggin keys."

"Not my keys, *your* keys."

"My keys? Why?"

"I'm taking your car."

"Fuck you."

James was surprised to hear Elmer stand up for himself; he was stronger than James had considered. It was an admirable quality, but Elmer's car was something James needed and acquiring it was a non-negotiable state of affairs.

"Elmer, listen."

"No. You listen. You've—YOU KILLED MY WIFE! How could you? How?"

James glanced at the crowd of people that was staring at him through the large tinted windows. He wondered what it would be like to start picking them off with the shotgun. It seemed like fun. "I have no time for this," he said.

"I really don't care."

"But the police are coming, and—"

"So? I want them to come. Don't you know that?"

"Elmer, give me the keys!"

"No."

"Now!"

"Go fuck yourself."

James lifted the shotgun. He pumped the chamber and aimed both barrels towards Elmer's chest. "I let you go man. Don't be difficult. Please… I'm trying to be a nice guy here. And I don't want this. I don't want to hurt you."

"Are you kidding me?"

Yes, James thought. I am kidding you. I want to murder you right now you bookish little small-dick fuck. I want it so bad I'm getting an erection. "Just give me your car keys and I'll walk away."

"You murdered my wife! Does that sound like something a nice guy does? You've got to be joking! You're not a nice guy… you're a psycho!"

James tried to say something but couldn't.

Elmer was right.

James wasn't a nice guy now. Maybe at one time he had been nice, like back in high school, or when he worked at the daycare center in his neighborhood. But that was a long time ago and he was a different person then. He was a guy without bills, a guy without debt, a guy without a string of cheating girlfriends under his belt; he was someone who trusted his friends and believed in people—but not now. Now he was jaded and cynical, now he was an adult.

"You're right," James said. "Murder isn't something that a nice guy does. But that doesn't mean I want to hurt you. I just want out of here. So give me those keys—"

James heard a siren.

It had taken a while, but the police were finally coming: it seemed the boys in blue had been sliced pretty thin today.

"Elmer," James said. "I'm going to shoot you and take the keys. Is that better somehow? Is that what you want?"

"Go ahead, shoot me. I don't care anymore."

"I'm not kidding."

"Neither am I."

James felt the muscles in his hands tighten and the gun shook apprehensively. He got into character and said, "Okay you stupid fuck. Change of plans. You're going to get up, go outside and drive me where I want to go."

Elmer laughed out loud, without a trace of happiness or enjoyment in his voice. "I'm not doing that," he said. "Why would I do that?"

"Because I have your wallet, and your address happens to be in it. And if you don't I'm going to murder you and your children."

Elmer could hear it—James sounded different this time, more serious, more insane. Elmer was at a loss for words. He wasn't so sure of himself now, or convinced that James was bluffing.

"You wouldn't," he said.

James unleashed a wicked grin. "No?" He asked, almost chuckling. It was clear: his sanity was slipping. "Why don't you take a good hard look at your stupid fucking wife? Maybe you should reconsider what I may or may not do. I loved killing her. I wish I could do it again."

Elmer looked at Tina, and the empty place where her head had been. He looked at her lifeless hands, the lumps of meat on the floor and the wash of blood that had sprayed the walls.

He was beaten.

Elmer made for the exit. His expression suggested that he was no longer interested in arguing, no longer interested in making a stand. The time for bravery had come and gone it seemed, leaving Elmer with nothing but the memory of failure.

54

As the two men got into Elmer's car a huge, voiceless crowd watched them leave. They stood—men, women, and children alike—around Elmer's vehicle in the shape of a horseshoe. They resembled spectators at a concert, where only the musicians and crew were permitted access to the performing area.

The performing area in this case was not the stage, but the vehicle, the open road and the faceless, inexhaustible journey.

Most people in the crowd took note of the car, the man with the gun, and/or the hostage. Many tried to snatch a glimpse of the license plate. One man even put his hands against the passenger door and his face to the glass. But no one tried to stop James, or question him with any sizable authority.

They weren't completely voiceless however—the crowd that is.

There was an underlying continuous murmur, the odd grunt, a rustling of feet and a hushing of lips. There were sirens in the distance, a child saying he was hungry and a woman asking a stranger, 'What's going on?' Another woman was caught in an annoying bout of muffled sneezing, and on the far side of the street, in a shop that sold t-shirts, glittery belts and other teenage-friendly items, a radio played Led Zeppelin's 'When the Levee Breaks' through a pair of small speakers with no bottom end. John Bonham's booming bass drum was lost in the mix. And finally, high above Debra's building—a commercial airliner ripped the sky in half with its blaring, knife-like, mechanical noise. The reverberation blanketed all other sounds nicely.

James looked at the horde and felt ashamed of them. Why didn't they say something? Why didn't they do something? He wondered if he'd be brave enough to stand against a madman with a shotgun if the situation had been reversed.

Not that he considered himself a madman.

Elmer put the car into gear and pulled away from the curb. He drove for a block and then turned left; people watched him go. He was heading for the highway, following all the rules and regulations commissioned in the International Navigational Rules Act of 1977. He drove without instruction, which was fine with James who hadn't quite figured on a destination.

After three green lights in a row, Elmer and James approached a poorly designed on-ramp, the kind that forces cars on the highway quick. Leaning on a yellow guardrail at the side of the ramp was a good looking man with a cigarette. The man saw Elmer and lifted a hand.

"Steel," he said with a rough voice. "Over here!"

Elmer spotted the man, nodded and cloaked a smile.

I'll call him later, he thought.

Elmer, who continued being a mystery, intrigued James. He showed signs of strength and courage in the face of death. And now a man with a cigarette calls him Steel. Why? Was this a reference to Superman, the Man of Steel? Ageless Elmer—with his odd-looking mustache and his long forehead? Really? Or was the nickname a jab, an inside joke. Perhaps it wasn't Steel at all—but Steal. Was Elmer a thief? Was Elmer a criminal?

While James chewed over the possibilities Elmer pushed a CD into the stereo slot. James recognized the band immediately. It was Slayer, 'Reign in Blood'. For some reason the music made James feel nervous.

"West?"

James shrugged. "Slayer huh?"

"Yep. The highway is here. You wanna go west?"

"Yeah, sure. West is good. There's nothing east."

Elmer turned onto the highway.

"You're a strange one Elmer, you know that?" When Elmer didn't respond James said, "Why did that guy call you Steel?"

"Is that what he said?"

"Yes."

"I have no idea. I don't know the man."

"But you nodded."

"It was a reflex," Elmer lied. "I've never seen him before in my life."

As James ran a hand across his chin, Elmer grinned like a shark—he loved lying. It was his greatest skill.

Needless to say, Elmer knew the man with the cigarette; he knew him well.

The man was Donald Markus McGivney. Until the age of fourteen, his friends called him Don. Then Don became Switch. He earned his nickname skateboarding in reference to a trick he mastered.

Elmer lived with Switch for two years; they had lots in common. They both liked boxing. They both liked women.

They were cellmates in prison.

They both committed murder.

55

Patricia walked into the hospital room and said, "Mrs. McGee, there's something you need to see.

Anne looked at the nurse apprehensively.

What is this? she wondered. This didn't seem like the same girl that brought her cookies and tea. She acted different and looked like she had been sucker-punched with a shovel.

"What is it dear?" Anne said. "Is something wrong?"

Patricia turned the television on and skimmed through the channels. Then she stopped skimming.

Anne watched the screen for a few seconds before she clued in.

The people on TV were talking about James—her James! His image was on the screen and they were saying he was a cold-blooded murderer. They were saying he killed a man and a woman with a shotgun less than fifteen minutes ago. They were saying he was responsible for the killings in High Park. They were saying a lot of things and none of it was good.

After an awkward moment, Patricia said, "The police are on their way here, Mrs. McGee. They're coming to see you. They want to ask you a few questions. I thought you should know."

"But I don't know anything about this!"

"I'm afraid that doesn't matter. They're on their way."

"But this can't be right! That can't be James, not my James!"

Patricia shrugged and left the room.

Anne never moved; she was shocked, and soon enough her eyes were glued to the screen. When she had seen more than enough she picked up the phone and called James. But of course there was no answer. He had turned his phone off.

56

Shortly after Elmer pulled onto the highway James phoned Debra on Mia's phone.

"Hello?"

"Hey," James said. "It's me."

"I just called you."

"My phone is off."

"Where are you?"

"Driving."

"Where're you going?"

"Not sure yet."

"Is everything alright?"

James leaned back, shifted the shotgun on his lap and considered jumping out of the car. He looked over both shoulders and then he looked at Elmer. Elmer was driving a straight line. "Yeah, everything seems to be okay. I'm on the highway."

"Are the police chasing you?"

"Not yet."

"What will you do when the cops see you?"

"I don't know."

"You need to think about that."

"Yes. I know." James took a deep breath. "You know Debra, I hate to say this but… you seem awfully calm, considering the situation."

"Well… I'm not calm, so don't get me started. I feel like strangling you, you stupid fucking asshole. What kind of life are we going to share now, huh? A life on the run? Wow, you're becoming quite a catch there, buddy. Lucky me."

"Okay, okay."

"You've pretty much ruined everything. Do you know that?"

"I'm sorry."

"I'm sorry? Is that all you can say? You're sorry that you walked into my apartment with a loaded shotgun and murdered some people, is that it? Jesus Christ. It's a fucking madhouse here. You've become Breaking News on CNN for crying out loud. Nice going McGee."

"What do you want me to say?"

"I don't know. That you didn't kill those innocent people, I suppose. But you can't say that, can you? You can't say that because you did it. You've lost your fucking mind and you're running around town with a loaded shotgun. Tell me I have everything wrong. Please, tell me you're innocent."

"No. I... guess I can't say that."

"They're finding bodies all over the place."

"I said 'I'm sorry'. What else can I say?"

"Nothing," Debra said. "Nothing at all."

"Don't be like this, please."

"Remember when we met? Do you? Remember how fun it was? We'd hang out day after day, just drinking and talking and goofing around. There was no stress back then, no real stress anyhow. What happened? Huh? What the hell happened to us? Do you know? Do you even have a clue?"

"I don't know."

"When was the last time that you and I were happy, can you tell me that? I'm just wondering, is all. I don't know what's been going on lately, and I'm looking for a few answers. Do you have answers James? Do you, because I don't. I'm all out of answers, and I don't have anything left in the tank. I'm spent. And this... this unbelievable stack of bullshit that you're unloading on me... it's too much. It's way, way too much. What the hell should I do with this?"

"Debra. I love you. I don't want to murder you yet."

"What? What the hell do you mean by that?"

James shook his head, confused.

Where did that statement come from? He wondered. Why did he say something like that?

"I just meant to say that I love you, and I'd never do anything to hurt you."

"Yeah. Right."

"I do."

"I don't care if you love me… not right now I don't. I've been think-ing…" Debra stopped talking. She hated her thoughts, and the situation. She was fighting a sea of tears—tears of anger, tears of frustration, tears of confusion and a future lost.

"What? What is it?"

"Never mind. But… I thought about what you said."

"What did I say?"

"On the phone, before you came over, before you lost your fucking mind… you told me that something was chasing you."

"Oh yeah. I forgot about that."

"You forgot?"

"I forgot that I told you, I've had a busy day."

Debra huffed. "You asked me to look something up on the Internet. Do you remember that? You asked me to look up 'Congo Basin Minkisi Bakisi'."

"Did you look it up?"

"Yes."

"And?"

"Tell me something first, was it an animal?"

James looked over his shoulder. "I don't know," he said. "Maybe."

"Was it a dog?"

"No, it was definitely not a dog. It was small and… I really don't know what it was. I couldn't make it out. Why? What did you discover?"

"I don't know why I do these things for you. I don't need this head-ache."

"Debra, please…"

There was a slight pause while Debra gathered up loose pieces of pa-per. She put on a pair of glasses and quickly scanned her notes. "This is what I found. You ready?"

"Yes."

"Okay. Listen to this…"

57

"The Republic of Congo is a country in Africa," Debra said. "The Congo River is the second longest river in Africa, next to the Nile. A basin is a body of water, not to be confused with the Congo Basin, which is the world's second largest tropical forest. It's huge. It covers seven hundred thousand square miles, across six different countries. So those first two words are pretty straightforward. The Congo Basin is a forest in Africa. You with me so far?"

"Yeah. Okay, what else?"

"And then there's that next word, Minkisi, and I've got to tell you, that's a tough one."

"Why?"

"Well… the English language has no word that's equivalent to Minkisi. The word 'fetish' is close, but not close enough—and everything I've read is confusing. A Minkisi seems to be a spirit, but it's also a mask and a medical treatment. It's considered a container, a ceramic vessel. Sometimes it can be an animal's horn, or an animal husk. A grave is considered a Minkisi, or more accurately, a portable grave is considered a Minkisi. And somehow, a Minkisi is a punishment. I've tried to find more info on that statement, but I haven't found much yet."

Debra flipped pages.

"What else do I have here? Oh yeah, here it is… a Minkisi is part of an African religious practice, you know, like voodoo shit? I've read a bunch of stuff about 'figures' too, but I don't understand what I've read. I wanna jump to the conclusion that a figure is a voodoo doll, but that doesn't quite fit. I read somewhere that a 'figure' can come in the form of an animal, which is why I asked you about that. Apparently dogs are tied to this Minkisi stuff, and they live in two separate worlds—the world of the living, and the world of the dead. I don't understand that statement at all by the way, so don't ask."

"Okay. I won't ask. Did you say a portable grave?"

"Yeah. A Minkisi is a portable grave."

"I think I saw one of those. This is making some sense, believe it or not."

"It is?"

"A little bit, yeah."

"You saw a portable grave?"

"I think so. It was at Sue's place, in the basement. There was an old wooden box. It reminded me of those black and white Dracula movies, where Dracula gets shipped around inside of a box of dirt. You know what I'm talking about?"

"Sort of. I'm not big on Dracula. You know that."

"Well… the box at Sue's place had strange markings on it. And below the markings, the words 'Congo Basin Minkisi Bakisi' had been burned into the wood. That's why I asked you to look it up."

Debra said, "You think this box is relevant somehow?"

James nodded. "I know how this must sound."

"Normally, it would sound stupid. But the stuff I looked up for you, well… I don't know. This stuff isn't folklore drivel. Its African history, you know? This is real. The museums are loaded with it. Jewelry, hooves, skulls, witchdoctor trinkets and charms… all connected to Minkisi. I have a quote here from somebody named Simon Kavuna. Do you want to hear it? This guy studied Minkisi in 1915."

"Sure."

"Okay. Here it is: '*The Minkisi receives powers by composition, conjuring and consecration. They are composed of earths, ashes, herbs, leaves, and of relics of the dead. The properties of Minkisi, is to cause sickness in a man—to destroy, to kill, to benefit. The way of every Nkisi is this…* Nkisi and Minkisi seem to be the same thing, by the way. Uh… okay, where am I? Oh yeah, here it is: '*When you have composed it, observe its rules, lest it be annoyed and punish you. It knows no mercy.*'"

"Huh. It knows no mercy."

"Yeah."

"Strange stuff."

"Yep. It is."

"And what about that last word? I gave you four words to check out."

"Bakisi?"

"Yeah."

There was a hard knock on Debra's door. "Miss McClure, open up. This is the Martinsville police."

"Oh shit," Debra said. "The police are here."

James gasped, "But what about that last word?"

"Miss McClure, open up now. We need to speak with you and it's urgent." There was another knock on the door, and this time it was louder than before. "Miss McClure?"

"I've got to go James. I'm sorry."

"But what about that last word? I need to know!"

Debra said, "A Bakisi is a spirit, an ambassador from the land of the dead." Then she hung up the phone.

58

James was shaken; the conversation didn't end on the best note.

He wondered if Debra was in trouble, if she was okay, and what it would be like to slit her throat. He wondered if she was still in love with him and what her blood would taste like. He wondered if the police would trace the phone call. Probably. This was serious business now. Tracing phone calls would be the first thing they'd do.

James tossed Mia's phone out the window and glanced at Elmer.

Elmer was deep inside his own thoughts—enjoying the silence and plotting his revenge.

***

After an hour, James felt a little better. His evil and obscure thoughts seemed to be less frequent, and since he hadn't told Debra anything—she didn't know anything. It was a comforting notion.

He contemplated his destination, deciding that Debra's cottage was the best plan. He figured the odds on it being empty were fifty-fifty. The cottage belonged to a bunch of people—her brother, her sister, her mom and dad, plus several aunts and uncles and the families they shared.

With the fingers in his mind crossed, James tried to summon a plan B.

He came up with nothing.

Oh well, he thought. If Debra's family is enjoying life at the cottage I'll kill them all.

59

The road had few travelers.

James attempted an open dialog with Elmer but it didn't work. Elmer had become a unified stack of negative emotions, indestructibly fused from within. He was tangled in a web of multifaceted thinking, with no desire to bite into the apple of conversation—at least, not yet. Not with his eyes on the road and his face expressionless. He strangled the steering wheel with his hands; his fingers were white-knuckled and unmoving. Sleeves covered in Tina's blood were crammed up to the elbow.

James sighed.

Having Elmer in the car was a big problem. It was kidnapping.

And although James didn't know it, CNN had connected him with the High Park Murders and his image was plastered on every News program in the country. His family, friends and acquaintances were talking—the last time they had seem him, how well they knew him, what they thought had gone so terribly wrong.

Back at the hospital Anne was crying again, and for the first time in her life she was none too proud of her family. And to make matters worse, the police were on their way, which was breaking her heart in two.

James hated people being upset with him, especially when he was in the wrong. And this time he was—there was no denying that. He had definitely made some mistakes.

But guilt was simple—Elmer wasn't.

James wasn't sure how to deal with the man. Should he shoot Elmer? Should he set the man free? It was hard to say. Bringing him along seemed like a good idea when Elmer was being a tough guy, but now it felt like another mistake.

So what now?

James was hungry. He wanted to eat something—a steak would be nice. Lobster would be better. A corpse would be best. But what could he do, sit down at an all-you-can-eat seafood restaurant, go to a drive-thru, hit the morgue? Not likely. Not with Elmer in the car.

He could lock Elmer in the trunk, he supposed. Or lock him in a closet once they reached the cottage—but why? So Elmer could starve to death? James didn't want to kill anyone—

He thought about Tina.

He thought about jumping in front of a train.

He thought about sticking his fingers into his eye sockets and biting off his tongue.

And what if Elmer escaped? What would happen then?

They drove past an old farmhouse, followed by several cornfields and an abandoned silo. Then they zipped past an unpaved road that ran along a sea of trees. The woodland seemed to go on forever, but James knew the area well and knew that it didn't. Twenty miles up the road there was a gas station sitting next to a greasy spoon. The gas wasn't cheap but the food wasn't bad. It was a fair trade.

James decided to make his move.

60

"Pull over."

"Why?"

"You're getting out."

You're going to kill me now, right out in the open. Is that it? Kill me on the highway? Jesus man, be reasonable."

"No, that's not it."

"We're going into the woods? Is that the plan? Will you shoot me in the back of the head? Will you bury me in the deepest hole you can dig? Is that what's happening now you sick, twisted bastard?"

"No. Just listen—"

"Then why should I pull over?"

"For one reason, I'm giving you an order."

"But why? Why here and why now? I don't wanna die today."

"I'm letting you go," James said, frustrated. He wondered if he was telling the truth. "Do you understand? There's a restaurant up ahead called King's Diner—if you care to go that way. But I don't really give two shits what you do; do what you want. Go bury yourself in the fucking woods if that makes you happy. I don't give a fuck. But know this, unless you hook up a ride it'll take a couple of hours to get to the restaurant, and forever if you walk the other way."

Elmer shot James an untrusting glance. "Yeah right, you're setting me free?"

"Yeah, but I got to be honest with you, getting a ride is tough. I ran out of gas one time; it took me three hours to flag someone down. So if I were you, I'd start walking the same way we're driving. You understand?"

"I don't believe you."

"That's okay; I don't care. Bringing you was a mistake, and whether you believe it or not, I'm sorry."

"Bullshit."

"I needed the car, that's all."

"You're so full of shit. You're gonna kill me and dump my body."

"Listen man… I don't know what to do with you. I've been thinking about killing you and eating you and to be honest, I don't know what I'm doing here. I have no plan. I said I didn't want to hurt you and I meant it. I know it's hard to believe. Trust me, I know. But what can I say? I didn't mean to kill your wife and I don't want to kill you, even if I do."

Elmer could see that James was losing it. "You're a liar."

"Just pull over."

"No. You're going to kill me."

"Yeah. Maybe I will. But pull the fucking car over anyhow or I'll shoot you while you drive."

After a few seconds, Elmer pushed the brake and turned the wheel. The brake pads touched the rotor. The tires slowed their rotation. The vehicle's speed diminished. Rocks, dust and sand found new places to sit, and soon enough the car came to a full stop at the side of the highway.

James coughed, still feeling the effects of the fire. "Get out," he said, holding the gun tight. "And leave the keys in the ignition."

"You're not going to kill me?"

"How many times do I have to say it?"

"Until I believe you."

"I don't care what you believe. I just want the car."

Elmer nodded, concealing a spiteful grin. He stepped outside.

"Okay." James said, getting out of the car with him. "Now give me your shirt."

"Why?" After a moment of silence Elmer said, "I have two or three shirts in the back seat of the car. If I were you, I'd wear one of those. They're clean—clean enough for you. No blood."

"Why do you have shirts in your car?"

"I don't know. They've been back there for a month. Can I go now?"

James nodded. "Yeah. Get the fuck out of here."

Elmer began walking down the highway, looking like he would return home on foot.

"Wrong way," James said as he slid into the car. Then he whispered, "I can't run you down if you walk that way." When Elmer didn't respond James yelled, "I'm sorry." Then he shrugged his shoulders and drove off.

Elmer heard the apology and kept on walking. Under his breath he said, "Not as sorry as you're gonna be you stupid psycho prick. You have no idea what I'm gonna do to you." A few steps later Elmer noticed a butterfly with a broken wing shuffling along the road. He killed it with his foot.

And in the sky above, dark clouds rolled across the horizon. The storm the weatherman had predicted was finally on its way.

PART FOUR:
HUNTERS AND THE CHASE

61

Elmer was a thief, a planner, a killer, an intellectual, a rebel, and a fighter. But most of all—more than any of these things—he was a liar. And he was good at it. He lied every day, rarely speaking a word of truth.

Most liars don't know why they lie. Some do it for the thrill and some do it because they lack courage. Others try to avoid punishment or save face. Some don't think clearly. Some don't think.

Elmer was different; he had a philosophy—not that he cared to share it: *the less they know, the better.* It was a simple philosophy—very straightforward, very direct. Not the viewpoint of a saint but it served him well.

Years ago, his mother was shot dead inside a Boston crack house. And on that day, after the news had made the rounds, Elmer changed. The idealistic young boy—who was known as David Timothy Camions at the time—disappeared. And in return the world received Dennis Wade, and Steven Beal, and Toby McBride, and Elmer Wright, and Michael Sapient.

Lately it was Elmer.

Elmer wasn't married to Tina. He barely knew her.

Tina was his customer—she bought pot from time to time. He had no feelings for the woman, no history either. They had been introduced one night in a bar. A nineteen-year-old drunk-punk named Terry set them up. He threw Terry a half bag of coke and a warped G. B. H. album and Terry landed him another semi-chronic. There was no late-night manger job at a coffee shop. No history of bingo. No Danny. No Beth. Every word that David Timothy Camions/Elmer said was a stone cold lie.

Tina looked confused when Elmer talked about the marriage and the children and the love that was fading between them. She was confused but knew enough to keep her big mouth shut.

Lot of good it did her, Elmer thought. Stupid bitch.

***

Over the ridge of a hill, Elmer noticed the growing shine of approaching headlights. The sky had not darkened much, and he could tell that the small blue car was fairly new, a Ford Focus perhaps. The young woman behind the wheel was twenty-two, maybe twenty-three. She was cute with short blonde hair; she had a thin face and a tan.

And she was alone.

62

Elmer walked into the center of the lane smiling. His arms were above his head, giving slow welcoming gestures. He showed no signs of urgency, no hint of stress or unpleasant dramatics. This type of carefree technique worked best, Elmer found. It set people at ease.

Elmer considered killing a dance, an exchange, a personal expression played out between two people. And Elmer loved to dance. If it were up to him he would dance all night, every night. And for years Elmer had been refraining, denying his instinctive, intuitive thirst for killing—but no more. Meeting James and seeing Tina's death put his finger on his past; it tweaked his thinking.

It was time to lace up those dancing shoes.

***

The car slowed before it came to a rolling stop.

The girl behind the wheel lowered her window. A puff of smoke escaped through the expanding aperture. She sat a cigarette onto the rim of the car's metallic ashtray and adjusted her designer shades with long, well-manicured fingers. She leaned her head to one side and smiled affectionately.

"Are you okay?" She said.

"My car," Elmer responded. He approached the window with slow moving feet. He pointed down the road, shrugged his shoulders and lifted his hands. Then he rolled his eyes and laughed, acting like a happy-go-lucky klutz. He couldn't help noticing the girl's white bikini top. It was the smallest he'd seen in a while. "What's your name?"

"Jennifer," the girl said with a giggle. Her laughter was not full-sized, but it was there. Elmer had the fish on the hook; all he had to do was reel her in.

"Hello."

Jennifer was a hottie. Her stomach was fit, a small ring pierced her belly button and her muscular legs were tanned brown. She had a bracelet around her ankle. She wore a pair of tight white shorts and leather sandals; perfect beach attire for a young woman wearing a bikini top.

Elmer smirked. He couldn't believe this dumb bitch; she was flaunting her body like a freebasing whore. He wondered if she was on a low dosage of MDMA; he wondered what it would be like to watch her die.

"Jennifer," Elmer laughed. "I'm in a bit of a spot. My car... well... it's a chunk of crap." And with that, Elmer laughed again, like he had said the funniest joke of the day.

Jennifer's smile expanded. She lifted her cigarette from the tray and closed her eyes while shaking her head playfully. "A chunk of crap huh? Well... that's not too good, is it?"

"No, I suppose it isn't."

"Where's the car? Down the road?"

"Yeah."

"And you need a ride, is that it?"

Elmer pointed. "You see those trees up there? You see that big tree... it looks a little bigger than the others?"

Jennifer squinted, looking at the trees swaying in the wind. "Yeah, I think so."

"The one with... ah..." His words trailed off. Frustration began to boil. He didn't have time for this shit, not with James getting away. He needed to make a move. He needed to get going.

Jennifer said, "I'm not sure where you're pointing, but I can help you out I guess. If you need a ride."

"Yeah. A ride would be great."

Elmer smiled—and suddenly Jennifer's smile fell from her face.

There was something wrong with this man, she realized, something dreadfully wrong. His eyes looked dead, and maybe they were. He looked like a corpse, like his insides had begun to rot and stink—and the eyes are the windows to the soul. She had heard that many, many times. And this man had the eyes of the dead.

A moment of insight came: *this man isn't a corpse*, she thought, *but a ghost*. He died long ago, or perhaps not so long ago. Perhaps he died today, and that car he's pointing at is wrapped around a tree. And he's there, bleeding from the stomach with a broken neck and chunks of his skull smashed into his brain.

Her eyes shifted; she looked at Elmer's shirt. It was covered in blood.

"Oh shit," she said, fearing the absolute worst. "What are you?"

Reading her face adequately, he said, "I am your death, my dear. But you know that. Of course you do."

It was a miracle she hadn't figured him out earlier.

63

Elmer reached inside the car and grabbed Jennifer by the hair. He cranked her head to the left and pulled as hard as he could. Jennifer's cigarette went flying and she screamed, thinking her skull would tear from her body. With her feet kicking the pedals, the floor, and that thing between the seats that guys working the automotive line call 'the doghouse', the car lurched forward and stalled. As it did, Elmer slammed Jennifer's face against the window casing. Her nose broke and her sunglasses fell from her face. A thread of blood and snot gushed down her chin in a long pink runner, soaking her white bikini top. The exposed portions of her breasts became shiny and red.

Elmer twisted Jennifer's head in an awkward, unnatural circle. Then he released his grip and opened the door.

Jennifer, crying and panic-stricken, scrambled to the far side of the car. Her neck was on fire and her eyes watered. Her nose was flowing blood, which rivered through her fingers abundantly. "Why are you hurting me?"

"Am I hurting you?" Elmer mocked with a heartless tone. He grinned like a shark. His eyes were coiled snakes. "I'm just getting started."

Jennifer begged and Elmer dragged her from the car by her feet. He ankle bracelet broke and fell to the ground in a ball, like a tiny mountain of gold. He straddled her, and pinned her shoulders beneath him. As he punched her face and neck she cried and screamed at the top of her lungs—but it was useless. Elmer wouldn't stop. He punched her until his knuckles were raw; he punched until he felt tired. And in time, when his muscles were sore, his stopped his battering and stood up. She didn't. She lay in a pool of her own blood, quivering and shaking. He began kicking her then; he kicked her as hard as he could, again and again. She did nothing to stop him; she didn't even raise a hand. He kicked until his feet felt numb—and when he finished he spat in her face and screamed in victory.

Elmer, panting, walked to the car and found the cigarette Jennifer had been smoking. He lifted it to his mouth and inhaled. The smoke didn't taste great but he didn't care. He had earned it.

He looked at his victim one last time. She was lying at the side of the road, unconscious. Her breath had grown unstable and wheezy. Elmer assumed she was dying.

"Sorry darling," he said, standing above her, not feeling the least bit sorry. "But I'm in a bit of a hurry here. If I wasn't we could spend all night together. I'd slice you into pieces."

He dropped the cigarette on top of her. Then he slid his fingers beneath her bikini-top and pulled with brute, careless force. Her top came off with ease and her breasts bounced free.

Jennifer's eyes opened. She mumbled, "What are you…"

"Shut up bitch," Elmer said. He slapped her in the face with the back of his hand. Blood from her broken nose squirted into the air in a thin red line.

Elmer felt himself getting excited. He ran a hand across her skin and pinched her nipples. He slid a hand beneath her shorts and assaulted her briefly, but he didn't have time for this. No. Time was short. He needed to get moving.

Elmer dragged Jennifer away from the road with heals scraping the asphalt; sandals fell from her feet. Blood clogged her nostrils and drained from her mouth. With five broken ribs and one bruised lung, she fell in and out of consciousness. Elmer released his grip; she fell, becoming submerged in the long, unkempt meadow.

He kicked her twice more and then returned to the car. An eighteen-wheeler roared past, followed by another. Elmer didn't care. The truckers probably thought he was taking a leak, if they thought anything at all. He considered waving but decided against it. Unnecessary attention could only bring unwanted trouble.

When he sat behind the wheel, he found a huge ball of Jennifer's keys hanging from the ignition and a pack of cigarettes sitting on the passenger seat next to an iPod. He lifted a cigarette from the pack and lit it. "Nice meeting you Jennifer. You're a stupid slut… your mother would be proud."

He drove down the empty road, scanning through radio stations. Most stations played crap: Celine Dion, Eminem, Garth Brooks, Madonna, Mariah Carey—it was all the same pointless shit, just different genres. He hated it. All of those lying assholes with their cowboy hats and leather pants, their satin and silk, their bling-bling and their ching-ching—that shit made him sick. Thank fucking God there was one or two stations that played something good, he thought. And on the edge of that notion he found AC/DC. It wasn't great but it wasn't bad either.

The song was Highway to Hell.

64

Elmer drove to King's Diner. He pulled off the highway, turned off the radio and nuzzled the car next to a pump. Even though he was in the middle of nowhere, the air didn't smell like nature; it smelled like cheap gasoline and greasy french-fries. He wondered which smelled worse.

Ignoring the oily scent, he pumped gas and sized-up his surroundings: there was an old woman with a dated yellow blouse sitting on a bench reading a C. S. Lewis paperback: the Silver Chair. There was a group of teenagers hanging around a dirty minivan. The van had a faded collection of Pearl Jam, Nirvana and STP stickers pasted to the back windows. He labeled the teenagers pot-smokers. Any other day he would have approached with an ounce or two, flashed it and offered a phone number.

Not today though, not today. He saw a dog tied to a flagpole with no flag, and a young couple that seemed to be lovers. The couple walked hand in hand, strolling past the only eighteen-wheeler in the lot. The guy looked about twenty, maybe younger; he entered the restaurant first. As his girlfriend followed him inside, Elmer saw the last thing he expected to see: his car sitting near the front door. He couldn't believe his eyes.

But where was James? he wondered. *Where has that psycho bastard gone?*

Elmer paid the gas-attendant with ten bucks he had tucked in his back pocket. It was the last of his money, not counting a handful of change.

A gust of wind nearly blew the bill from the attendant's hand.

He started the car, cruised across the parking lot and parked next to a dirty white pick-up that had seen better days. The pick-up sat next to a pay phone.

He stepped out of the car, keeping an eye on the restaurant's large windows. He dialed directory assistance and began sinking change into the slot.

How many germs are on this thing? he wondered. Must have been a hundred million of them.

The operator came onto the line sounding like the live version of a bleak recording. "Business or residential," she said.

"Residential."

"City?"

"Martinsville."

"Who are you trying to reach?"

"Donald McGivney."

"One moment please."

As Elmer waited, he pumped more quarters into the phone. From where he was standing he could see James.

James was sitting in a booth eating lunch, drinking a beer, and looking out the window. He was dressed the same, no clean shirt. Looked like a maniac.

Elmer smiled.

The operator returned. "Hello, sir?"

"Right here."

"I have the number, would you like me to put you through?"

"Yes please."

"One moment."

Elmer heard the tone adjustment in the line before the phone rang twice. "Hello?"

"Is Don there?"

"Yep. You've got 'em."

"Hey Switch, it's me."

"Steel! Is that you man?"

"You know it."

"What's going on brother? Hey, I saw you a couple hours ago."

"Yep."

"You were getting on the highway. Did you see me?"

"Yeah, I did."

"Well thanks for waving, buddy. What's up with that? You're too cool for me? To cool for school… is that it? We used to be tight, remember…"

Elmer interrupted. "Switch, I need your help."

The two men fell silent. Then Switch said, "You do?"

"Yeah."

"Why? What's up?"

"It's a long story."

"I've got time. I'm waiting for my coffee to brew."

"Yeah?"

"Yeah man. Let's hear it."

Elmer took a deep breath, wondering how to explain the day's events. He wasn't sure if he could do the story justice; everything had been too crazy. He said, "You know what's been happening, right?"

"No, what?"

"You don't know?"

"You mean around town?"

"Yeah."

"Oh… yeah, I know a little, but I don't know much. I saw a couple cop cars with their cherries flashing. Why, are you in trouble again? You did something bad and you need a place to hide out. Is that it?"

"I'm not in trouble, not this time."

"Well that's good."

"Switch," Elmer said, shuffling his feet beneath him. "I need your help. I need to kill a man."

65

Switch chuckled. "Oh man… it's like that, is it?"

"It's like that."

The conversation fell into an awkward lull. Then Switch changed his demeanor and spoke like a disgruntled high school teacher that was giving the gears to the school bully.

"Get your head out of your ass," he said. "The last thing you need is another murder rap. You want that kind of heat, really? What are you, stupid? Forget it man; forget it. Burn the fucker's house down if you have to but don't kill him. It's not worth it. Trust me on this, will ya?"

"I have to kill him. There's no other way."

"Why?"

"I just do."

"No you don't, you can walk away. Remember all those books and seminars that we—"

"Fuck that," Elmer retaliated. He suddenly felt a surge of anger.

"Why?" Switch asked with a voice that was forceful and controlling. "You can walk away man, you know you can."

"Not this time."

"Okay," Switch huffed. "Fine. But you can do this without my help."

"Sure I can, but I don't want to. I want to make it last, you know what I'm sayin'? I'm gonna enjoy killing this bastard, and I wanna share the moment with a friend, with someone I trust."

Switch laughed and softened his approach. "Holy shit man, you're pissed."

"Yeah. That's why I'm callin' you."

Taking a deep breath and the time to reconsider his values, Switch said, "You know I'll be there when you really need me. I'm always there for you. You're like a brother to me, and my mother thinks the world of you. But… I need a good reason to help you out on this one man, 'cause I'm clean, you know? I'm not risking my future the way you've been. No offence, but you know what I mean. I'm not buying, I'm not selling and I'm not wearing any colors. I'm clean man; I'm clean. They've got nothin' on me these days. Nothin' real anyhow... and it feels good. I feel like I've got my life back."

"Yeah right."

"Honest."

Elmer rolled his eyes. "Well, that's good to hear. Good for you, brother. Good for you."

"So tell me... what did this guy do?"

"Say hello to your mother for me."

"Fuck," Switch said. "You're impossible. Don't give me that courtesy bullshit and don't change the topic. What did this guy do to get you so upset?"

Elmer raised an eyebrow and looked across the parking lot. His car was still there, unoccupied, and James was still inside. Things were still in order; he still had time.

"The asshole put a gun to my head and threatened my life. Then he killed two people and lifted my wheels."

"He killed people?"

"Killed the girl I was hangin' with right in front of me, the fuckin' prick. He's going down. With or without your help, I can't let this one slide. This bastard has got to go."

"He killed your girl?"

"She wasn't my girl, but he didn't know that. He thought the bitch was with me and he didn't care. He smoked her with a shotgun."

"Oh man... that's crazy shit!"

"That's what I'm tellin' you. This motherfucker... you know what else he did? The prick took my phone and my wallet. He probably snaked a thousand bucks!"

"For real?"

"Uh-huh. I made a couple sales today. There's no doubt about that."

"Oh shit, did you see him do it? Kill the girl I mean—did you see him?"

"I was standing right there, man. I was standing right fucking there. This is front-page news; you know what I'm sayin'? He probably killed five people today. The guy's a psycho."

"Fuck me."

"That's right, now you're getting' it. Now you're catching what I'm telling you."

Switch had to admit, he was beginning to see a whole new picture. "Okay, okay. So, assuming I help—do you know where this guy is?"

Elmer laughed. "That's the good news bro. He's right in front of me."

66

James finished his meal, scooted out of the restaurant and drove.

Elmer followed at a safe distance, making directional notes along the way. He checked Jennifer's purse, which had been sitting in the backseat. It was loaded with all kinds of junk including a wallet and a cell phone. The phone had plenty of juice. The wallet had sixty-five bucks and a Visa card. Elmer figured the Visa would be safe for a day or two, if he was smart about it.

After an hour, James made two sharp turns within a mile of each other and pulled the car onto a dirt road that led to Debra's cottage. Elmer trailed him until the very end. Then he called Switch.

"Hello."

"Hey Switch. It's me."

"You get there yet?"

"Yep."

"Great... where are you?"

"It looks like I'm at this guy's cottage. Have you left yet?"

"Yeah," Switch lied. "I just walked out the door."

"Did you get everything?"

"I got everything you asked for and a whole lot more."

"Nice. I'm guessing you want directions, so call me when you're closer and I'll give 'em to you."

"Sure buddy. Whatever you say."

***

After the conversation, Switch called his mother. He told her the situation and she gave him some advice. She was good like that, always had been. She said, "Donald, I love you and I don't want to see you getting in more trouble. But you should do what's right and calling the police is something that needs to be done. This is a police matter; it's big-time. Problem is, the police aren't going to be careful or delicate. They're going to jump to some unmerited conclusions and connect poor David (she knew Elmer as David) with these murders and the press will have a field day. His life will be ruined… again. And he's come such a long way since they've released him. He's tried so hard, you both have. Calling the police would be like sending your friend back to lockup. Somehow it doesn't seem fair. But like I said, this is big-time. I think you should try and talk some sense into him. Go to the cottage and straighten him out. And if that doesn't work, do what you must… call the cops before he does something he'll forever regret."

The conversation went back and forth awhile, and when it was over his mother wept. "A good boy, that Donald. He sure is a good boy."

67

James parked near a large birch tree, not thirty feet from the cottage door. He killed the engine and stepped outside. The summer air had a sweet, unsullied eminence. The grass had grown long and green. And best of all, the driveway was empty. It was a good sign.

He walked to the porch and then tilted a large stone on its side. He reached his hand beneath it, retrieving a single key. Then he looked over his shoulder and opened the door. The cottage was empty.

"Thank goodness," James whispered.

After a quick bathroom break, James cracked a beer (the cottage always had plenty of beer) and called Debra.

"Hello?"

"Hey," James said. "It's me."

"Oh, hi. You still at the restaurant?"

"Nope. I'm at the cottage now. Just got here. Are you still coming?"

"Yeah. I just left."

"Cool. How long 'til you show up?"

"It'll be two hours, maybe longer. It might rain tonight you know."

"Oh yeah, I know. That sucks."

"Yeah, it does. And I had to deal with the police… so, I'm running late."

"How was that?"

"It was awful."

"Are you okay?"

"Yeah, but I don't want to talk and drive. I hate doing that. I'll talk to you when I get there, alright? I'll tell you everything."

"Sure babe. Whatever you say."

"'Kay. See you soon."

"Love you."

"Love you too. Bye."

"Debra?"

"Yeah?"

"Thanks."

"No problem. I'll see you in two hours."

When James hung up the phone he thought about killing Debra with a chainsaw; he thought about it for a long time. Then he went outside and looked in the shed. There was no chainsaw; all he found was an axe. It would have to do.

He decided to chop off her head.

68

Jennifer McCall's face was swollen; she had bruises on both sides of her neck. When she opened her eyes, her sight was blurry and shadowed. The dirt and blood in her mouth was thick enough to create paste.

As she ran her fingers along her belly, she began to cry. She rolled onto her side, taking the pain the best she could. Seeing her chest exposed, she feared the worst. But she didn't remember being raped. Of course, that didn't mean that it didn't happen. Anything could have happened, anything at all.

A car drove past.

With a great deal of effort Jennifer pushed herself to her elbows. The grass beneath her was sticky with blood.

My blood, she thought. This is my blood. I'm at the side of the road, bleeding and beaten. How did it come to this?

She could see the forest, and the highway that was less than forty feet away.

"Where am I?" She tried to mumble, but it came out all wrong, like her mouth was filled with cotton. She tried to stand but it was impossible.

Memories came in a lump: she had been attacked. She had been— raped? Is that what happened?

Another car zipped past.

Jennifer rolled onto her stomach and the pain became worse. Five minutes later a wave of darkness came, taking Jennifer away.

69

The Bakisi followed the scent of the man into Debra's complex. It entered silently, following the blood that perfumed the air. The building had so many confusing smells, more than the ambassador was accustomed to. But the pungent scent of the man that it hunted was strong and the Bakisi stayed on track. Through trial and error it found its way to the fifth floor.

The man-scent was strong on the fifth; fresh blood had been spilled.

It approached Debra's home. The gateway was closed but it did not matter. The Bakisi was capable of entering through the smallest openings. The insignificant space beneath the door was more than sufficient.

It entered the dwelling, and ingested a new scent—the woman scent.

The woman scent was strong here, inside this man-dwelling. It was stronger than all other scents. It was stronger than the man scent. But the man, it knew, had been here many times. The man spent days and nights; he had loved here—but the man had gone.

The Bakisi re-entered the hallway. It detected a man with a loaded gun inside his holster. This armed warrior was protecting something familiar, something that was masked heavy with imitation aroma.

It was a woman; she was filled with terror and dread.

Now the Bakisi understood.

The woman had been with the man today. And feared the man. And hated the man. And couldn't stop thinking about the things he had done, and the things he was still doing, for she had a brush with death. And death, the Bakisi decided, would come to the woman. It would come to the woman and to all who had crossed paths with the man the Bakisi was hunting.

70

Officer Gentry felt his head bob. For a moment, he had fallen asleep. He repositioned his feet and pushed himself into a more stable position. Then he shook his head, rubbed his face and tried to sit straight.

He checked his watch.

Gentry had two more hours before his shift would end, two more hours before he would be free to go home—and fight with his wife.

Sigh.

He hated days like these. They were so boring. And today shouldn't have been boring. Today, the town had fallen apart. There had been murders and fires and mass hysteria. Today was a big day—and he was bored to death.

Suddenly the hallway became cold.

Gentry saw a shadow creep across the floor. But that couldn't be right. He was alone and tired. It was nothing—had to be nothing. There was nothing in the hallway. He was sure of it.

But it *was* cold.

The door rattled and the coldness dissipated.

Maybe it's me, Officer Gentry thought. Maybe I've lost my way.

71

The Bakisi entered the apartment. The frightened one sat alone on a couch; the hunted-man was not here. The hunted-man had never been here. But his scent was here. It was with her, with the frightened one—even though she had washed him away.

There were two more—a man and a woman—hiding within organic scents: vegetable scents, plant scents. They were veiled in the smoldering essence of animal death. And the animal was inside a machine, a hot machine. The man and woman called this machine oven.

The Bakisi did not recognize the word 'oven', but it recognized the scent of the slain beast. And thus, it felt anger.

72

James was tired. He finished his beer, sat on the couch and leaned his head against a decorative pillow. The pillow, like most throw pillows, wasn't comfortable. It was old and hard with strange, dirty lumps inside. But that was okay; James didn't want to sleep, he wanted to be awake—and aware.

After a few minutes passed, James removed his pants; they were filthy. His legs had cuts, scrapes, bruises and bites. He ran his fingers across the wounds, the physical proof to the day's events. He considered Johnny's words—A Bokor Incantation.

Jesus, he thought. What a mess.

James grabbed another beer. After swallowing half the bottle he wrote 'Bokor Incantation' on the back page of a newspaper, so he'd remember.

Maybe Debra would know the meaning.

He sat his beer on the coffee table and held the axe close to his heart.

He thought about chopping off some fingers and toes and flushing them down the toilet. He thought about disconnecting the toilet and throwing it in the lake. He thought about drowning himself in the lake and putting an end to it all. Then he placed his head on the rough edges of the pillow and felt his consciousness fade. He chewed on the pillow. As his eyes narrowed he remembered the warning—*try not to dream. Whatever you do, try not to dream...*

Johnny had said that before pulling the trigger.

Johnny...

James began to weep. Not because he was in pain, or because he was afraid—but for Johnny, Mathew, and Tina. He killed Tina; he shot her dead. And killing Tina was no accident. It was an impulse. It was desire. Robert Frost would call it design—*the pull of his finger was the spider of the appalling darkness, governed in a thing so small.*

He wept for twenty minutes; then fell in terrible slumber.

73

Mia Powell sat in a comfortable change of clothing, wedged into the corner of her designer couch. She drank coffee and watched television, thinking about James—or more specifically—about what James had done.

James pulled the trigger accidentally, she thought. Maybe.

She saw the flinch in his eyes and the surprised look on his face. It seemed possible that he didn't mean to kill the man that looked like a cowboy. The cowboy was in the wrong place at the wrong time, and James was startled. Not that it made things better, it didn't. A man was still dead. And so was Tina, from what the police had said.

She wondered—why did he kill her? Did he mean to do it? Was it an execution? Did she attack him?

The killing was by far the most violent thing she had ever witnessed. His stomach exploded like a bomb had gone off. She was glad she didn't see Tina die.

Stories of tragedy: life flashing before your eyes; time falling into slow motion.

It was different for Mia—everything happened so fast. The explosion of blood and guts, the unexpected pain, the terror, the boom of the shotgun and the sudden face of death—it was all over before she knew what had happened.

She sat her coffee down. Feeling a little cold, Mia pulled a blanket over her legs. Then the temperature fell drastically.

"Hey Mom?" She said, raising her voice so her mother would here. "Is it getting cold in here, or is it just me?"

74

Elmer waited for the sun to set and the moon to rise. Then he traveled from cottage to cottage until he found his car sitting beneath the birch tree.

This was the place.

Not wanting an unexpected phone call, Elmer turned off Jennifer's cell and snuck between two buildings, which were sixteen feet apart. Walking across a slight slope, he headed towards a pair of windows and then peaked inside. He found two empty bedrooms. After checking a third window he found James in plain view. He was in the living room, asleep on the couch.

Elmer smiled; he wondered if he should wait for Switch or make a move.

Making a move now would be fun, he thought. But waiting for Switch would be safe.

Although the decision had not yet been made, he put his hands on the window and pushed. The window didn't budge. He pushed a second time.

Then a twig snapped.

An old man with a heavy German accent said, "Who goes there?" This was Franco; he lived next door.

Elmer spun around, grabbed Franco by the throat and clutched his windpipe with sadistic intentions. Being unexpectedly attacked, Franco staggered back and fell.

Elmer held tight and stayed with him. "Shut the fuck up," he whispered, now lying on top. "You'll ruin everything."

As Franco kicked his feet and waved his hands, Elmer squeezed his neck harder. He could feel grease on the man's neck and hairs scattered around his fingers.

What am I doing with this guy? he wondered. *What do I want to do with this guy? Set him free? Knock him out? Say sorry?*

The instinctive voice inside his head answered: kill him. Do it now. Do it quickly. Kill the bastard and drink his blood.

Elmer squeezed his fingers tight, making them hurt. Then he bit Franco's face like an animal. The aged flesh tore easily; veins bulged and his eyes widened. Soft tissue became the ruins of waste. Elmer bit into him again and his teeth scraped across cheekbone.

Franco squirmed. Blood ran down his face and pooled beneath. His heart was pounding and he couldn't breathe. His neck was under great strain, due to the strange position he was laying. He knew it would soon break. This was the end. He could feel it in his soul.

Then came a voice. "Franco?"

It was the voice of his wife, but was she strong enough to save him?

***

Helga wore pink slippers and an old robe. Her gray hair was sitting in a bob high upon her head. She was eighty-four years old and spoke with a slight stutter. Some days the stutter was non-existent. Other days it was so bad that she hardly said a word. Tonight was a good night; her stuttering was running about 20% less than usual, which was fine by her. The doctors all agreed that her condition was caused by genetics, although she didn't see how that was possible. As far as she knew no one else in her family had every suffered from such an affliction. And she never stuttered as a child. It was only now, living in these twilight years. She often wondered if she had suffered a stroke and somehow missed it.

"Franco," She repeated. "Are you here? Are you au-alright?"

Elmer shifted his weight and snapped Franco's neck. Then he loosened his grip, letting the corpse settle. He could smell the last breath the old man released; it smelled nice, like mint. With the back of his hand he wiped a string of blood from his face, smudging it along his arm.

He never intended on killing these people—these old people. But sometimes life is funny; sometimes things get handed to you on a blood-drenched silver platter, sometimes life offers a deliciously wonderful gift. Or two.

Thank you, he thought.

But like all atheists, he had nobody to thank.

75

James was on security tapes, identified, sought after and awaiting conviction. So when the police arrived at Debra's door, she allowed them to search her apartment. When they asked questions, she gave answers, telling them about the phone calls, the car accident and her limited knowledge concerning the murders. She didn't really care one way or another, and figured it made no difference. The police were not wondering who did it—they were wondering how and why and where is the suspect hiding.

Debra drove to the cottage thinking these things and more. An arrogant, loud-mouthed officer had told her to stay close to home, enjoying his authority and grinning like he owned the planet. Debra quickly agreed, and assured the man that she was not going anywhere—not that her word meant anything.

As she drove the empty back-road highways, she kept her eyes on the rearview mirror. She assumed the cops were following her and that keeping an eye on the suspect's girlfriend was standard police procedure. Maybe it was and maybe it wasn't, but either way, she was not being followed. There was nothing behind her but the road. But Debra—being a mildly creative person—constructed scenarios inside her mind: the sky was loaded with helicopters, a roadblock awaited; she was being monitored by satellite.

Of course, none of these things were true. Debra was alone.

She watched the road meticulously, with her stomach tied into a ball of nerves. Still, there was no police chase, no roadblock and no swat-team flying helicopters in the satellite-monitored sky. She was free to run, free to hide, free to tie a noose and hang—and for what—a boyfriend that was going to jail, a relationship that was about to end, a love that didn't exist?

She deserved better.

Tears formed in her eyes. She felt the first of many sobs and a quiver inside her chest. Crying was inescapable. She had earned it, or to be more accurate, she had been given this grief without request. It was a gift from her problem-ridden asshole boyfriend, a gift she did not want.

The pain was hers now. Tears came in thick beads. They dripped from her face and blurred her vision. Her chest was heaving; her throat began making those awful, horrid noises that can only come from anguish. The make-up she applied so carefully had become a smudged, nightmarish mess. And as she cried, she began to hate him. She hated what James had done and what he had reduced her to. It was his fault she was like this. Everything was his fault.

How could they spend a life together now? It was impossible. The damage was done. The future they planned had fallen apart.

"You're such a jerk," she whispered between sobs.

Then the lights of her car hit something unusual.

Crouched into a ball at the side of the road was an animal. No. Not an animal—a young woman. And she wasn't crouched; she was sitting. Sitting at the side of the highway with bruised legs that were spread wide. One hand covered her naked chest. Her other hand was held up in a sad, struggling wave.

Debra drove past the woman and her sequence of odious thought was lost.

76

After two high-pitched screams in a row, Officer Gentry leapt from his chair and pulled out his gun. He opened the door to Mia's condo looking strangely comical, like a character from a 1970's TV show that was exaggerating his movements for the camera. He saw Mia standing near the kitchen; her hands were shaking and trembling. Then came a third scream and Mia backed away from the room.

"Oh God," she said. "Look."

Gentry ran to the kitchen and saw Mia's mother lying in a runners pose. Her neck was twice broken and her head was cocked against the wall. A rope of blood had drained from her mouth, leaving an almost black, opaque, lumpy puddle.

Seeing this, Gentry's stomach turned. He had never seen a dead body, at least, not in the line of duty.

In the corner of the room Mia's father William was fighting a losing battle. He had a shattered leg and several broken fingers. Unseen razors shredded his face. He tried to speak but his voice had taken on a rumbling, machine-like quality, reminiscent of a lawnmower coming to a gagging halt.

"Do something," Mia whispered.

Officer Gentry turned towards her; his face was pale and grave. "What can I do?"

"Stop it," she said. "Stop this from happening."

Officer Gentry hesitated; he was afraid. This wasn't a chapter in any police book he read or the topic of dispatch discussion. This was a whole new thing. And he was a paycheck cop, not an unsung hero.

Gentry pointed his gun towards William and the violence suddenly ended. William's hands dropped to the floor and Mia ran to his side. A second later cold air brushed by Gentry, who felt goose bumps cultivating his legs.

"Oh dad," Mia was saying. "Are you alright?"

The Bakisi was standing on the counter now, sizing up Mia and Gentry. They didn't know they were being watched; they didn't know what was happening.

Neither Mia nor Gentry had considered the notion that 'something unknown' was with them. Mia was too shocked and Gentry figured William had killed his wife and then sliced himself up somehow. Of course, this didn't quite fit; it wasn't what he'd seen. But then again—what he saw was impossible. And he was tired. And his wife was making him crazy. And his mind was playing tricks on him. And his shift was almost over. And he wanted to go home.

With so many excuses ready for action, Gentry's memory turned against him. He tried to find something logical to believe in. He tried to find a suitable answer. He couldn't. There was a battle. And William was in the corner with blood across his face and chest; he had broken fingers and a shattered leg. How could a man do that to himself Gentry wondered, and why on earth would he?

As Gentry lowered his gun, William opened one of his eyes. The other eye was puffed shut and would not open. Ever.

William said, "We're not alone."

Then Gentry made a decision, the wrong one. He pointed his gun at William's chest and said, "Sir. Don't move."

"What?" Mia barked in anger. "Are you crazy? My father's hurt and my mother's dead! Call the hospital!"

As Gentry considered her words, the Bakisi attacked.

77

James dreamt as he slept. Inside his dreams he could see those he had killed, and those he watched die. He also suffered a discovery of fatality, a discovery of bereavement. The journey started at Johnny's house...

***

The gun went off and Johnny died. He sat there in the chair for a moment, unmoving. He didn't fall; he lifted his head. His eyes were red and bulging. Smoke drifted from his nose and the bubbly hole on the flipside of his skull. A stream of blood, teeth and charred tongue ran from his mouth, his gums, and down his chin. It seemed to flow forever—like a film clip, edited and looped.

Then the image changed; the loop changed.

Johnny stood up. He stepped away from the chair that had become soaked in blood. A lump of soft, wet tissue fell from the back of his skull. As the meat hit the floor his feet began moving with strange, uncharacteristic ineptness, as if his intellect had fallen below any logical level, below the echelon of instinct. He walked past the police officers that stood in his living room drinking coffee, taking notes and snapping photographs. They didn't see him; no one could see him. Only James.

He fumbled outside and walked along Tecumseh Street alone. The street was quiet, the air was still and sound was non-existent. There was something on the road ahead: Doctor Anson. A car had run him down; his chest was crushed.

Johnny laid his hand on Anson, then continued walking.

Anson's dry unmoving eyes opened. He stood up, put a hand to his chest and hobbled along behind Johnny. His back was clearly broken; he was in agony.

On the road ahead a crowd had gathered. Johnny and Anson entered the swaying mass of men, woman and children, walking past an excited dog, a lanky black man who was dialing a number on his cell phone and two teenagers who seemed ready to fight. They walked past a fat man who rubbed his giant knuckles into an open fist. They walked past a man with green eyes who was close to hysterics. Still, there was no sound. Not even a trace of noise could be heard. James could see that people's eyes were focused on a single house; the bungalow James had crashed into. The fire was out. Only the smallest threads of smoke filtered into the heavens through the blackened wreckage.

Johnny and Anson stumbled up the hose-wet driveway. The crowd didn't look, didn't notice. James—the only person who could see the dead staggering into the bungalow—watched things happen from a perspective that swung from viewpoint to viewpoint, changing with independent will. Sometimes he would be above Johnny and Anson, a bird's eye-view. Other times he would be in front, watching the blood flow down Johnny's mangled face. But now—as Johnny and Anson entered the home—James seemed to be floating behind them. He watched streaks of smoke that was drifting through Johnny's skull.

The men slumped past officers, firemen and a man that looked like a politician. They entered the living room through the clutter of the front door and stood near the wreckage.

James could see the car, the debris, and the nearly incinerated bodies of two children that were lying among the soot in strange undefined heaps. He could see the children's mother, her fried corpse.

Johnny touched his hand upon each of them, one at a time. The skeletal remains revealed the mysteries of their ruins. The bones and blackened innards that had endured the fire came together. Bodies without flesh began standing, shifting, walking.

James continued floating; he watched from a new angle.

The dead walked into a room where two more children lay—a four-year-old boy and a five-year-old girl. James hadn't seen these two before; this was new. They were not burned. No—these two children had suffocated; they had drowned inside the poisonous air.

Johnny laid his hand upon each child, first the boy, then the girl.

With Johnny's touch the children opened frozen eyes, aloof with unquestioning death. Behind the stone glare James saw a congregation of fear. It was a fear unknown to the living, a fear that was as deep as the sky above the sky and the universe that encased it. The children, alive but dead, were afraid and pathetic. Their faces and hands were charred from the smoke. Dried tears had carved lines in their cheeks.

Johnny held the youngest by the hand and led all seven from the house. They moved down the driveway and through the crowd. They crossed the street and entered a backyard.

Stan and Emily were lying in a bloody, tangled pile. Stan's throat had been torn from his neck and his right leg had been broken. Emily's eyes had been pushed into her brain; her bottom lip hung severed from her face.

Both husband and wife awoke from their slumber and followed in silence, limping in Johnny's shadow and guided by Johnny's hand.

Nine bodies now, they walked through the backyard in a cracked row and crawled the fence in anguish. They crossed the schoolyard and entered the school. Inside the gymnasium four more waited in death. A thirteenth and fourteenth rose from the hallway. A fifteenth came from the school-yard; a sixteenth and seventeenth joined from the parking lot.

Then came Nash, the tattooed man who had been pulled through the car window. His neck had been broken; his head was twisted in circles and pulled free. It hung by a thick, meaty thread. His face banged off the small of his back as he walked and blood poured onto the ground behind him, leaving a trail.

The dead walked across town; they entered Debra's complex.

Johnny extended his hand twice more.

As Tina stood, the Johnny Cash wannabe opened his eyes. With a broken spine he lifted himself to his feet. The pair followed this grisly spectacle holding hands, for Cash had no center of balance, and Tina—no eyes to see.

There were twenty-one bodies in all, moving in a scattered cluster. Johnny no longer gathered corpses, no longer hunted the dead. That part of the journey was finished now; a new chapter had begun.

They walked from town together, leaving Martinsville behind. They walked the empty roads and the dark highways. And James recognized those long terrible roads, those thin, empty highways. It was the path to Debra's cottage.

The dead were coming.

The dead were coming tonight.

78

As Elmer stood up, Helga saw Franco. His eyes were open and blank; blood was smeared across his face.

She gasped, "What have y-you d-d-done?"

Helga couldn't believe what she was seeing. She never heard the struggle between the two men, and the last thing she expected was this. Moments ago she was making tea; she wondered if Franco had wanted a cup and stepped outside. Truth was, he always said yes. Asking was just a formality.

"Franco's dead," Elmer said.

"But why? W-why would you d-do this? He did nothing to you!"

Elmer stepped over the corpse and stepped into the moonlight. Then the clouds moved and the light all but vanished. The wind blew a forceful gust and Helga stepped back. A fly landed on her face and she swatted it away.

"What are you doing?" She asked. "Get out of here. Leave me a-alone!"

She saw Elmer's mouth. Blood was dripping from his chin; he looked like a vampire. She considered running but it didn't take a genius to figure out that an elderly lady running from a psychopath in the dark was a pointless endeavor. He was too young and she was too old. He'd catch her quickly and kill her soon after.

But what other options did she have?

She could fight, but she'd lose. She could scream, and hope to be saved. Or she could talk to the man. She could try to reason with a psycho. Her choices were terrible.

"Listen," Helga said nervously, backing away as she spoke.

"No. You listen," Elmer said, keeping pace with her footsteps. "I'm going to kill you and I'm going to enjoy it. I'm going to snap your neck."

"You don't h-have to do that."

"I know."

"Then why do it? For the th-th-thrill?"

"I can't let you go, lady. Not now. You've seen my face. You've seen my work."

"I can't see anything. I'm old… and it's dark out here. I don't nu-know who you are or what you've d-done. I don't know a-anything."

"That's too bad, 'cause it doesn't matter."

"Sure it does!"

"Not to me."

"You can turn a-away right now. You can leave me a-alone. The Lord will p-punish you if you don't follow in his f-f-footsteps."

Elmer giggled; the woman was hilarious. Sometimes her cheeks puffed out and sometimes her eyes bulged and sometimes her lips looked like they were pinned together with a clothespin. She needed her own sitcom.

"The Lord's not here, lady," Elmer said. "He stays away from me most of the time. In fact, he's never around when I need him and I don't think he'll be around when you need him. Honestly now, do you?"

"Oh yes… he is h-here! The Lord is here. And he's wa-watching you. He's watching us! The Lord is everywhere. He's here right now and he p-pap-punishes the wicked!" Helga couldn't help it; she spit in the air trying to say the word 'punishes'.

Elmer smirked. "I'm afraid not."

"His word is not to b-b-be questioned!" She continued backing away, with small careful footsteps.

"You're trying to talk me down, scare me a little… is that it?"

"I'm trying to reason with you. For G-G-God's sake, think about your soul! You're better th-than this. Don't think for a minute that you can do a-as you please, killing and terrorizing and d-doing all the terrible things that you've been d-doing, and then what? Will you sit among the faithful at the end of your d-d-days? It doesn't w-work that way, although so many think that it does. You can't say, Lord I'm s-s-sorry… Sorry, on your deathbed and expect all to be forgotten. You can't. You just can't. Repent now and be saved now, for the Lord punishes the wicked. He saves the m-merciful. Beg his forgiveness right here, right n-n-now, for it is not too late to follow in the footsteps of the Lord. Once the bell tolls there'll be no more f-f-footsteps to f-follow, can't you see that? You can't follow his word when your time is done. Follow his w-word now, and he will l-l-lead you to the Promised Land!"

"Fuck that. You're trying to escape. But you're too old to run, and too smart not to know it. Frankly, I'm impressed. But I'm not falling for it."

"But the Lord—"

"It's not going to work lady, you need a new angle."

"I don't want to die," she blurted out, more afraid now than before. She didn't realize it, but she had stopped thinking about her husband. The shock of his death had come and gone very quickly. And religion, she discovered, wasn't the solution she was looking for. It was a tool that wasn't working. It was the wrong approach. He was right; she needed a new angle. "I don't want to die. Not here, not b-by your hand."

"I don't know if you realize this or not you stupid stuttering whore… but I don't care. This isn't about what you want. This is about what I want."

"Please, b-be reasonable."

"But it's your time to die. And I am being reasonable. Let me enlighten you on a thing or two. First of all, there is no God."

"O-oh yes th-there is."

"No. There isn't. Think about it. This planet has been here millions of years. People have been evolving for millions of years, long before organized religion. You say that 'two-thousand years ago Jesus came!' But two-thousand years ain't squat. What happened to all of those people that were born before Jesus, huh? No heaven for them I guess. What a rip-off."

"You d-don't under... s-s-s-stand! It was Jesus th-that—"

"No! You don't understand. I'm going to kill you, and when I die there won't be a bearded man standing at the golden gates wondering why. End of story."

Helga kept walking. She didn't know what to do. She didn't know what to say. This guy wasn't kidding around. He was planning to kill her, and was going to enjoy it.

How do you reason with that?

"Where do you think you're going," Elmer said with a smirk. "You're going to walk all the way to New Jersey? Is that it?"

"I don't want to d-d-die today."

"But you're going to."

"What c-c-can I do to change your m-mind? Tell me, and I'll do it! You can ha-have anything that you want. You can h-have everything."

"You can stop walking. How about that?"

"No. I can't do that th-that."

"Why not?"

"You'll grab me, and with the Lord as m-my witness, I believe you'll kill m-me."

"That's inevitable, I'm afraid."

"It doesn't have to be."

"But it is." Elmer wrinkled his nose and slowed his pace. "Can I ask you something?"

"Yes."

"This is your house, right? This isn't some summer home, you're here all year around, aren't you"

Helga swallowed back her lies, then nodded. "Yes."

"Do you have any guns inside?" As Helga's expression changed, Elmer knew the answer. "You do, don't you?"

"No."

"Yes."

"No."

"You're lying."

"Stay out of m-m-my house."

"Where is it?"

"I'll n-n-never tell you anything. I'll never tell you w-where they are."

Elmer giggled. "They? How many do you have?" He said. "A whole trunk full, apparently."

Helga took one step too many. She fell off a three-foot ridge, landed hard against the beach and expelled a grunt. Elmer, who laughed as she fell, stood at the edge of the drop off. As his laughter tapered, he watched Helga in admiration, feeling his excitement building inside; he loved anticipation. It was the best.

"You're a smart woman," he said, nodding his head. "Very smart, and very well spoken for a stuttering whore. A bit too church-lady for me, but I'm impressed."

Helga was moaning now. The unexpected fall injured her back.

"Any last words?"

Helga inhaled a deep breath and said, "The Lord is my Shepard; there is n-n-nothing I shall want."

And then she screamed.

79

Debra drove another eight seconds before she finally stopped the car. Then, with her arm resting behind the seat, she backed up. She had just driven past a woman on the road, and the woman needed help.

But the road was dark; she couldn't see much. And Debra wasn't a great driver, at least not when driving in reverse, without her glasses—at night.

She expected to see the girl but never did. Finally she stopped the car, opened the door and stepped outside. The wind was blowing, causing her hair to fall in front of her eyes. She hated it when that happened. She hated when her hair became muddled by the wind.

She held her hair with her hand and said, "Hello! Is anybody out there?" No response. "Hello!"

Debra eyed the side of the road, the trees and the dark, haunting branches they were swaying in the not so gentle breeze, thinking—*what did I see? Maybe it was an animal, or maybe...*

She jumped back into the driver's seat and turned the car around. She drove along the darkening highway slowly, watching the side of road the best she could. The glow of the headlights brightened the grass and all that was around it. Then, when she was beginning to think that she had imagined the girl, she saw something. It looked like a ghost. She held her breath and turned towards the image. No—it wasn't a ghost. It was the girl; she was sitting at the edge of the road, holding her knees against her chest.

Debra parked the car. As she stepped outside Jennifer looked up. Her body was shaking, her cheeks were swollen, her nose was broken and her eyes were puffed.

"Save me," she said. "Please... save me."

"Oh my," Debra whispered. The girl looked liked she had been attacked by wolves.

Debra put her hands beneath Jennifer's arms and lifted.

Jennifer stood with a grunt, with legs shaking and breasts exposed. Fresh tears formed in her eyes.

Debra said, "I'll get you something to cover up with, as soon as you're in the car. What's your name?"

"Jennifer."

"Hi Jennifer. My name is Debra."

"Thank you."

"Don't mention it."

Debra helped Jennifer into the car. Then she looked through the trunk and found a shirt; it was big and dirty but it was better than nothing.

80

James shouted. That's how he woke up from the nightmare: he shouted. His skin was drenched in sweat. His clammy hands clutched the center of his chest. His hair was matted and tangled. He had lines across his skin from the ribbed nap of the corduroy couch and a thick aluminum taste had made camp inside the back end of his mouth. For some reason the taste reminded him of napalm.

James sat up, rubbed a numb hand across his face and coughed. Soot from the fire sprayed into his hand. Then he became worried.

The dream wasn't fading, as dreams usually do. Instead, it was becoming clear. He remembered everything about it, every last detail—Johnny's hand, the bodies coming to life and walking the lonely road. The nightmare felt less like a dream and more like a premonition, a forewarning. Something was coming—twenty-plus dead bodies, dragging their broken remains along the dark desolate highways. They were coming to get him. Coming to kill him.

"Fuck," James said, shaking his head and rubbing his neck.

He got off of the couch and laid the axe on the floor. Then he put his pants on, rubbed the sleep from the corners of his eyes and wiped a hand across his mouth. He walked to a window and looked outside. Darkness had fallen. And seeing the darkness, he felt scared.

They were coming.

James pushed the destructive thought away.

Now what? He wondered. What should I do?

He poured a glass of water, plunked himself into a chair and emptied his pockets. He had a handful of change, two sets of keys, two wallets and two cell phones: trophies of the day.

Two phones, he thought. *That's weird. I should have three.*

What happened?

Oh yeah. Mia's phone was thrown out the window.

It was a shame Mia ran away from him, terrified and screaming, thinking he was psychotic and wishing he were dead. Mia was cute and she couldn't be more wrong about a person. James was a good man, a caring man. He was honest and decent and loving. And he'd love to know Mia better—maybe take her to diner and a movie. He thought they'd make a great couple. He wondered if they'd be married. But these weren't fair thoughts; he knew that—he had a girlfriend that he loved very much. But still, it would be nice to spend time with Mia. It would be nice to have sex. It would be nice to crack her head open and eat her brain. He saw that in a movie once: people eating brains, monkey brains. Was it Faces of Death, Mondo New York? He couldn't remember, but he did remember Japanese businessmen and their wives sitting around a table as a half-dozen screaming monkeys had their skulls smashed apart with a hammer. The people, dressed in their Sunday best, ate monkey brain while the animals died at their feet. It was a delicacy, very posh. The wives didn't seem to care for it but their husbands did.

James picked up Elmer's phone and dialed Debra's number. Then he ran a butcher's knife across his forehead. He thought he was a monkey. He also thought he was a Japanese businessman.

As the blood began pouring down his face Debra answered the phone.

81

The Bakisi killed Officer Gentry quickly. It sliced a deep and fatal laceration across his throat with its fingernails, causing blood to flow down Gentry's chest, belly and groin. As it happened, Gentry dropped his gun, which landed barrel down on the floor before falling onto its side. Gentry came next, toppling onto his back.

Seeing this, Mia released a high, shrilling scream, threw an arm around her father's neck, and held him tightly.

William coughed out the word, "Run…"

"What?"

"I said run! Get!"

Mia looked her father in the eye. "I can't leave you!"

"Run or you'll die!"

"What's happening?" she asked.

Suddenly William was alive and forceful, pushing Mia away with power and dominance. The look that filtered through his working eye said more than words ever could.

He was trying to save his daughter.

"Look around you!" William barked. His heart was beating so fast it could generate electricity. "Things have gone bad here! Satan is with us! Get out! GET OUT OF THIS PLACE!"

Mia was stunned. Her father looked insane.

She glanced at her mother, who was still lying in a runner's pose with her head cocked against the wall. She looked at the fallen officer as he snatched his last breaths and clutched his throat with twitching fingers. She could smell the blood. She hadn't noticed it until then, but now the odor seemed overwhelming. She realized then what the room had become—it had become a killing box.

Her eyes sprung open; a profound sense of horror awoke inside. It was a fear she had never known—not today, not ever. She felt like she had been submerged into a pool of bloodthirsty sharks while bleeding at the feet. And the predators were snapping thousands of teeth inside massive jaws. She felt like a feeding frenzy had begun and she was part of the meal, part of the reason the sharks were bloodlust crazy. And instead of kicking her feet and escaping the danger—instead of saving herself—Mia was doing the opposite. She was floating in the water, waiting her turn, waiting to be ripped apart.

With spittle hanging in a thin line from his chin, William shouted, "What are you waiting for child? Run!"

Those seven words snapped Mia from her daze. She looked at her father with understanding eyes. She whispered, "Okay." It was the last word she would say to him.

The invisible Bakisi jumped on her back. Falling forward, she smashed her head on a cupboard door. As pain and confusion mingled together the Bakisi sliced William's neck with that same move it used on Gentry. Then William gasped and gagged. Blood rolled on top of blood. The air became thicker still.

Dying, William pushed Mia with the last of his strength, and gurgled, "GET OUT OF HERE!"

Then Mia stood up. She backed away from her father, watching as he died, feeling the fear devour her, feeling the sharks circling. If she didn't want to become part of the meal it was time to start swimming.

82

The phone rang three times before Debra answered. "Hello?"

"Hey, it's me," James said. He placed the butcher's knife on the kitchen counter next to a toaster; blood dripped down his face. He no longer thought he was a monkey or a businessman. He wondered what the toaster was thinking. It was probably sneaking around behind his back when he wasn't looking, devising a plan, stealing his thoughts. He would have to keep an eye on it, because the toaster was clearly keeping an eye on him.

"Where are you?" he said.

"Driving."

"Are you going to be here soon? How far along are you?"

"I have a bit of a problem."

"Oh no, no. What is it? Are you still coming? Did the cops stop you or something?"

"No. It's nothing like that."

"Then what is it?"

"I have to go to the hospital."

"Why, what happened?"

"Don't worry, nothing happened. At least, nothing happened to me. But I've got this girl here, her name is Jennifer and she's hurt. I need to get her to a hospital."

"Oh." James said, sounding a bit surprised. He realized that he was bleeding and wondered what had happened. Looking over his shoulder, he had the feeling that he was being watched. But it was probably nothing. It was probably just the toaster playing tricks on him. Toasters do that sometimes. Everybody knows that.

Debra said, "Yeah. Sorry. I picked her up along the way."

"Is there any other way... not that I don't understand, because I do. But can someone else take her?"

"I'm on highway sixteen now. What do you think?"

"You're close."

"Yeah, I'm right around the corner... but I need to take care of this first."

"Yeah, I guess."

"Okay, so listen. I'm getting off the phone, I'm being rude to Jennifer."

"Is she hurt bad?"

"She has a broken nose, and maybe a broken rib or two. She pretty beat up."

"Oh really."

"Yeah."

"What happened?"

"Jesus James, you're fucking impossible... I'll tell you everything when I get to the cottage, okay? I can't talk now. Like I said, I'm being rude. You know how it is."

"Okay, okay. Sorry about that. I just feel like talking."

"Well, I'll be there soon."

"I love you."

"'Kay. Bye."

"Bye."

Saying I love you felt wrong. It felt like a lie.

It wasn't that James didn't love his girlfriend; he did. But dragging her out to the cottage seemed reckless; it seemed like the wrong move.

Debra should be home or somewhere safe. James was no good now; he was a fugitive, a wanted man. He was ten gallons of trouble in a five-gallon drum. He was a killer, a waste of effort, armed and dangerous—

The train of thought hit an unexpected way station.

"Armed and dangerous," James whispered with a cursing tone.

Damn, he thought. I forgot the shotgun in the car.

James set the phone on the counter next to the butcher knife. He unplugged the toaster and covered it with a blanket (to keep it from biting him; sometimes they do that). He put the toaster in a bedroom closet and placed a stack of books in front of the closet door. Then he placed a lamp on top of the books, took the lampshade off the lamp and placed it on the desk where the lamp once stood.

That oughta hold it, he thought, referring to the toaster. *Now where did I put that shotgun?*

83

Debra hung up the phone and said, "That was my boyfriend. His name is James. He's an idiot."

"You have a boyfriend," Jennifer said flatly. She was feeling a little better now; she was able to talk. "I kind of figured."

"Yeah... well he's sort of my boyfriend. I still have a good time if you know what I mean. I do what I wanna do."

"Oh, you have one of those relationships."

Debra smiled. "I do. He doesn't. At least, I don't think he does." After a little thinking she said, "He better not have one of those relationships or I'll kill him."

Jennifer nodded. She realized that she didn't care much for Debra. She figured the girl was a selfish bitch. Having sex with a multitude of people was fine in her books, but lying and cheating on someone that thinks you love them is another. It was the lowest of the low. A relationship is special thing, based on trust. Assholes like Debra gave sexually driven girls a bad name.

With obvious distaste, she said, "But it's okay for you to do... whatever, right? As long as you don't get caught."

Debra smirked. "What can I say? Guys love me and I've only got one life to live. Am I right or am I right?"

"I suppose." Jennifer forced a smile, disgusted. She clapped a hand softly against her knee. "I appreciate this you know. I really do."

"I know."

"Yeah but, I want to say it again, now that I've got my head on a little straighter. Thank you."

"Don't worry about it. You look better… now that you cleaned up a bit."

Jennifer shrugged, wordlessly explaining herself by gathering a handful of paper towels that were covered in dirt and blood. She put the paper towels in plastic bag, and tucked the bag beneath her feet. While she did this, Debra turned on the radio and hit some buttons. Snippets of music, static, commercials and news reports came and went. After a brief search they found a station proclaiming to be the 'home of the hit makers', playing Elton John.

"Tiny Dancer," Debra said, laughing and resisting the urge to sing tunelessly. "I love this song."

Jennifer smiled without forcing it. "So do I."

As the song played, fingers tapped and Jennifer's spirits lifted. She listened quietly, allowing the hook of the melody to take her away. It was the beginning of the healing process, a therapeutic moment. It came much earlier for Jennifer then it does for most assaulted women. She was a tough girl.

The song finished and the car passed a hospital sign; relief washed over both of them.

"Finally," Jennifer said, turning down the volume of the radio.

Debra smiled. "We've only been driving forty-five minutes or so, and we're in the middle of nowhere. We found a hospital sooner than I thought. To be honest, I'm surprised we found one at all."

"Yeah, I guess you're right. It just hurts, that's all. I want this to end."

"Where does it hurt most?"

"My nose."

"Did those painkillers I give you kick in yet?"

"I don't know. My face is killing me."

"How about your ribs?"

Jennifer lifted an eyebrow. "Sitting this way makes me feel better. The ribs don't hurt too much. They do, but… you know. It's just my nose that's bugging me. It's throbbing. And this chipped tooth keeps stinging. It hurts when I inhale."

"That sucks."

"Yeah."

They drove past a farmhouse that had a dozen cars in the long gravel driveway. A bonfire surrounded with people, laughing and drinking, could be seen at the side of the barn. Both girls fell silent as they drove past. They stayed quiet for several minutes.

Jennifer was the first to speak. "You know what? Those pills you gave me are working. I do feel better, now that I think about it." Jennifer touched her nose delicately. "Why would someone do this to me?"

Debra shook her head and said, "I can't believe it happened. I'm shocked." There was a slight pause, then, "It makes me nervous."

Jennifer nodded her head lightly. "Me too. If I ever see his face again, I think I'll lay down and die."

"I hope they catch him."

"Yeah. I hope he gets what's coming to him."

"Which is?"

"I don't know, getting his balls cut off?"

Debra snickered. "Is that all?"

Jennifer changed radio stations. She found a college station with poor reception. The inexperienced disk jockey was fumbling his words, trying to be cool while explaining that he was about to play an instrumental version of How High by Redman and Method Man, followed by a bunch of classic hip-hop: A Tribe Called Quest, Fu-Schnickens, Goodie Mob, Nas, N.W.A., Slick Rick, The Roots, and Kurupt. He was a terrible DJ but it was a good string of tracks, not that either girl knew it. They listened for a while then Jennifer changed stations. Now Otis Redding was singing a cover of the Beatles. The song was Day Tripper, which seemed to fit their mood.

"Is this the original version, or is it a cover?" Debra asked.

Jennifer shrugged. "What is this?"

"It's that Beatles song, I think."

"I don't know; I don't recognize it. It sounds old."

Eventually, Debra said, "You know... you're holding yourself together better then I would. I'd be a mess. I've been through a few things; nothing like this mind you... nothing close to this. But I know how I'd be. I be thinking about everything over and over again, making myself crazy, making myself upset. And I'd imagine every nightmare I could. The, 'what-ifs', you know? What if this, and what if that... I get that way. Sometimes I can't let things go. But you're different then me, I can tell. This doesn't seem to be bothering you at all."

"It's easy when you don't remember what happened."

"You don't?"

"Nope. Not really. I remember stopping the car and talking to the guy... the guy that attacked me. He seemed normal enough, kind of like a used car salesman. He seemed nice, natural. He didn't come off like a weirdo or anything, so I wasn't worried. Then I noticed that he had blood on his shirt. I thought, oh my—you're hurt. Then I looked at him, and realized he was insane. His eyes seemed to be spinning in their sockets. His face looked like a corpse's. And before I had a chance to say anything he reaches into the car and grabs me. He slams my head against the window. I remember telling him to stop, and I remember the pain... I remember getting dragged outside. I thought he was going to kill me. And he was kicking me... I remember that. But that's it. When I woke up I figured he was still around. And I thought I'd been raped. But the guy was gone; he took my car. And... I don't know. I don't think he raped me."

"Really?"

"Yeah, really. I mean... I know my shirt was off, but... I think it came off by accident."

"Yeah right. How is that possible?"

"I was wearing a bikini top. It was nice; cost me sixty bucks. It might have been sitting in the grass." Jennifer took a few seconds, arranging her thoughts. "Yeah. It probably came off by accident. Or maybe he wanted a cheap thrill; I don't know. Hell, if he had of treated me better I would have shown him my tits for nothing."

"Oh yeah?"

"You wanna see 'em?"

Debra laughed. "I've seen them."

Jennifer nodded and smiled thoughtfully. In time she said, "After I woke up I checked myself out... you know, down there. It was one of the first things I did. And, I don't think he touched me there. It doesn't hurt, and it's not wet or dirty or anything. It feels the same."

"You're lucky."

"Yeah, " Jennifer said sarcastically. "I'm real lucky. It's my lucky day. I should buy a lottery ticket."

"You know what I mean."

"Yeah, yeah. I'm just... you know, fucking around with you."

"I know."

"I'm pissed off though. He stole my car. I had a huge CD collection in there, a nice pair of boots and an iPod. It took me forever to get all those tracks and the boots were gorgeous. What an asshole."

"No kidding."

They drove without speaking for the next couple minutes, following the signs to the hospital. When they arrived, Debra went inside, leaving Jennifer in the car. She spotted two empty wheelchairs next to a vending machine.

The waiting area was nearly empty; it smelled like medicine. Three women sat in one corner, and on the other side of the room, two men sat alone. A Chinese woman sat behind a computer.

Debra shouted across the lobby, "I'll be back in a minute." Then she rolled the wheelchair beside the car and locked the wheels in place. She helped Jennifer change seats and brought her inside.

"Thanks again." Jennifer said.

"No problem."

"You've been my guardian angel. I'll have to repay you some time."

"Don't mention it."

As the big wheels stopped rolling a television captured Debra's attention.

"Oh God," she said, nodding towards the screen. "That's my stupid boyfriend. What a jerk off."

Jennifer looked up at the monitor and her mouth dropped open.

The television displayed a CNN split-screen. On the left half of the screen was James. On the right, Elmer.

Below the men it said, MARTINSVILLE HOSTAGE CRISIS.

84

Elmer leapt from the edge of the bank. Helga lifted a knee and raised both hands. When the two bodies connected Helga's knee caught Elmer in the groin. Her right arm missed its mark completely and her left arm connected with Elmer's chest; it shattered like an eighty-four-year-old brittle twig. They both screamed, but it was Helga that kept on screaming. Her arm, now snapped in eleven places, had a large chunk of bone sticking through her forearm like a blunt stick. The agony was unlike anything she had experienced. It didn't come and go; it consumed her body and submerged her in a galaxy of physical suffering. When Elmer regained his wits he slapped a hand over Helga's screaming mouth and punched her in the stomach. Helga's eyes popped opened and mucus shot from her nose. Her feet kicked and her arms waved. Her broken arm flopped like a fish but she couldn't stop moving it; her body was going into shock.

Keeping his hand on Helga's mouth, Elmer slid his index finger and his thumb over her nose and pinched. Now her air was cut off and her face began changing color. It turned pink, then red; then blue. Her eyes opened wide and grew dark. The veins in her neck bulged and her arms and legs kicked with more urgency. Blood ran along her elbow, like it was attached to a pump. A small pool formed and Elmer freed a hand and punched her twice more. He looked fanatical now, dedicated to the art of murdering this unfortunate soul.

Helga was desperate. She slammed her knee into Elmer's groin a second time, hitting him square. It didn't hurt much, but the blow threw Elmer off balance and his hand slipped from her face.

Sucking huge mouthfuls of air, Helga began screaming, "Oh God! OH G-God! OH DEAR GOD, SAVE M-ME!"

Instead of covering the woman's mouth, Elmer positioned himself better and pinned her arms with his legs. He pummeled her in the face with his fists. First a left, then a right, then another left, then another right. The onslaught never seemed to end. It went on and on until her face was crushed and trodden, packed into itself like a pair of rolled socks. When Elmer was finished, which was none too soon, his knuckles were bloody and his victim was dead.

85

James moved furniture into the bedroom for various insane reasons: something was too big, too small, too old, too new, it smelled funny, it wasn't to be trusted, it was stupid, it was smart, it was thinking, it wasn't thinking, it was alive, it was dead, it was gross, it was clean, it was dirty, it was a sworn enemy, it reminded him of his mother, it *was* his mother, it was his father, it talked too loudly, it didn't say enough, it was listening, it was watching, it wasn't watching, he didn't feel like being around it, he didn't like it, he thought it was an alien.

As James removed a painting from a wall (the painting was too old, too big and had too many colors) he remembered Suzy's shotgun. It was sitting in the car.

Shotguns can get lonely, he told himself. Very lonely. That's what makes them dangerous.

He dropped the painting and made for the door. Then he heard Helga scream, "Oh God! OH G-God! OH DEAR GOD, SAVE M-ME!" He stopped dead in his tracks and a shiver rolled down his spine. That scream could only mean one thing:

The Bakisi had arrived.

James ran outside and opened the car door. He grabbed the shotgun and the box of shells and he ran between the two cottages. In the blackened alley he tripped and fell. The shotgun slipped from his fingers and he grunted loudly—loud enough for the Bakisi to hear. Of this he was sure; all hopes of a sneak attack were lost.

James stumbled along the ground, trying to find the weapon. But it was dark and his eyes hadn't adjusted yet. Fingers tickled rocks, dirt and grass with urgency, before ultimately, his fingers found Franco's warm, bleeding corpse.

He knew Franco; he liked the man quite a bit.

The Demon is here, James told himself. *The Demon is here!*

Suddenly he was shouting, "FUCK, FUCK, FUCK!" But that was no good. He needed to stay quiet. And more importantly—he needed the shotgun.

86

Mia ran from the kitchen as fast as she could. The need to escape her apartment had come at last, in a great, all-consuming heap. As her feet began moving she felt the cold air at her heals. It felt like death itself was chasing her, which wasn't far from the truth.

She made her way out the front door and down the hall staying close to the far wall. Her ankle twisted slightly, and she thought for sure she would fall on her ass and before she could say uh-oh-spaghetti-o she'd have her eyes pulled from her head and her arms ripped off and her legs broken into a hundred thousand pieces. But she didn't slip, she didn't fall, and her ankle held tight.

When she arrived at the elevator she hit both buttons. But how long would she wait, and how much time did she have? The answer was simple: she had no time to spare and waiting was suicide.

So what options did that leave?

Changing the gears in her mind, Mia decided on the staircase. She took the stairs two, three, sometimes four at a time. The steps soared past. She didn't know she could move so quickly. Her knees pumped and her hands held the railing for balance. It seemed that her feet never even touched the floor. She sped past a NO SMOKING sign and a fire extinguisher. She wondered if the extinguisher would make a good weapon but the answer didn't matter. She ran past it before her thoughts had time to find a conclusion.

She came to her first obstacle at the bottom of the staircase. It was a discarded newspaper. The headline read: MANHUNT FOR MARTINSVILLE KILLER GOES ON. She slammed her foot on top and it cost her. The paper went one way and she went he other. The railing slipped from her hand and suddenly everything changed: her feet were in the air and her mouth was open and her eyes were facing the ceiling.

After landing hard on her back she jumped up like a rabbit and ran towards a door that led to the underground parking lot. Any other time she would have stayed right there, with her mind convincing her body that it was broken; but not today. Today she didn't have time for a broken body so she kept moving. She passed through a door and five long seconds later she was standing at her car—without her purse, and more importantly, without her car keys.

Panicking, she shouted, "What am I DOING?"

Then she began running again. This time, her feet moved her body towards a door she hadn't used before. Hopefully it wasn't locked. But it had to be, right? Isn't that the way these things usually ended—with a screaming girl pounding both fists against a locked door? (Sure it is, **her** inner child warned. Everybody knows that. You'll have your throat **cut** before you know it. It's pine-box time, my dear. You and your parents **will** be buried together now! Isn't it wonderful?) Mia tried the door; it was unlocked. She cranked it open and ran up six stairs, through another hallway and out another door.

Outside seemed surreal. Everything was calm, quiet, dark. Nice.

"Hey!" she shouted, and a few people turned their heads. They seemed curious, but not helpful. She raised her hands in the air and tried to wave down a car.

But the driver in the car wasn't having it. He saw her standing there, but he didn't slow down. Truth be told, he sped up.

87

Switch drove alone listening to punk rock and classic metal. Today's music of choice included The Ramones, Judas Priest, Dio, S.N.F.U and NOFX. It was music he knew well and played often. He was smiling and singing and in a wonderful mood, which was common. He was a good guy to be around. And just the other day he downloaded a handful of Blondie tracks that were recorded live at CBGB's, back in the day. They sounded like shit but were cool to hear. He enjoyed his music for a long while, and then clicked off his iPod and took pleasure in the silence.

As Switch closed in on his destination, he stopped for coffee and pie at King's Diner. He chatted up a teenage girl that was working behind the counter and when he was done, he returned to his car with slow, dragging feet.

The fact of the matter was this: he didn't know how to approach the evening.

In fact, he didn't really want to go. But he did go. And if you asked him why, he wouldn't be able to answer. Switch was like that. He did things that his instincts hated, and often felt that he had no choice.

He thought to himself—Elmer's pissed off. There's no doubt about that. But killing a man, well, that's something that shouldn't be taken lightly.

He decided—at some point after his second coffee was gone, and his pie was gone, and the waitress had stopped talking to him—that he would make Elmer see things a different way. Show the man logic, talk him down and cool him off—for a day, maybe two. Then if Elmer still wanted to murder a man, Switch would listen to him, and maybe, just maybe…

No. Switch wondered what he was thinking.

Elmer was a friend, sure he was; he was a good friend, an old friend, a friend that he respected—but Switch would take no part in the killing. Killing was wrong.

It had to be stopped.

88

Elmer looked at the blood on his hands and at the trodden face of the dead woman. She was lying in the sand near the edge of her family's property line. Her right arm was slanted upward and her left arm was folded onto itself near the wrist, showing bone in two places. But Elmer wasn't enjoying his visuals; he was more concerned with a different slice of his acuity: his sense of hearing.

Elmer, all ears now, listened for the intruder that had become aware of his presence. Somebody was near; he was sure of it.

On the far side of the cottage he heard a voice, possibly two. He assumed that one voice belonged to James, which it did. He didn't rule out the idea that James was alone, but Elmer heard more than a voice or two. He heard a door slam and a scuffle. Stuff like that didn't happen without reason. No sir. Stuff like that happened when somebody was trying to get somewhere fast. Odds were, James came outside quickly wanting to know who was screaming and why.

Slowly, carefully, Elmer pulled himself off of Helga's body, trying not to make a noise. Wind blew dirt in his face. He put his hands down and shifted his weight; his fingers sank into the sand, which had turned cold. And beneath the top layer, the earth was colder still. Holding his breath, he started moving. First he shifted his right hand and right leg. Then he shifted his left hand and left leg. Each time it did this, he could hear his jeans rubbing against the sand. He assumed that his knees were leaving a good-sized trail. He didn't care about the trail—it was dark now; the trail meant nothing. The sky had blossomed into the night and the moon had shown itself to be small and powerless; it looked like a sickle. And that was before the clouds had erased it completely. No, he didn't care about the trail; it was the sound that was bothering him.

As Elmer moved, his pants seemed unacceptably loud. He figured the entire beach could hear him. And people were nosey. That was one thing Elmer knew for sure. People were nosey.

Hell, he thought. Just look around. Two dead bodies on the beach don't lie. If the old couple weren't so fucking nosey—why, they'd still be alive!

After crawling thirty feet, Elmer allowed himself to breath a little. He looked over his shoulder. A half-mile away or so—it was hard to tell for sure—a campfire was lighting up the beach. It looked like a pack of teenagers, from his position, four or five of them.

One was playing the guitar and singing a song that sounded like Bob Dylan. But that couldn't be right, could it? Did teenagers like Bob Dylan? He doubted it. He also wondered if they heard Helga screaming. If they did, they didn't seem to care and more importantly, they didn't act on it.

Elmer pushed on, making more noise then before. Up ahead he spotted a man and a woman walking along the shoreline, holding hands. The couple had a dog, which ran circles alongside them. Elmer stood up and began walking towards the people, thinking—kill them. But why? And how? He didn't have a knife or a gun. He also didn't have a reason. These people weren't looking for trouble, or suspicious of him in any way. They were just another twosome walking along the beach. Just walking, he thought—a husband and wife, perhaps. They were probably in love. Married. Kids. Families. But he wanted to kill them. And they were closer now, twenty feet away.

Nineteen.

Eighteen.

Seventeen.

He still wanted to kill them.

The dog ran away from the couple, towards him. It barked once, then twice. Then, as the dog bounced and leapt and wagged its tail, Elmer considered the way that he must look after killing the old couple. Like a lunatic, he thought. His face and shirt, covered in blood, his knuckles sandy and raw; his hair matted to one side. It was the aftermath of combat.

He mumbled, "Where the fuck is Switch?"

Shouldn't Switch be here by now?

Fifteen.

The dog was at his heals, still barking.

Whroof. Whroof. Whroof.

"Hello!" the lady on the beach said, nodding her head and smiling.

Then the man waved.

Twelve.

Elmer raised a hand as his shoe clipped a sandy wave in the beach. He ran his tongue across the grime of his teeth and could still taste the salty aftertaste of Franco in his mouth.

Ten.

"Hello," Elmer said with a grin. "Nice night for a stroll, isn't it?"

Nine.

Eight.

The couple didn't say another word. Their faces were blank and ex-pressionless.

89

The man in the car was old and tired and hung-over and wanted no part of Mia's bullshit. He hit the gas, flipped Mia the bird and drove around her. Fortunately for Mia, a second car was right behind the first. It stopped and without hesitating and Mia jumped into the back seat.

"What are you—?"

"DRIVE!" Mia shouted. "SOMETHING IS CHASING ME!"

The driver's mouth popped open and he hit the gas instinctively. The car shot ahead with tires squealing. Mia spun around and looked through the back window as the area shrunk away. She was breathing heavy and panting.

It's over now, she thought. *It's over.*

Then she thought, *isn't that what James said? Something is chasing me?* She felt her skin crawl.

"Who's chasing you?" the man behind the wheel asked. He was confused, but not upset. His name was Alex; he was a nice guy. He was thirty-something, good-looking. He worked with a web development company and was quite gifted. He was also single, talked like a teenager and couldn't help noticing the curves of Mia's body. She looked voluptuous; he liked that. Most thirty-something teenagers did. Then again, Alex liked most women that gave him the time of day and he took what he could get more often than he'd like to admit.

"I don't know," Mia said. "Just go! Go!"

"But where am I taking you? I don't know what you want!"

"Get away from here! Turn right and keep going!"

"Do you, like, mind telling me what's going on? I can drive you somewhere, as long as it's like, close and you're not an asshole, but I wanna know why I'm doing it, ya know? That's just the way I am."

Mia gazed out the window. It was amazing how normal everything seemed. The houses were all sitting in a row, cars were either parked or driving, traffic was smooth and people were going about their business. She pulled her eyes from the scenery and leaned on the front half of the seat. Her heart was racing.

She said, "Do you know what happened today?"

"I sure do," Alex said. "Everything's been happening today. It's been nuts and crackers around here. Or are ya, like, talking about what happened inside that building you came running out of? Because if you are, then, yeah. I know about that too. I live there. I've lived there for six years, or is it seven? I don't know. Six or seven. I live on the fifth floor. It's a pretty nice place if you ask me. It's fancy. I can see half the town from my balcony, and that's alright by me."

"You live there, huh? So do I."

Alex snatched a better look at Mia. Even in her frazzled state she was gorgeous, which went a long way with Alex. He liked hot women. If only he could find one to love.

He said, "Really? You live there? Do you live on the fifth?"

"Yeah."

"Oh wow. Jesus dude, what are the odds of that? Do you know Debra? I live next to her!"

"No, I don't."

"Oh you should meet her. She's great. She's a cute girl, dark hair, smoker, likes to dress like a slut." Alex suddenly stuck his knuckle in his mouth. He looked embarrassed and fumbled his words, trying to undo the statement. "Well, come on, like, you know what I mean. She wears loose tops and stuff. Half the time you can see... well, you know."

Mia didn't care about Alex's careless tongue. She didn't care about anything.

She said, "Up until a couple weeks of ago my time was divided between my job and my boyfriend. Now they're both gone and I have a dog."

"What happened?"

"I don't want to talk about it. Not now."

"I thought you looked familiar," Alex said. He was lying of course. He was just trying to impress her, land a date. Land a wife.

"Oh?"

"Yeah, after a while you get to know the people in the building. Some people I see all the time. I don't see you all the time, but I recognize you."

"I'm the girl that escaped from the killer today. My face has been all over the news. Maybe that's why."

"You are?" Alex was shocked. "Why aren't you at the police station?"

"I was there for three hours."

"That's wild. I heard that bad stuff was happening today. So, like, who's chasing you? Is it the killer? Is he like, in the building again?"

Mia shrugged and rubbed a hand across her face. For the first time since she jumped into the car she thought about her parents. She had forgotten somehow. During her getaway all she could think was: RUN. And that's what happened. She ran. But now a back-catalog of sorrow and horror was re-surfacing and it hurt like hell.

Alex said, "Someone told me the killer was Debra's boyfriend, but I don't know about that. I know him pretty well. James is his name. It doesn't seem to fit if you ask me."

His words seemed to be a question that Mia didn't answer. A breath of silence came between them, and although Alex had plenty left to say on the topic he held his tongue as long as he could. The silence lasted three seconds.

"Yeah, I know James," Alex continued. "He's quiet sometimes, he's loud sometimes. We went to a Halloween party together. Debra likes him quite a bit and I bug her about it all the friggin' time. She takes it well. You'd like Debra. I'll like, introduce you, if you want. I'll introduce you to James too."

"No thanks."

Alex made a dumb face. "Come on. Don't be like that. They're good people."

"I need to go to the police station," Mia said. Then she put her hands over her face and cried her eyes out.

90

The Bakisi left Mia's apartment and killed two boys. They were standing in a hallway, talking video games. The incantation took them both on a once, exterminating them quickly by crushing their hearts. Later, the medical teams involved would list the deaths as suspicious, but autopsies would show something different and force the unlikely assumption of natural causes. Not that the Bakisi would know this—or care. The Bakisi had no interest in the thoughts or politics of man, for the beast was untouchable and eternally alone. And man could do nothing to stop the instinctive nature of the creature, or condition it to the will of the human race. Nor could man understand the Bakisi's unchanging and ageless temperament, which never faltered and never modified.

After the Bakisi killed the boys it searched the building—floating but not floating, touching walls and floors but not touching walls and floors. The molecules inside the being separated; they stretched over several meters. It was in this way—with condensing and expanding molecule densities—that the Bakisi was capable of traveling through its surroundings, suspended inside the atmosphere, drifting through the physical objects it encountered. Its science was indistinguishable to the human eye.

The Bakisi floated high above the building. It could see the trees, streets, people and cars. It could see the buses, buildings and sidewalks. It circled Martinsville like an eagle, in a wide tracking ring. It searched the beaches of the south and the forests of the north. It searched the hills, valleys and roadways of both east and west. Then it swooped down, gliding though the streets of Martinsville, checking the houses, schools, swimming pools and parks.

Hunting the woman scent which, for the time, seemed lost.

91

Alex pulled the car to the side of the road, bumping the curb, forty-five feet away from the mammoth doors of the police station. As the curb and rubber met, Mia wiped a hand across her chin and looked down. She eyed her legs for no distinguishable reason, thinking about the things she had seen. She noticed a smear of blood on her left knee, and drops of blood on her right. She couldn't finger the moment it happened, but it did happen. All of it; the bloodstains on her clothing were proof—solid, undeniable proof.

A deep, ugly sickness threatened to consume every last morsel of her being. But she didn't want to be sick. She didn't want to cry more. She had cried enough and wanted to get going, see the police and try to understand what the hell went wrong.

Keeping her eyes on the bloodstain, Mia said, "Thank you, Alex. You've been great." Then she lifted her chin, placed a hand on the door handle and applied some force. The door opened. Mia slid one foot outside.

Alex twisted towards her.

"No worries," he said with a soft, disadvantaged tone. "I'm glad to help you out."

But the truth, Alex knew, was slightly different than he wanted to admit. The truth was—he was glad to have met her, regardless of the circumstance. He needed a woman in his life; he needed one bad.

Somewhere overhead, the Bakisi detected Mia's scent. It changed course, and began moving in a straight line, faster and faster. Plummeting.

Alex said, "Hey Mia?"

"Yeah?"

"I know this is a bad time and everything, and I'm not trying to make you uncomfortable. Honest I'm not. But if you want to hang out later and you like, need someone to talk with, I'm right down the hall. I'm less than sixty feet away. And I'm a good guy, a good listener. At least, that's what my friends tell me."

"Thanks Alex. I appreciate that. You've been great."

"You know which door is mine, right?"

"Five-fifteen."

"Five-fifteen. That's the one. Don't hesitate to give me a ring, any-time, day or night. I'd love to see you again, under different circumstances of course. Maybe we could like, get together for a drink or something."

Mia nodded, stepped outside and closed the door tight.

Alex rolled the window down and leaned out. "And don't worry," he said. "Things are bad now, but like, things will get better. I promise. Things always get better."

"Thanks again Alex. I'll talk to you soon."

"Do you want me to come inside with you?"

"No, no. I'll be fine. Thank you."

Mia walked a staggered line towards the giant police station doors, feeling a significant amount of sadness. Her parents were dead, murdered. But why—and what the hell had happened?

Two police officers rushed past with shoulders wide and stern. They moved like they were in a hurry. Mia snatched a quick, careless glance, and realized that both cops had thick mustaches and wore dark, thick-rimmed sunglasses. With the uniforms, the men looked almost identical. And gay. It was a stupid observation, but for some reason it prompted Mia to stop walking and turn around.

Alex was still there, watching.

She looked at Alex and her thoughts changed direction. She felt her fingers tighten and her muscles tense. She hated it when guys offered too much attention. It made her feel like a piece of meat. And today, that was the last thing she needed. Guys were always hitting on her, it seemed. And after a while it felt less and less flattering; it felt insulting.

But Alex seemed different than the others—somehow.

Sure, he wanted to get laid, of course—but he was sweeter than most guys she encountered. He was cute, and he had a youthful quality she hadn't seen in a while. And he did help. He did. That had to be worth something—a knock on the door, a cup of coffee, an open mind.

Looking Mia up and down, Alex waved.

Mia returned the gesture, just as the image of her father came to her. He was propped up against the counter. His face was swollen and red; blood ran down his neck.

Satan is with us, he had said. Satan.

Jesus.

Mia wanted to think that her father had gone crazy, but she didn't. Something happened; something she didn't understand.

Alex, who had no idea that Mia was so upset, opened his mouth, preparing to unleash one last mouthful of words, one final awkward attempt to bring Mia into his life. But the words never came.

The Bakisi came instead.

Mia was thrown to the concrete ground. Her neck snapped twice; it tore open and a jet stream of blood cascaded into the air like a fountain.

Alex found himself jumping out of the car and running towards her.

What's happening here? He wondered.

Then ice-cold fingers circled his neck and a pressure he had never known crushed his throat. He heard a woman scream. His eyes bulged and his face was forced into his chest. With knees buckling, Alex fell to the ground and rolled. And in his final moments, before the police would come running (those same two men that Mia assumed were gay), he watched blood gush through a growing hole in his dress shirt, knowing—but not quite understanding—that his ribcage was being pulled apart.

92

Three bedrooms, one bathroom, one common room and two exits: that was Debra's cottage. The common room was a kitchen, a dining room, a living room, and the gateway to the outdoor patio (which overlooked the beach) all in one. And on the other side of the cottage, a hallway with a door at the end of it divided the four remaining rooms: two bedrooms on one side, bed and bath on the other.

It was in this hallway that James found himself hiding.

After James had fallen, he searched until he found the shotgun. Then he ran inside the cottage, threw the box of shells on the dining room table, opened the box and pumped shells into the chamber. This took time, lots of time. And when he was ready to step outside again—to save the screaming woman, or shoot the screaming woman, or do whatever he was thinking of doing—he felt that it was too late. The screaming had ended.

James stepped outside slowly, and his heart rate stabilized. He no longer felt a sense of urgency. He felt something else—something comparable to stupidity. Creeping outside, into danger, into a dark open space—it wasn't exactly the play of the day.

He returned indoors like a coward and swiftly locked both doors. Then he turned the lights on, closed the bathroom door and the bedroom doors. It was all about the common room and the hallway now, nothing more. The common room was almost empty; the hallway was as clean as a whistle. The other rooms were shut off and were no longer an issue.

He looked over his shoulder, scratching his head. Where was it? Where was the killing machine? What was it waiting for? Where was it hiding?

Come on—

After sneaking from window to window, James cowered in the hallway. His fingers gripped the weapon like he was trying to kill it. His eyes were wide and glossy; his hair was a damp and tattered mess. He could smell the oak and pine of the cottage, and occasionally he would mumble, and give himself warning: Stay quiet... stay quiet... stay quiet...

Because it was here, the killing machine was here.

93

Thoughts and conversations swirled through Debra's mind in sporadic isolated chunks. A surge of anger and frustration raced throughout her frayed and battered emotions.

She hated James. Hated him!

She slammed a hand against the steering wheel before pushing on the gas pedal. The engine awoke from its half-slumber, pitching up two notches. The trees blurred in the darkness; the road raced beneath the wheels. Small drops of rain bounced lightly against the windshield, and then the raindrops grew—size and weight doubling, tripling, quadrupling. Just as Debra flicked the wipers on, a crack of lightening thrashed against the skyline.

Debra, alone now, took her eyes from the road and looked into the sky. She heard the rain before seeing it, like angry fists pounding against a steel drum without rhythm. Titanic drops of rain slammed the car. She blinked twice, astounded by the sudden downpour. She pulled her foot from the gas pedal, pressed the brake and threw the wipers on full blast. But her vision had narrowed. It was becoming non-existent—even with the vehicle slowing, even with the wipers blasting and her body arced towards the windshield—the rain was in control now. The rain had taken the land.

Noticing that her window was down and water was getting inside the car, Debra lifted a hand from the steering wheel and crushed a finger against a button on the door. The window hummed, then closed. Alone in the car, the dusty seats and stale air caught her senses. Her finger tapped the button, once, twice. She opened the window a little bit, just a crack, and then closed it again. Her thoughts turned to smoking—the taste, the smell. But why smoking, she wondered. She hated smoking, and had given it up long ago, so why here? Why now? She hadn't smoked in weeks.

But what about girls-night, when was that? Last night?

She pushed the thought away. Girls-night didn't count.

She thought about the rain. She thought about driving and considered stopping at a convenience store. Yeah. Stopping at a convenience store. That would be nice—a nice little break—but not to buy cigarettes, of course. No. She just wanted to get out of the rain for a minute or two, pick up a bottle of juice, or a cup of coffee, or maybe one of those super-fattening but terribly delicious chocolate ice-cream bars, but not cigarettes. Buying a pack of cigarettes would be stupid, a total waste of time and money. The pack would go stale. She wouldn't even smoke it. And besides, she didn't enjoy smoking now. It tasted bad, like the bottom of an ashtray. Hell, she wasn't sure why she started in the first place.

Her (smoking) fingers tapped the window button.

Tap; tap; tap.

Well, maybe she knew why she had started. Yes, on second thought—of course she knew. She was young and foolish. It was the cool thing to do. Her friends were doing it, and even if they weren't they thought she was cool when she was doing it. Wasn't that right?

Yes. Of course it was.

Tap; tap; tap.

Whatever. Who cares? Who fucking cares if smoking is cool, or not cool, or good for you, or bad for you… she was a non-smoker now, and nothing would change that, no matter what.

Tap; tap; tap.

She liked the sound of that, a non-smoker.

Tap; tap; tap.

And yes, she had quit before, and then started again. It was a stupid thing to do. She knew that, everybody did. Why start again, she wondered. Why would anyone start again? Smoking was a stupid thing; it was mind-less and unnecessary. It gave you bad breath. It gave you cancer. It turned your skin into a bowl of spaghetti wrinkles and made your (smoking) fingers (tap; tap; tap) yellow.

Debra pushed on the button. The window dropped an inch. She pushed the button again. The window raised an inch.

Tap; tap; tap.

Still, she thought. One cigarette would be nice; just one, for old times sake.

A shot of vodka would be nice too—with a cigarette.

After two minutes, Debra slowed the car to a sluggish crawl and turned a corner. Picking up speed, she clicked the radio on—static—then off. Ten minutes after that, she turned another corner. At the side of the road, standing next to a large green and purple bush (which reminded her of a meadow, or maybe a marsh) Debra spotted a man with his hands raised. He was smiling and looked friendly and helpless.

Although she didn't know it, the man was Elmer.

Elmer, soaked to the bone, waved and smiled like he needed assistance.

Debra ignored him. She didn't have time for strangers. Not now. Not today. She didn't even have time to stop at the convenience store to get a bottle of juice, or a cup of coffee, or maybe even an ice-cream bar (tap; tap; tap). She needed to see James. She needed to keep on moving, because she was twenty seconds away from being there.

"Sorry buddy." Debra mumbled, as she pulled the car into the cottage driveway. "Some other time."

***

Elmer watched; then turned away with a grin.

Deep inside the gloom of the rain, another car was approaching. He figured it was Switch.

Let the games begin, Elmer thought. *Let the games begin.*

94

James saw headlights in the driveway. He leaned the shotgun against the wall, opened the door and stepped outside.

Debra parked her car in the center of the lane and ran towards the cottage. "Get inside James! It's pouring out here!"

As they stepped inside, Debra said, "We need to talk."

James closed the door and locked it. Then he put his arms around her, ran his fingers down her back and kissed her.

Debra, standing in the hallway, quickly pulled away. The kiss seemed forced, strange. Wrong.

"James—"

"I know, I know. We need to talk. Trust me, I get it. I need to tell you a few things too. And I need you to understand something, because I didn't lose my mind this afternoon, and I didn't mean to kill anyone. I've been a victim all day and I've made a few mistakes. I'm really sorry for everything I've done. I need you to understand this, okay baby? Please. Can you understand? I'm sorry."

"Shut up a minute, will you? Fuck. I just got here and you're being a dickhead. Give me some breathing room. What the hell is wrong with you?" Debra raised her eyebrows and laughed, but not in a happy way. It sounded like a laugh of frustration, annoyance and resentment.

She needed a fucking cigarette.

James watched her expressions, her emotional release. She needed time and didn't want to jump into the thick of things. He could understand that. He could sympathize. But the clock was ticking and he needed to explain the situation: explaining seemed essential, the key to everything.

"Yeah," James said. "You just arrived, but Debra... we need to talk and we need to do it now. Something's out there... I know it."

"What the hell is your problem? I've never seen you like this."

"I've never been like this.

Debra walked down the hall, shaking rainwater from her hands. She opened the fridge door, squatted, and pulled a bottle of water from the bottom shelf. After a quick drink she stood up, leaned against the counter, ran her fingers through her hair and said, "You lied to me."

"What?"

"You heard me."

"I didn't lie to you."

"Did you take hostages? Yes or no?"

James looked down. He put a hand on his face and pushed his fingertips into his brow. With a mind full of lies and a heart filled with truth—and the urge to blast her head clean from her body—he wondered what to do. The truth wasn't good and he knew it. The lies seemed like an easier road. And blowing her head off seemed to be the best of the bunch. He wondered how her brains would look dripping from the ceiling.

Debra took another drink of water. "You did, didn't you? You've taken hostages today. Why? Why the fuck would you do that? Have you gone crazy?"

"It's not my fault."

"Are you kidding me? How can you accidentally take hostages? What are you, some kind of terrorist now?"

"How do you know this? How do you know I took hostages?"

"It was on the fucking news asshole, on CNN. I saw footage of you—"

"Footage?"

"Yeah, from security cameras in my building."

"Oh my, really? You said your building didn't have cameras!"

"Well... whoops. I guess I was wrong." After a long, ugly pause, Debra said, "What the hell is going on today? Honestly, have you gone mad?"

James, biting his tongue, said, "Debra... Franco is dead. Someone, or something, killed him. And I heard screams, screams that didn't come from a man. I think the beach has a few more dead bodies lying on it. You want answers. I get that, but you need to know a few things first."

Squinting her eyes, Debra said, "You mean Franco—"

"Yeah."

"Franco... my neighbor?"

"Yes."

Debra stepped away from the counter. "Did you kill him?" She asked, thinking he had.

"No, Debra. I swear on my life, I didn't touch him."

"Honest?"

"Of course! Don't you know me?"

Debra realized that for the first time ever, she was afraid of James. Wondering if she was in danger she said, "Not today I don't."

"Debra..."

"How come everywhere you go people are dying, and how do you know Franco's dead? How do you know that he's dead if you didn't do it?"

"I found him outside, and look at me..." James opened his arms, as if to say, "I didn't do it." But with the shotgun in his hand he looked like a creep.

"I don't know why I came here," Debra said flatly.

"Neither do I," James said. Then he pointed the gun in her direction.

"James?" Debra stepped back. "What are you doing?"

"You know what I'm doing."

Debra felt her nerves tighten. James was about to kill her. She knew this now; it was so completely obvious.

On the driveway, headlights cut through the pouring rain.

The game was about to begin.

PART FIVE:
THE GATHERING

95

The hot August temperature was gone. Lightening cracked, thunder roared, and between the two events clouds pushed out wave after wave after wave of rainwater. The water flooded the ditches and overwhelmed the lanes. It drowned the flowers and shrubs while submerging the grass. The wind, which had come and gone throughout the day, had returned once again in all its powerful glory. Trees were swaying, branches were cracking and animals, both large and small, were hiding or finding shelter. On the far side of the cottage, where the beach had transformed into sludge, the lake had become a volatile place where no sailors dared to set sail. And beneath the instability and regimented confusion of the rocky waves, the fish and the sea-creatures found refuge in deeper, colder waters, where the storm had little, if any, effect.

James lowered the weapon and ran to the window. Debra, confused, followed. Together they stood in the hall watching the downpour drill pockmarks into a driveway that had become a mucky, mud-drenched nightmare.

"Who's here?" Debra said very softly, almost whispering. She nodded her head towards the light on the driveway.

James spoke quietly too, not that it was necessary. The rain was loud on the roof. "I don't know. Maybe it's your parents."

"My parents? I doubt it."

"Why?"

"Look at the weather. Nobody comes to the cottage on a day like this. Why come when it's raining?"

James scratched his head. "I don't know, but who is it? Who else would be here, if not your family?"

"Maybe someone's lost, or in the wrong driveway?"

"Yeah, maybe."

The headlights turned off. Two doors opened and the car's interior lights came on. Two figures stepped into the rain and both doors closed together. CKH-UNK was heard in stereo and the yard fell into a darkness that seemed absolute.

"I can't see anything now," James whispered. He reached out and held Debra's hand. "Can you see? What are they doing?"

Debra considered resisting his touch but thought better of it. She didn't want to fight or upset him; she didn't trust it. "No, I can't see a thing."

"Where are they?"

"I don't know. Are they coming this way?"

James lightened his grip and allowed Debra's hand to fall away. He held the shotgun against his chest. "Who are they? Cops? Do you think?"

Debra shrugged. She looked at the gun and felt a nervous spike. With caution she asked, "What's that for?"

"What?"

"The gun. Why do you have it?"

"I told you. Things aren't right. We're in danger."

"Why did you point it at me?"

"I didn't. I was pointing it at them."

Debra considered his words. She didn't believe him, but she had to. The only other possibility was that he was about to kill her. And she wouldn't think that, although it seemed like the truth.

"Okay," she said distrustfully. "But do you really need a shotgun? Haven't you gotten into enough trouble with that thing?"

"You just don't understand."

"Make me understand."

James shook his head in frustration. "Whatever."

"Where did you get it, anyhow?"

"Sue's place."

Debra, thinking terrible thoughts, said, "Oh, James."

"What?"

Debra didn't respond. Instead she moaned.

"What? What's wrong now?"

"Just... don't."

"Don't what?"

"You're scaring me. That gun is scaring me. Why the hell did you bring a gun? Do you really want to kill more people today?"

"No."

"Did you kill Franco?"

"Debra," James said, with a heartrending expression. "Come on."

In the past, when Debra was upset, James knew what to say. He could make things better with a few simple words. He could make her smile; make her forget the concerns and dilemmas that plagued her mind. But here, now, James couldn't manipulate the conversation in his favor. Truth was, none of this made sense. He was as nervous as she was, a nervous wreck. And he wanted to shoot her. He really did, more than anything else. He wanted to shoot her and stab her and pull out her eyes. And he would. Oh yes. He would; he promised himself that. It was just a matter of time.

Debra looked outside, feeling the goose bumps surging on the back of her neck. "Where did they go?"

James rubbed a hand across the window in the door. Then he coughed twice, still feeling the effects of the fire. His lungs had taken quite a beating; they seemed to be filled with a coat of dust. He could hear his throat producing a thin wheezing noise, reminiscent of a child's rubber squeak-toy.

"I don't know where they are," he said. "I can't even see the car. Can you?"

"I think so."

James put his hands against the glass like binoculars. A few seconds later he said, "How is that possible? My eyes are better than yours and I can't see shit."

"I have my contacts in."

"Still…"

Ignoring James and his complaining tone, Debra tapped her fingers together. Tap; tap; tap. Something felt wrong, something she couldn't express or explain. It was like she was standing on a landmine.

She looked at James, wondering if his eyes were always so dark.

96

"There's so much rain," James said. "I can't believe it."

"We should call the police now, right?"

"What's that?"

"I should call the police now."

James reflected on the fire, the burning children, and the emergency vehicles that raced to the scene. He remembered the school and the chaos that was inside it. He blocked his thoughts and said "no" without realizing it. Then, with his eyes closed, he stepped away from the window feeling a light yet painful twinge inside his chest. He wondered if he would have a heart attack.

"Why not?" Debra asked.

"What?" James opened his eyes. He wanted to shoot Debra more than ever. But he wasn't ready yet. His thoughts were swaying. He thought about the Bakisi and the urge to kill came down a notch.

"Why not? Why shouldn't we call the police? If you're innocent I mean. If you're really innocent, explain it to the cops. It might be a pain in the ass, going to court and everything, but I'll stand by you. I promise."

"I don't think we should get the police involved Debra, at least, not yet."

"If we're in danger, we should call them."

As the words were spoken, Debra realized that the police had told her to stay close to home. She questioned her actions, her words. *How much trouble have I caused myself?* she wondered. *Will I be charged for something? Have I gone that far?*

As Debra's mind rehashed her conversation with the police, James was up to his eyeballs in his own thoughts. He wanted to explain; he wanted Debra to understand that before anything else happened—before the police were involved—he needed to kill the Bakisi.

Lightening blasted the sky, startling both of them.

"Who do think is out there?"

Debra shook her head. "I don't know. Maybe it's the police."

"Did you call them?"

"No."

"Honest?"

"I wouldn't lie to you, James. But you're being stupid."

James felt his shoulders slump. "Listen Debra," he whispered. "There's something you need to know."

"What is it?"

The sound of breaking glass filled the air, followed by an unusual, awkward TH-THUMP. One of the bedroom windows had just been destroyed.

James smiled, finished his thought and whispered, "You're going to die, you stupid fucking whore."

But Debra, who had just released a small, sharp yelp, didn't hear a word of it.

97

They shuffled down the hall together; James opened a bedroom door. He clicked the light on and stepped inside. Rain fell through the gaping hole where the window had once been. There was broken glass everywhere.

"What's this?" Debra asked. The room was loaded with furniture from the living room. And it wasn't just the furniture. It seemed like everything was in there. "Why would you do this?"

"It doesn't matter. I'll explain later."

"Explain now! What the hell are you doing?"

James stroked the gun. *Now*, he thought. *Do it now. Shoot her in the face. Shoot her in the face and then rape her. Pull the bones from her body and set her hair on fire. Chop off her head. Do it! Do it now!*

"I'm phoning the cops," Debra said. She had enough. "I'm not playing this game any longer; you've lost your fucking mind."

She rushed into the common room, aiming for the phone.

James spun around; he lifted his arms and said, "Don't Debra! Please! Let me deal with something first!"

Debra couldn't believe it: the phone was gone—almost everything was gone. Only a couch, a table and a chair remained. She wondered what to do, and then she remembered that her cell phone was in her purse, which was in her car. But did she want to step outside? No. She didn't. Not a chance.

"James, give me your phone," she said. "I'm calling the police."

"No! No police, not yet."

"Give me your phone, you psycho!"

"No!"

Before Debra had a chance to escalate the confrontation, another bedroom window smashed. The sound of rain became louder.

"Oh shit," James said. "It happened again!"

He scooted down the hallway and opened another door. Firewood was lying on the floor in a pool of broken glass. Without hesitation, James moved across the hallway and opened the third bedroom door.

This time he watched it happen: firewood smashed through the window; hundreds of tiny shards blasted apart and three large hunks of glass fell from the sill. Large pieces of glass exploded on the floor, becoming small, dangerous projectiles that bounced in every direction. The firewood landed on a carpet and rolled across the floor spinning.

With the shotgun raised, James walked to the window. He fired a shot into the darkness. The sound was enormous.

"Debra! My phone…" James reconsidered his words. Did he really want the police here?

"Where is it?" Debra shouted.

Firewood smashed through the kitchen window. Seconds later the bathroom window suffered the same fate.

Debra ran across the common room with tears forming in her eyes. "Come on, she said. "We're under attack! Give me your phone!"

Look on the table, James secretly thought while saying, "No Debra! No phones!"

Then the gunshots blasted. It was hard to say how many shots were fired; it sounded like a dozen or more. And as the patio doors shattered and glass went flying into the near empty living room, James thought he was hit. But he wasn't. Not yet.

98

Debra dropped on her hands and knees, and then rolled onto her belly. Tears streamed down her face. Her hands shook and her lips trembled.

She could feel the air blowing through the cottage now, and the rain seemed louder than ever. She was confused and afraid; she wished she had stayed home. Everything was happening too fast.

Holding the shotgun high, James stepped past Debra. He walked towards the door, the danger, and whatever else lay waiting. A growing puddle of rain was on the floor now, and James realized that every room would be wet. Not that it mattered. After all, a wet floor wasn't a concern. Living to tell the tale, on the other hand—

"Where are you going?" Debra mumbled, trembling on the floor. A mountain of thunder shook the world around them. "James?"

"Get down and stay down!"

He imagined that he was the masked executioner, and that she was a witch. He imagined a crowd of thousands watching and cheering as he raised the blade above his head.

Where is the axe? he wondered.

And there it was, lying on the floor near his feet. He set the shotgun down and lifted the axe up.

Now, he thought. *Chop off her head now.*

He knew it would be easy. Debra was lying face down with her hands over her ears. She was perfectly still. This was the moment he had been waiting for.

James raised the axe above his head.

Another two shots were fired. Both bullets came through the doorway, catching James in the shoulder. He spun in a circle and stumbled back. Pain tore through his body; blood squirted through the air. The axe slipped from his grasp, narrowly missing Debra's head.

And Debra screamed.

James, still standing, felt strange and distant. He wondered where he had been hit. Then another ripple of pain came, and his thoughts were lost inside a swirl of agony.

Another shot was fired. And another.

More glass fell.

Then came silence. Not total silence. No—not with the storm ripping the neighborhood a new asshole, but for James it seemed like silence. Or death.

Yes, he thought. *Perhaps death has come.*

He fell then. He fell against the wall and slid down it. And that's where he stayed—leaning against the wall with his legs folded together, the axe lying across his lap and his head resting against the pinewood wall. Blood bubbled from the double hole in his shoulder, staining his dress shirt red. His eyelids fluttered. Then his eyes closed and he began fading...

Debra scrambled towards James on all fours. She ripped open his shirt and rammed a finger into his wound.

James opened his eyes wide.

"Man oh man," Debra said, trying to whisper. "I need your phone you fucking idiot. I need your phone and I need it right now. Where the hell is it?"

She twisted her finger in a circle, scooping meat from his shoulder.

James felt the pain, heard the words, and sensed that something was rooting around inside his flesh, but he didn't understand. He was adrift within the pain and the confusion. The infection was getting worse now. The beast seemed to be taking control.

"Who would do this? He whispered, tasting blood in his mouth. "The police?"

"I don't think so asshole, but... oh God... I need the phone. Where is it? I need to call 911. This is an emergency James. This is an emergency!"

She rammed her finger in further.

James coughed and moaned. Soot-flavored blood filled his mouth. He didn't know if he was bleeding internally or if he had bitten his tongue. Perhaps it was both.

"Come on, come on!"

Debra heard footsteps. She felt the aura of an unfamiliar presence and looked up. She was hoping to see a uniform.

Elmer and Switch looked down at her; they were soaking wet. Switch held a baseball bat in the tight swirls of his hand. His eyes seemed to be filled with unstable, stressed-out shame. Elmer had two of Franco's guns tucked between his leather belt and his jeans. He had a sinful grin on his psychotic face; he looked like a gunslinger.

"What do you want?" Debra said. She pulled her finger free of James and pushed herself away from the two men.

"You'll see," Elmer said. He yanked the bat from Switch's grip and raised it high. Grinding his teeth together, he took a swing.

And James began laughing.

99

First came nothing, then a terrible, lonely darkness.

Footsteps.

Wind.

Cold.

A long empty road…

No… not empty.

Not empty.

Thunder.

Rain.

Lightening. And with the lightening came a brilliant sliver of light. And inside that brilliant sliver of light, that sliver of simple clarity, an image appeared. An image of people, dead people, a marching band that struggled to march, a band without music, without rhythm or happiness, moving together, walking in silence. They were the walking dead.

It slipped away.

Nothing.

Darkness.

People.

Dead—with feet dragging.

Tattered remains.

Clothing torn.

Broken bones. Crushed limbs. Missing teeth. Burning flesh.

Blood.

Fading.

Fading away to nothing, to red, to dust.

"I'm going to save you," a voice said. It was the boy. It was Mathew. He was sitting on a park bench with a balloon in his hand—a red balloon that seemed to be dripping blood.

"How can you save me?" a voice asked. The voice belonged to the person James had once been, before the infection. He sound normal and nice; he sounded sane.

The boy took a deep breath, as if discouraged. "All I can do is try. I can't promise you, James. It may not be within my power. But I'm on the other side. I'm with them. I will try."

Mathew released the balloon. It floated into the air, still dripping blood.

Drip; drip; drip.

James opened his blurry eyes and heard Debra crying—and begging. She sounded like she was in danger. He wanted to help her. He wanted to save her. He wanted to chop off her head and eat her body. But he was hurt. Blood was running along his face, falling to his legs.

I'm sitting in a chair, he thought. I'm tied up. Tied to the chair. But I've got to help Debra, because Debra's hurt. They're hurting her. Some-one is hurting her, making her cry, making her scream. I need to chop off her head.

I owe her that much.

Where have the gunshots gone?

Where are the guns?

James closed his eyes. He wanted them to stop hurting her. He needed them to stop, but... they didn't. They kept going; they kept doing whatever it was that they were doing. She was crying, begging, screaming.

She was suffering.

Suffering. Suffering.

He was drifting away. Drifting.

Drifting into the nothing, into the darkness, into the black.

Into the abyss—

Blackened.

Red.

Blood.

Dead bodies.

Tombstones.

Pain and suffering.

Vengeance. Retribution.

Walking, living scarecrows.

Rain. Thunder continuing.

Lightening. Two times. And with the lightening James saw Johnny among the scattered few.

Johnny.

Johnny walking.

Walking to the cottage—walking with the dead. Leading them to him.

Johnny, with a self-inflicted bullet hole in his head and blood dripping endlessly—he was bringing the dead through the darkness, the rain, the thunder and the lightening. Johnny was bringing the dead.

The dead were coming.

The dead would be here soon.

And a single red balloon floated above them.

Drip; drip; drip.

A single red balloon.

100

The Bakisi circled the town until it picked up another scent. This time, it found the scent inside the hospital. It traveled floor to floor, searching. It moved past the elevators and along the patterned floor. It moved past a row of vending machines and an open concept waiting room. Finally it found Mathew's room.

It entered.

Mathew was in the same position he had been in all day. Anne was beside him in the chair, asleep.

The Bakisi didn't wait; it didn't hesitate. It killed Anne quickly, making a five-inch incision in her throat. Anne fell to the floor with her rosary wrapped around her fingers. Blood pooled around her head. A string of spittle hung between her lips, which opened and closed until the end. She never said a word. She never even opened her eyes.

As the Bakisi turned away, Mathew sat up. He reached out with his mouth wide; he took hold of the Bakisi and squeezed it inside his tiny bruised hands.

Then everything changed.

**

Mathew was sitting beside an old man on a park bench. The sun was shining and the air was warm and still. The old man looked to be a hundred and fifty years old or more, and older still if you saw into his eyes. They were black pools of what seemed to be infinity. He was dressed plainly, in a long thin coat without color. He wore dark shoes and dark pants.

Mathew said, "Why are you doing this?"

The old man turned towards the boy. His teeth were long and sharp, like the teeth of an animal, like stained pitchforks. He said, "It is nature's way."

Mathew pondered this. This was not the nature that he knew of. He wondered if he was being told a fib.

"Surely," he said, "there is nothing natural about you, whatever you are."

"But there is." The old man replied, flaunting a terrible smile. "It is nature's way, and I'm a part of nature. I am as natural as the air we breathe, the sky above, the water in the ocean and the serpents within it. In days gone by, I was considered a God. And as a God, an old God, I can tell you quite surely that there can be nothing good without something bad, happiness without sadness, heaven without hell. I would think that you understood these basic principles. This is not the deliberation of genius."

"Then you are from hell, yes?"

"There is no hell."

"I don't understand."

The old man stood up and walked across the yard. Mathew followed. Soon they came to an ice-cream stand and the old man said, "Would you like an ice cream?"

"Yes please," Mathew replied. He was handed the cone and he licked it immediately. "This is delicious."

"Of course it is. It is a taste that you enjoy, more than all others."

Strange, Mathew thought. He had never tasted it before.

They walked a little further. The park was near empty. And it was a beautiful day; the type of day that Mathew lived for.

Something occurred to him: he created this world, this environment that surrounded them. This was his heaven, his sanctuary. Nothing bad could happen to him here.

He wasn't sure how he knew this, but he did.

Testing this theory, Mathew wished for a green balloon. A balloon appeared; the string was comfortably wrapped around his free hand. But it wasn't green, his favorite color. It was red. He tried his luck again. This time, he wished for a baseball hat. One appeared on his head, New Jersey Devils. It fit perfectly.

"Third time's a charm," he said, and he wished that the Bakisi would be gone forever, erased from reality, non-existent.

"I'm afraid your petty tricks won't work on me, little one," the old man said.

"And why not?"

The old man grinned. "I have some terrible news for you. This is not your world; it is mine. I allowed you to think that you had captured me. But it was I that captured you. I brought you here, and I had you believe that you were the dominant one. You and I are connected now, here in this world of darkness. And in your own world, you are at the mercy of those around you. You will never wake—and I will not harm you. Not now. Not ever. We are connected. We are as one. You will see what I see. You will go where I go. You will know the things that I choose to teach you. And I will reap the rewards. I *know* what you know. And now, little one, I know where your uncle is hiding. You have shown me the way. We shall travel there together. It's time to get going."

The old man began laughing, with his long teeth clicking concurrently.

The world, that was a shining paradise for the child, began changing. The sky turned black, the ground turned to flame, the ice cream cone became a handful of scattering insects with mouths hungry and snapping.

Mathew screamed. The string that was attached to the red balloon tightened around his hand like a snake. He screamed again. And again.

He screamed for a very long time.

He screamed forever.

101

James opened his eyes; the room was spinning. He tried to lift a hand and couldn't do it. He was tied to a chair.

Fading in and out of consciousness, the room blurred. Sounds that seemed muffled and strange seeped into his brain. An overtone of ringing and buzzing was heard. He looked through the broken patio door and noticed the rain. It seemed softer, less severe. The storm was dying; soon it would be over. Without looking around, James drew the conclusion that the room was empty. And perhaps the cottage was empty—except, he could hear voices and laugher coming from one of the bedrooms. He could also hear Debra crying. As it turned out, the room wasn't empty. Debra was beside him, tied to another chair.

"Debra." James whispered.

Debra's lips were ripped apart on one side. She had scrapes on her knuckles, and one finger was missing. It had been crudely bandaged with a cloth. The cloth was bright red. Her eyes were puffy and she had large bruises down both sides of her face and neck.

James swallowed. It tasted like acid. His eyes watered; his heart skipped a beat. This wasn't right. No matter what she had done, this was definitely not right.

"Are you okay?"

No response.

After a long silence, James realized that Debra's clothing had become dirty and wet. She looked like she had been dragged outside.

Debra mumbled, "You're awake." Her tattered lips quivered.

"What's happening?"

Debra's head rolled to one side; a line of blood pooled on her chin. Struggling to speak, she said, "The guy you kidnapped is here, but be quiet. Don't let them know you're awake. If they find out, they'll come. I don't want them to come out here. Not again."

With the lowest possible voice, almost like a high-pitched wisp, James said, "The guy I kidnapped? Who are you talking about?"

Debra coughed gently. "I don't remember his name. Is it Alan?"

"Do you mean Elmer?"

"Yes, that's him. Elmer. He has two friends with him; don't you remember? They shot you; and smashed us with a baseball bat. Then they beat me up, and…"

Debra closed her eyes. She didn't want to say it or admit it. She didn't even want to think it. But she knew what they did. Oh yes. She knew.

First it was the big guy—the guy she hadn't talked about yet; the guy with his chest covered in tattooed skulls, spiders and dragons; the guy with the nice clothing and foul breath. He was the violent one. From the very beginning, he was sadistic. He wanted to cause pain; he liked it rough. He forced her to say things, forced her to do things, terrible things, things she would never do again. And before he was finished—before he punched her and kicked her and tore her finger off with his teeth—he dropped his seed inside of her.

Then Elmer joined in.

Elmer wanted to abuse Debra, just like the big man. He wanted to drop his seed inside of her too, and show Debra what a real man was about, but he couldn't. He couldn't keep himself excited. He tried and failed, which made him embarrassed and angry. He turned violent and became an animal, a monster.

But monsters don't exist, Debra told herself while it was happening.

But sometimes they do.

Sometimes they do.

Debra fought back the tears. She didn't want to tell James that Elmer forced her to suck his cock until he was so angry—and embarrassed—that he spit in her face and pulled her bottom lip three inches from her mouth. No, she didn't want to tell James that. She didn't want to admit it either. But it happened. Oh yes, it all happened.

"I don't remember," Debra said, pushing away the thoughts.

"What is it?"

Debra swallowed, struggling to speak. "There's another man, a third man. He's big… and mean. He has tattoos on his chest."

"Elmer's here?"

"Yes, I'm trying to tell you…" Debra closed her eyes. "You remember the girl I brought to the hospital? Her name is Jennifer."

"Yeah."

"Elmer beat her up."

"When?"

"Jennifer said she found Elmer on the highway and she stopped to help him. And then Elmer attacked her and took her car."

"How do you know this?"

"Shhh. You've got to be quiet!"

"I am being quiet. How do you know this?"

"Inside the hospital we saw the news reports on TV. She saw his face on CNN. He was with you."

A silence fell between them; James remembered dumping Elmer on the side of the road. He remembered treating him poorly and thinking that Elmer was a hard book to read. Looking back, he sure as shit had done some misreading. "How did he find us here?"

Debra whispered, "I don't know."

Dizzy. Lightheaded. It became hard for James to stay focused. Thoughts of Elmer drifted, replaced with nothing.

Then—

Leaning his head back, he thought about the two of them, James and Debra, peas in a pod. He thought about the fun times—lazy Saturday afternoons, lying in bed, naked and playful. Laughing, with smiles on their faces and contentment in their hearts. He thought about the nights they had spent, the good times and the bad. Jokes, boisterous laughter, drunken fights and bliss; the face Debra made while sleeping, with her mouth open and the unseen hinge of her jaw wide. Like a soldier, Debra had once said, and he knew what she meant. Debra would lie under the covers like a soldier, not moving, not disrupting the perfectly tucked, ultra-clean sheets. And in the morning the sheets would be flawless on her side. In contrast, the sheets would be destroyed on his, like he had jumped on the bed for hours. He thought about all this and more—the day they met, birthdays and dinners and everything else that the relationship had been. She had made him a better person, a more complete person. She had seen his promising side, his confidence, his drive, and the diamond that was lying within his undeniable rough. She loved him, and he loved her. He loved her so much that it hurt.

"Debra," James whispered. "I'm really sorry. I never wanted things to happen this way. Please forgive me. I love you. Since the day that I met you, I've loved you like no other. You're my world."

Debra began crying. She hated hearing James giving his last rites speech. It didn't make things better. It made things worse, solidifying the reality of the situation.

"Oh God," she said, pulling air deep into her lungs "You kidnapped the wrong guy, James. Now it's payback time. We're in serious trouble here. I think they're going to kill me. I really, really do."

James didn't know what to say. He knew she was hurting. Truth was, he was hurting too.

A thought came, clear and simple: if Elmer doesn't kill you, I surely will. I fucking hate you.

And then he smiled and consciousness drifted away.

102

In the master bedroom, Switch and Elmer sat on a bed, drinking beers and snorting fat lines of cocaine off an unread Sèphera Girón novel. The Girón cover displayed a naked woman holding a knife, which was the reason Elmer had picked that particular book off a shelf loaded with fifty or sixty unread novels—most of them being James Patterson, Michael Crichton or Tom Clancy. It was the first time he had ever seen so many unread books in one place, with the exception, of course, being inside a bookstore.

For the occasion, Switch brought thirty-six beers, a bottle of Scotch, two bottles of Vodka, a couple joints and two eightballs of coke—each ball being the equivalent of three and a half grams. It was enough drugs and alcohol for a very good-sized bender, as long as the party was small. He also brought two bags of greasy, low-end Chinese food, a bottle of Pepsi, two bottles of Ginger Ale and a bottle of orange juice. Elmer ate a few chicken wings and a half plate of noodles before knocking back three rails, one after another. After that, the food wasn't nearly as appetizing and it sat in the dresser, largely untouched.

And even with the alcohol, THC and cocaine in his system, Switch felt a terrible guilt eating at his thoughts.

When Switch arrived, he expected to find Elmer waiting for him inside a car. He figured he'd talk Elmer into renting a motel, or perhaps one of those cheap rental cottages that gets used and abused by college kids. After all, they needed a home base. Didn't they? Of course they did. How could they live without one?

He figured talking Elmer into renting a place would be easy, but it didn't happen. In this plan of his (that seemed as clear as the sky above, which wasn't all that clear—if he remembered correctly), he could see Elmer sitting on a motel bed, restless and anxious, more than prepared to go James-hunting. He could see Elmer's impatience, anxiety and annoyance growing with every minute that slipped by. He could see Elmer's irritation turning to anger, his frustration becoming fury. But he could also see something else, something small and simple. He could see Elmer's eyes widen when the food came in, realizing, perhaps for the first time, that he had not eaten a bite in the last five or six hours. We shouldn't go out there on an empty stomach, Switch would say.

Queen takes Knight.

And when the beer came in?

Queen takes Queen.

And at the end of the meal, after a second and third beer, Switch would pull out the cocaine, drop six lines on the table and roll a fresh bill.

Queen takes King.

Check and Checkmate.

Game Over.

Instead of murder, it would be a night of drinking, talking, inhaling lines and gaining a new perspective. Thoughts of murder and revenge would be put on hold, and in time, replaced with consumption. Murder would seem like the wrong approach, and if it didn't seem wrong—it wouldn't matter. Switch would have secretly called the police by then and James would have been caught.

Unfortunately, all this came to a crashing halt when Switch found Elmer at the side of the road, covered in blood, saying he killed five people in the last few hours. To make matters worse, Elmer phoned Moore, the biggest, meanest asshole in the world. Switch hated Moore. Always had.

On a brighter note, Elmer hadn't actually killed five people. It was only four.

Jennifer had survived.

103

Moore stepped out of the bathroom. He was a big man. His clothing was stylish and expensive. He had money, drugs and power; he had muscle and the desire to use it. Weighing in at two fifty-five, Moore looked like a football player—with a neck larger than his head. He enjoyed the good things in life and he felt right at home when people looked at him with a mix of fear and admiration. His skin was dark and smooth, if you didn't take into account the long scar beneath his chin. There was nothing smooth about that place; someone had cut his throat with a broken bottle, attempting to saw his head from his body.

Moore entered the common area and realized that James had opened his eyes. This seemed to be what he had been waiting for. He smiled an evil man's smile, pointed a thick, non-calloused finger and licked his lips.

"Oh lookie-here," he said with a deep, upsetting voice. "Look who's coming around… it's the man of the hour, the dickhead I've been waiting to meet. The one and only: James the jerk-off. He's back and ready to join the party. Wait 'til guys hear. Things are about to get interesting, I reckon. Yep, things are about to get real good."

Moore dragged his fingers along the center of his scar. He opened the fridge, lifted a beer and spit on the floor. Closing the refrigerator, he began to laugh.

James wondered if laughter had ever sounded so cold and cruel. He also wondered if Moore was an alien.

Debra started to cry.

104

"Do you know what time it is?" James asked, while he had a moment alone with Debra. His eyes were glossed over, his hair was matted to one side.

"I'm not too sure... it's close to five am, I think. Why?"

"The sun will be coming up soon. If we get lucky, someone will find a corpse on the beach, or in the grass, or wherever. Then the police will be involved. That's our only chance, really."

Debra groaned, holding back her tears. "Don't say that."

"Sorry."

"I wish I had never come."

"I wish you called the police when you had the chance."

"You wouldn't let me."

"I know. I'm kicking myself for that."

"When will you learn that I'm always right?"

"A little too late, apparently."

For a while neither of them said anything. Then with a nod of her head, Debra said, "This sucks." Her mouth felt dry and sticky.

James said, "I think they killed Franco's wife." He sounded a lot like Johnny now. His voice was flat and empty.

"What makes you think that?"

"I don't know. It's just a feeling I guess. I'm thinking this: the neighbors on the left side are never home. And if one of those guys didn't kill Franco's wife, she would have come over... or something. She would have been looking for Franco, right? But she didn't come over. At least, I don't think she did. And I heard a woman scream. I know I did. I figure it was her."

"Maybe she came by."

He looked at Debra then, with dark eyes that were rolling in their sockets. "When?"

"I don't know."

"Wouldn't you have noticed?"

"Elmer... beat the shit out of me. Then he tied me up. I passed out for a while after he tied me. I don't know what happened. Anything is possible, I suppose."

Time crawled a while, and then Debra said, "Listen James, I'm pretty upset with you. To be honest, I wish we had never met. But when I first got here, you said Franco was dead. Well... I thought you killed him. I was sure of it. It seems now that you didn't. I guess I'm trying to say this: I'm sorry. For what it's worth, I'm sorry. Not that I don't want to kill you right about now, 'cause I do. I fucking hate you, but I'm also sorry. I wanted you to know that. I had to get it off my chest."

"That's so funny," James said. "I want to kill you too."

Debra nodded. She thought he was kidding.

Inside the bedroom the men shuffled their feet; they were about to join the party.

"I guess this is it," James said.

"Yeah, I guess so. I love you, James, even when I hate you."

It seemed that James didn't hear. And a moment later, the bedroom door opened. This was the end.

105

As Moore and Switch walked into the common room, Elmer stepped outside. A few minutes later he returned, dragging Franco's body inside by the wrists. Franco's head hung back. He was dripping wet; all but the sockets of his eyes were covered in dirt.

Elmer plunked the corpse on the floor near Debra's feet. Then he stepped outside again, and returned with the body of a woman that neither Debra nor James had seen before. Elmer laid the woman next to Franco. He rubbed a dirty foot along the side of the corpse and unleashed a terrible grin. "You see that?" he said to Debra. "That's you, an hour from now. Dead. You like that?"

James bit his tongue; Debra thanked God for small miracles.

"Hey bitch," Moore said. "You were asked a question. Do you like what you see?"

"No," Debra said. "Of course not. What kind of a question is that? Nobody likes that. This is terrible."

"I bet your boyfriend likes it," Elmer said. "He likes that sort of thing. You know that, right? Of course you do. He's a sick fuck. Maybe you are too."

Moore sipped his beer, and said, "He's a stone cold killer."

James moved uncomfortably in his chair. His shoulder throbbed. He wasn't sure if the bullets had passed through him or if they were still inside. If he had to guess, he would say they were still in there. But what did he know? He had never been shot before.

Elmer stepped outside again, and then tossed a dead dog into the hallway. After that he dragged the dog's master in by the scruff of his neck. The man's water-wrinkled face had turned as white as the ceiling he gazed at. His teeth were covered in dirt. On his fifth and final trip, Elmer dropped Helga's dead body on—what was now—the pile.

106

James had seen enough horror flicks to imagine Elmer's next move. He figured Elmer would prop the bodies up on the couch; perhaps he would try to feed them or have a conversation with them.

Of course, Elmer wasn't thinking that way. He wasn't crazy. James was the infected one. Elmer had simply brought the bodies inside to hide them. Nothing more. Nothing less. Dropping the corpses in front of Debra and James, that was for the dramatic aspect, sure it was, but the dramatics would end there. And after a few minutes, a damp, pungent smell began creeping around the room, making people nauseous and woozy. It smelled like old meat.

Nobody liked that.

Ultimately, Elmer dragged the bodies into a bedroom. He sprayed air freshener; Moore poked fun and Switch said nothing. Elmer didn't care what either one of them thought. The bodies were grossing him out, and besides, they were getting in the way.

"How do you want to do this?" Moore said.

Elmer shrugged. "I don't know. What do you think?" The question was directed at James.

James shook his head and said, "How about you let us go?"

The remark earned a few laughs, not that James was trying to be funny.

"No son," Moore said. "I don't think so. In fact, I think it's time we get started."

"Any last words?" Elmer said. "Final requests… anything like that? If so, now's the time."

Debra looked nervous.

James wondered if she knew she'd be first to die.

Since the moment that James opened his eyes, he knew Debra would be first. And worse than that, he knew it wouldn't be pretty. He took a deep breath and tried to be strong.

"Are you being serious?" he asked. "Or are you just talking shit?"

Elmer's grin faltered. "What do you mean?"

"What I'm saying is this: are you talking shit right now, reciting cool dialog from a movie you didn't understand, or are you actually offering me a final request?"

The room fell silent.

Moore crossed his arms and leaned against a counter. Switch lifted an eyebrow. The weight in the room shifted, if only for a moment. Pressure had fallen upon Elmer's shoulders. Was he a man of his word, or just another asshole with a mouthful of bullshit?

"I don't know," Elmer said. "Why? Do you have something important to say? You gonna talk your way out of this or somethin', douchebag?"

"No," James said. "I don't think that's possible. And if you're reciting lines from a second-rate action movie I'll save my breath. But if you're really offering me a final request, then I suppose, I do have something worth asking. The thing is… I haven't figured you out yet, Elmer. I'm not sure if asking is worth my time."

"You don't have much time," Elmer said. "And I'm not so sure you figured *that* out, hotshot."

"Yeah, I figured as much. I might be stupid but I'm not that stupid."

Moore leaned in; he rubbed his hands together. "Listen son," he said. "I'd love to hear a final request, a final plea, your famous last words. And I'm sure the guys would love to hear it too, right guys?"

Switch faked a laugh. "Let's hear your famous last words."

"Without meaning disrespect to you two cock suckers, I'm asking Elmer. He's the one with the problem. He's the one that wants to kill me."

"No son," Moore said, reading James with his eyes. "I'm the one that wants to kill you. Steel just wants it more. Ain't that right Steel?"

As James waited for the Elmer to supply him with an answer, he couldn't help notice that the word 'Steel' had been used again. Things became clear: Elmer had lied. Truth be told, James knew it all along.

"What's the request?" Elmer asked.

James shifted his weight; his shoulder throbbed. From where he was sitting, he could see his shotgun sitting on the table, next to his wallet, his keys, and a couple phones. Then he noticed a handgun on the table, and a knife. The weapons seemed so close. If he could break free of the chair, the gun would be in his hand within seconds.

"What's the request?" Elmer asked a second time.

"Should I ask? Will you—"

"If it's reasonable," Elmer barked. " I'll consider it."

"Okay. Fair enough. I'd like a couple of beers, for me and Debra."

"Is that all?"

"Yeah. That's it."

"Why do you want beers, to ease the pain? Is that what you're thinking? Because if that's what you're thinking you're fucking stupid."

"We're talking about a beer or two each, like the condemned man's last meal. How much pain can it possibly ease?"

Elmer shook his head.

"Not much," he said. "Not much at all."

107

Moore pushed a gun—a different gun, not the one sitting on the table—against Debra's temple. Switch untied her, and re-tied her moments later, allowing one hand freedom below the elbow. They did the same for James. Within a few minutes James and Debra were drinking what they thought to be, one final beer. As it turned out, they were offered a second.

James thought things were starting to swing in his favor, at least a little. Then Elmer said, "Let the games begin." And without hesitation, Switch re-tied their hands and Moore made a trip to his car. He returned with a large, black toolbox. The very sight of the box made James nauseous.

"It's getting bright out there," Moore said. "It's getting hot too. Looks like a nice day is brewing. What do you think of that? It rained all night long, now it's beautiful. Strange weather, huh?"

"Sure is," Elmer said. "We're standing on the edge of a wonderful, and memorable day. Are you guys ready?"

James said nothing. Debra said nothing. Switch opened his mouth and then snapped it shut.

Moore said, "Fucking right I'm ready."

And with that, Elmer began to laugh.

108

Elmer opened the toolbox and lifted a hammer. Turning to Moore, he said, "Do me a favor?"

"What's that?"

"Can you gag this woman? She's about to start screaming."

"Sure buddy. How about duct tape? We've got plenty of that."

"Yeah, whatever. But put a towel in her mouth, will ya? Duct tape alone won't do."

"Listen guys," Debra said. She knew she had nothing to bargain with, and they weren't going to listen. But she had to try. She had to. This was it. "You don't have to do this… I can give you money. I'll do what ever you want!"

"Oh God," Elmer said, sounding bored. "Hurry up, will ya? She's starting to gush."

"Yeah, yeah. Hold on."

"Come on!" Debra cried. "Don't do this! You don't have to do this! I won't tell, or say anything! I'll be good! I won't—"

"SHUT UP!" Elmer screamed, slapping her across the face.

Shock claimed the room. Nobody was prepared for Elmer's violence. Not James, not Debra, not even Elmer's goons. Somehow—until that moment—everything seemed unreal, like a joke without a punch line. But now the punch line was revealed. Elmer wasn't fucking around. He was planning on killing James and Debra, and he was planning on being mean about it.

Switch said, "Hey Elmer, buddy. Take it easy. You don't have to do this. Let's have another beer. Let's chill out a while."

Elmer spun around. His nostrils flared. "No! No! No! Don't you dare pull this shit! I knew you were getting soft on me! And you knew what this was, you knew right from the start. Do you think I'm kidding, Switch? Do you think I killed those people and that stupid dog because I was joking around? Get your head out of your ass or I'll tie you to that fucking chair as well!" Pointing at James, he said, "This is what we came here for! This pile of shit, right here! It's time for this bastard to get what's coming! And he knows what he did! He knows! Now hand me that fucking duct tape and a dish towel."

Without hesitation, Moore tossed Elmer the tape, along with a rag he found under the sink.

Debra, still stunned by the slap in the face, looked James in the eye.

"Oh shit," she said. "Don't let them do this to me! Help me! Do something! Do something!"

James struggled in his chair, cursing and swearing. He would have given anything to be somewhere else at that moment, and he would have given anything twice over to bring Debra with him. His place, Debra's place, they both seemed like a dream now, a dream that was slipping away.

It was then, at that very moment, as Elmer was wedging a dirty fingernail into the duct tape, trying to find a corner, when James wished—with all of his heart—that he didn't love her. Love was doing nothing for him—nothing good, anyhow. Love stinks, love is a drug, love is for suckers, love is the enemy—and all the rest of it. If James didn't love her, his heart wouldn't be getting tossed into the wood chipper and his thinking wouldn't have been clouded and diluted with forthcoming bereavement. But the fact of that matter was this: he did love her. Oh yeah, he loved her always and he loved her forever. She was his everything—his reason to get up in the morning, his reason to smile. He would have traded places if he could, not that it would have mattered. After those bastards had their way with Debra, James would be next. And by that time, they would be all warmed up and ready for more.

James struggled, noticing that the ropes were not as tight as before. For some reason, unknown to him, Switch had left them loose.

"Easy there son," Moore said. The rasp in his voice was like ugly on a gorilla. "Don't struggle that way or you'll be dealing with me sooner than expected. And you don't want that, son. I'll rip off your head, open up my ass and shit down your neck. I'll drink gasoline and piss fire. I'll slit your throat and call it happiness. Don't think I won't."

"Oh please don't do this!" Debra kept begging, "I'll do anything! I'll do anything!"

Elmer swiftly and crudely stuffed the rag into Debra's mouth. Then he ran the tape around her head, making it tight, making it hurt. He said, "Of course you'll do anything bitch. You'll do anything I want. But it doesn't matter, 'cause your time is up." He punched her in the face once, which dazed her. It became a little easier to roll the tape around her head, finish what he was doing.

"You fuck!" James shouted, twisting and kicking and thrashing about. His insanity seemed to be coming and going in waves now. Love, hate, fear and anger swirled together improperly. His feelings were all over the road. "Leave her alone," he said. "YOU LEAVE HER ALONE!"

Elmer reached inside the toolbox and pulled out a hammer. "Are you ready James? You ready for a little payback? Huh? Are you? Are you? You ready motherfucker? Watch this!"

James felt the ropes give, not completely, but some.

Escape seemed possible, perhaps likely.

109

Elmer swung the hammer around in his hand. The double-claw end was face down, like jaws of a rattlesnake. And for a brief moment, before the hammer came speeding through the air, before Debra closed her eyes, before she felt the pain, before James screamed and Moore laughed and Switch wondered why he couldn't stop what was happening, Debra felt her bowels twist into a knot and release. Her muscles, which were as tense and rigid as a painted door hinge, unexpectedly loosened and relaxed. She felt faint. She felt the room spin and her eyes flutter, and she became aware of a warm, wet sensation running through her legs and onto the chair. For the briefest of moments she felt embarrassed, but the feeling was short lived. The hammer came rushing down with terrible mind-numbing speed and precision. And as the hammer fell, her knees never moved, never flinched, never flexed or pulled away. They just sat there, waiting for the violent and blunt amalgamation between tool and flesh.

The rounded claw hit her left knee. It tore through her jeans, skin, muscle, veins, cartilage, and snapped her bone—making a SKQUAT sound as it hit. And although her legs never moved during the course of this union, the rest of her body did. Her shoulders jumped and her fingers clenched; her stomach flipped and her eyes tore open as her head fell back. Debra's mouth, which was a good size, turned into a gapping O that an eagle could had nested in, if not for the rag that was stuffed inside her mouth. Her teeth snapped after she screamed. Then she whined and gasped. And the room continued swirling. Hair clung to her head. Blood mixed with urine began draining to the floor, like she had sprung two leaks at once, which was not a far cry from the truth.

With a grunt, Elmer pushed the hammer towards Debra's belly care-lessly. He looked like he was trying to remove a stubborn nail from deep inside her knee. Then he pulled the hammer towards himself, wiggled it back and forth several times, and eventually, yanked it free.

To say that Debra felt pain would be an understatement. Debra felt pain, more than pain in fact. She felt a taste of hell.

Debra was in hell now, and James had a front row seat. And his ropes were loose, but not loose enough. Escape seemed possible, but it wasn't happening. At least, not yet.

A furious and senseless look passed through Elmer's eyes as he raised the object a second time. He looked as though he was having a religious experience. It was terrifying; he seemed more animal than man.

As the hammer went up a string of blood quivered between the claws and Debra's head came snapping forward. She knew what was coming; she recognized the motion. Silently she begged and inaudibly she screamed.

The creature that Elmer had become didn't notice, didn't care.

She begged for mercy with her eyes, knowing none would be received. And she continued begging as the hammer came roaring down, like it did the first time, with sick precision and a noise that was nothing short of ghastly. The claw hit the same muscles, crunched the same bones and mulched the same veins and arteries. But this time, her feet kicked and her legs slapped together, blood shot across the room and pooled around the chair. Her face dripped sweat. She turned as white as the glue she used as a child, during those pre-school Arts and Crafts classes. What she wouldn't give to be there now.

Elmer pushed the claw back and forth until he yanked it free. A piece of meat fell into the expanding shores of the fresh red pond. He swung the hammer again, grinning like a lunatic as he hit the same knurled spot— again. And again. And again.

In the back of regions of Debra's mind, she thought the hammer felt like thunder and sounded like a wave crashing against a rock. She wished she had never come. She wished she were dead.

James couldn't turn away.

He had been screaming, cursing, begging, threatening, all the while, fighting the ropes that held him. But the ropes were too strong. They were strong and loose at the same time—and he couldn't break free. Lying, he told himself it didn't matter. It didn't matter now, because all this was happening; he couldn't change it. Nothing could change it. Debra was suffering and quietly screaming and it didn't matter—but it did matter. It did. Debra was being murdered one kneecap at a time and it was his fault. His reckless behavior created the situation, created the terror. And now he was strapped to a chair. Watching. Oh God, he couldn't stop watching.

His eyes were glued to the hammer—and the hammer kept going, and going, and going. And he loved it. That was the strangest thing. He loved it, even though he was the next in line and Debra was his girl. It didn't matter. He screamed like he hated it but was lying to the world. He loved it, oh God. It was making him hard.

What else, he wondered, would the son of a bitch do? Chop Debra into pieces? Pull out her eyes? Boil her alive? Drill a screw into her forehead? Cut a hole in her stomach and remove her intestines, one bloody loop after another?

"FUCK!" James screamed. He blamed himself.

And he loved it.

He didn't need hostages. Oh no. He didn't need hostages and he didn't need to threaten strangers with a shotgun. He didn't need to pull the trigger two separate times, kill two separate people, destroy lives and property and God only knows what else. But he did. Oh yes, he did it all. And this was the punishment. But it wasn't being handed to him; it was handed to the woman he loved: Debra.

It wasn't fair.

He wanted to be the one that killed her. He wanted to chop off her head.

Debra stopped fighting. Stopped watching. Stopped feeling the pain—at least for the moment. But the hammer kept coming, and coming, and coming.

How many times? Ten? Twenty? Fifty? Two-hundred-and-fifty? She didn't know. Her body was in shock now; her internal motor had turned off, like her mind, her thoughts and all of her survival intuitions. She was on other side of the violence now, not seeing, not listening, not caring or knowing.

James watched the claw as it made its way through her leg; it began hitting the chair. Wood splintered. Lumber cracked.

James and Debra were in hell.

110

Switch didn't like it. He didn't like it at all.

He stepped outside and walked along the driveway, away from the cottage, the blood, Elmer, and that goddamn hammer that came crashing down on that poor, unfortunate woman. He felt absolutely terrible.

What Elmer was doing was wrong. Not a little wrong, like telling mom your homework was finished when you had four pounds of it waiting in your room. It was really wrong; Charles Manson wrong, Ted Bundy wrong, John Wayne Gacy wrong.

Switch had no idea that Elmer was a lunatic. He always considered Elmer a friend, another misunderstood soul that rolled the dice and came up shy. He thought they were alike.

He was mistaken.

It was no secret that Switch had killed a man and went to prison, but it had been… well, different. Refined. Gentleman-like. Not like this.

This was madness.

***

Richard Tokay was the man's name, the man Switch had killed. And Richard Tokay got what he deserved, which was punched out and left in a parking lot. The only problem was, he suffered too much, timing was wrong, and Richard froze to death on a cold February night. This happened nine years ago.

Switch had just turned twenty-four; he had spent the night getting drunk with his buddies on the east side of town. Club Crow Bar, it was called. The bar showcased local bands for almost ten years before it finally went under, like so many venues before it. Switch was a musician back then, and his band Skulls & Daggers had played there many times.

At 2:30 a.m., Switch walked to his car with a guitar in one hand and a girl he almost considered his girlfriend in the other. The girl's name was

Carrie Holbrook; she was a real cutie. Red hair. Tight body. Soft voice. Full lips. Great personality. A woman like that—no wonder Switch was smitten.

Switch and Carrie had been drinking for hours. They were both loaded, and Switch shouldn't have been heading towards his car with driving on his mind, but that was beside the point.

Richard Tokay, who enjoyed picking fights and was considered the town asshole, followed them outside. He asked for a ride. When Switch said no he took it personal. He called Carrie a whore and began suggesting that she had slept with half the men in town, including him and all of his friends. He also called her a band-slut. He said the only reason she liked Switch was because he played guitar. This didn't sit well with Switch, who feared it was the truth. He had been harassed by Richard twice before, and this time he wasn't having it. Words were spoken, followed by pushing and shoving. The guitar was dropped. Then came the fists. The fighting went back and forth violently. If a referee had been present he would have called it a draw. But then fate stepped in; Richard slipped on a patch of ice and went down hard. He banged his head off the bumper of a rusted-out Plymouth and Switch put the boots to him, kicking the man more times than he would like to admit.

After that, Switch and Carrie jumped into the car and drove back to Switch's apartment worried about drinking and driving and rehashing the fight. And if memory served them correctly, five minutes after they arrived home Switch passed out on the couch, blowing what was otherwise, a night of drunken, smutty sex.

The next day he realized that he left his guitar in the parking lot. It was a four thousand dollar Les Paul in a twenty-five dollar case. He never forgave himself for losing it.

Two days after that the police came calling. They arrived at Switch's front door with cuffs in hand; Switch was arrested. After a short trial, the sentence was dropped from second-degree murder to manslaughter. But with the admittance of drinking and driving, plus a few other misdemeanors, Switch was sentenced to six years, which seemed high to both him and his parents, who, not surprisingly, loved him very much throughout the ordeal and never lost faith in their boy. He ended up serving three and a half.

And that brings us here.

Yes, Switch had left a man out in the cold, and yes, the man had died. Richard Tokay turned into a human Popsicle the night Switch tried to beat the shit out of him. But no, Switch was not a killer. He didn't have the killer's mentality, the killer's instinct. He always wanted to do right, and yes, he made a few mistakes along the way. His prison time, mixed with his upbringing (which wasn't bad, but wasn't illustrious or thick with wealth by any means) hardened him. Made him rough around the edges. But all that is neither here nor there. What it comes down to is this: Switch was in the wrong place at the wrong time on that cold February night, making the wrong moves under the wrong set of circumstances—nothing more, nothing less. He could have been someone you know. He could have been anybody. Which is why—as Switch stepped off Debra's driveway and onto the wet and mucky dirt road—he released a sigh of relief.

The boys in blue had arrived, with guns aimed and ready.

Too bad one of them was itching to pull the trigger.

111

When Elmer finished his business with Debra he stepped outside with a beer in his hand. He walked across the large wooden patio that overlooked the beach. He rested his beer on the railing. He could still hear James shouting, cursing and swearing. He ignored it. Somewhere, beneath the sounds of James, Debra moaned. Elmer ignored that too.

The sun was up, shining bright. Picturesque ripples fluttered across the water. The rain had stopped falling and the clouds had moved on. But he could see them; Elmer could, like dark mud puddles in the sky, hanging above the lake at some mysterious and unknown distance. Perhaps the rain was still falling on the far side. He did not know, or care. But here, now, standing on the patio as the sun sparkled across the water, everything was beautiful.

A seagull squawked as it flew overhead. It landed on the sand, some fifteen feet away from where the waves made their final touchdown. On his left, Elmer could see something that looked like tiny mountains, if there were such a thing. After further inspection, he noticed that the mountains had been compromised. The hills were thin on trees and thick on ski runs. The ski runs sat empty and alone, waiting for the summer to end. If ever there was a more objectionable sight then ski runs in the summertime, Elmer did not know what it was.

On Elmer's right, two cottages away, some asshole in a pink shirt and a bright blue thong was playing fetch with a poodle. The unfashionable man seemed to be having more fun with his dog then any man in his right mind would. Elmer wondered if the guy was into bestiality. He didn't care, mind you, but the more Elmer watched the man, the more likely the bestiality scenario seemed.

Elmer took a drink of beer and thought; this fucking guy sleeps naked with his dog, guaranteed.

Whatever. The poodle loving ass-buffer did nothing to suggest that he had heard James screaming, which was pretty important, considering. But the man was close by. Close enough to hear something, and that made Elmer nervous—nervous enough to consider talking with the man, and getting a better understanding of the situation.

Elmer reached into his pocket and pulled out his wallet. He had found it sitting next to his phone on the dining table, with every dollar tucked safely inside. Nothing could have surprised him more.

Remembering the moment that he found the wallet, Elmer smirked. I should thank James, he thought. Give him a reward or something.

Still smiling, he opened the wallet and pulled out a credit card. Then he dug into his pocket with fingers scrambling. A little baggy sat beneath some change. Inside the baggy was cocaine. With the wind all but gone he decided to bust out a line—outside. This was a dangerous move. One slight breeze and bye-bye, no more coke.

After drying part of the railing with his sleeve, he crushed the rock (and lost a point-one into the moist cracks of the wood) and shuffled the coke into a long line; he rolled a twenty-dollar bill into a straw and cranked the powder back. The coke burned his nose faintly and his eyes watered a tad, but overall, the coke was strong enough and smooth enough to be considered above average quality.

He dropped another rock on the railing, crushed it and shaped it and stuffed the baggy into his wallet. After that, he stuffed his wallet into his pocket. Then he turned away from the beach and the coke and noticed a small AM/FM radio sitting on a table beneath a large patio umbrella. The umbrella could easily cover six people. The radio, which was old and dirty, wasn't plugged into the wall or anything. It worked on batteries or it didn't work at all.

Elmer approached the radio, which was still wet from the rain. He clicked it on, assuming that it wouldn't work. He was wrong. Somehow, the radio worked fine and when he heard The Who singing My Generation, he left it at that.

After knocking back the second line, Elmer looked through the broken patio door. Moore was inside, drinking a beer, sitting close to James and Debra, rubbing the fingers from his left hand over the knuckles on his right, while talking.

James was quiet now; his face drained of expression.

Debra's head was slumped forward. She looked dead. Blood drained from her... stub?

To Elmer's surprise, the bottom part of Debra's leg had come free, and sat on the floor beneath her. How is that possible? Elmer wondered. Then he looked at Moore—and at his blood soaked hands and legs.

That crazy son-of-a-bitch must have pulled her leg off after I walked away, Elmer thought. *Good man, that Moore, crazy, but a good man indeed.*

112

"Put your hands on your head." Officer Scriber said with a calm, tranquil voice. "Do it slow, do it quiet and don't make a sound. I'm not going to hurt you."

Switch stopped walking. His jaw unhinged.

"Listen," he said.

"You shut your fucking mouth or I'll shut it for you," the other officer said, loudly. This was Officer Layton, the rookie cop that nobody wanted to be partnered with; the rookie cop who was a bully in high school with a history of fighting, and wouldn't have been on the force at all—if not for some heavy financial contributions within the small town political world; the rookie cop who was inching to pull the trigger.

Officer Scriber, curbing the urge to tell Layton to shut up, closed his eyes briefly. It was something he was going to do, sooner or later, because—like any man with half a brain—he hated David Layton. He hated him enough to ask for a new partner, or a transfer, or seriously consider quitting the force, or maybe—just maybe—accidentally putting a bullet in David Layton's head.

Scriber huffed.

No. He would never do that. He would never sink a bullet into another person, not unless he had to. And even if Scriber could get away with it—which he couldn't—it would still never happen. Scriber was a good man, a family man with spiritual leanings. He was a man with morals, ethics and good-natured principles. And no matter how much he disliked his partner he would never cross the line. Not like that. Not in a month of Sundays, as his mother sometimes said.

"Shhh," Scriber said, looking in his partner's direction with frustration brewing. "Everyone, just relax a little. There's no reason for any of us to get excited. Now sir, I've already asked you nicely, and I'll ask you again. Please put you hands on your head, and do it slowly. I don't want any trouble. I'd like to do this by the book."

Switch slowly held his hands up, so both officers could see them. While doing this, he looked past the two men and the police cruiser. The road was nearly empty. Their only company was a squirrel.

With his fingers wide, he raised his hands to his head.

"I don't want any trouble," Switch said. "And I won't give you any trouble. But I didn't do anything wrong here, so please take it easy on me. I'm the one that phoned the police." At this point, Switch realized he had an eightball of coke in his front pocket. His eyes shifted in a guilty sort of way. He felt his temperature rise and his composure slip.

Being a veteran cop, and a good cop, Scriber caught it.

Layton didn't.

"Is everything okay sir?" Scriber asked.

Switch quickly accepted the fact that he was going to get busted on possession. He wasn't thrilled about it, but considering what he had witnessed, it seemed like no big deal.

"Yes," he said. "Everything is fine. I don't want any trouble. In fact, I'd like to help you gentlemen out, if I can."

Officer David Layton jumped up a foot, thrusting his gun in Switch's face. "Do you have any weapons on your person, sir?" Again, his voice was loud and inappropriate.

"No officer." Switch said, flinching back a step. "I don't."

Scriber was becoming furious. "Hey Layton, do you mind keeping it down a bit, or do you want to yell a little louder, maybe fire off a few warning shots?"

"Very funny."

"I'm not trying to be funny. I'm trying to be quiet."

"I just want this dickhead to know who's in charge here, that's all."

"Don't worry," Switch said. "I know who's in charge. You are."

"Fuckin' A I am. Now turn your ass around, get on your knees, and keep your mouth shut."

"It's pretty muddy."

"I don't give a flying rat-fuck if it's muddy. Turn around and get on your knees."

Switch turned and dropped to his knees without any sudden movements. Within seconds, his face was pushed into the mucky ground and he was cuffed. With his hands behind his back, Layton read him his rights.

Once Layton had finished his cop speech, Switch said, "Can I say something?" His face and body was needlessly covered with mud now, and his anger just was around the corner.

"Sure—" Scriber began.

Layton's body language shut him down.

Most of the time, Scriber could deal with Layton being an asshole. But here, standing within spitting distance of a murder suspect, Layton had snapped; he was impossible to handle.

It was the license plate number that did it. As soon as Layton called it in—and realized that they were dealing with the 'Martinsville Terror', which was what the cops were calling the whole string of High Park Murders in this part of the country—Layton went nuts, turning all his imperfections up ten notches. Scriber figured Layton had dreams of being a hero, and dreams of fast tracking his career if he played his cards right.

Not that he was heroic.

"Just keep you fucking mouth shut or I'll shut it for you! Do you get me? Or do I need to show you the long arm of the law?" Layton's meathook hands were in fists now, with his gun almost hiding inside his right one. Layton wasn't tall, but he was big—two hundred and thirty pounds. His hands looked like they could strangle a bear.

"Can you hear me out?" Switch said. "I'm trying to tell you, there's a woman inside and she needs your help!"

Switch was still on his knees with a face full of mud when Layton slapped him across the back of the head. After that, Scriber lost his cool. Harsh words were spoken and soon enough, Layton began shouting.

Scriber shouted back.

Switch thought the two cops were going to drop the guns and fist-fight, right there on the road. But as it turned out, six more police cruisers showed up before the situation had a chance to mature.

And after that, all hell broke loose.

113

Moore thought he heard something, an argument perhaps. He leaned back, listening, and after a moment of silence and reflection, he looked through the broken patio door.

Elmer was standing on the patio, gazing across the water and listening to the radio. If Moore had been able to see his face, he would have thought the man was in a trance. His eyes were locked in a cold, motionless stare.

After considering his options, Moore decided not to tell Elmer about the noises on the other side of the cottage. Elmer had lost his mind in the last ten minutes or so, at least on some levels, and Moore figured he needed time to regain his wits.

Looking at Debra, he said, "Don't go anywhere, beautiful. I'll be right back." Then he chuckled, winked at James and picked the shotgun off the table. "You want some of this, tough guy? Do you? I don't mind blowing off a few of your fingers before I step outside. How would that suit ya? You down with that, or maybe I should unzip my pants and let you blow me. Huh? You feelin' me, son? You feelin' me?"

James sniffed. His nose was running and his eyes were red.

"What's wrong buddy, cat's got your tongue?"

"Why don't you fuck off?" James said, pulling his eyes away from Debra's non-existent breathing.

"Yeah, yeah," Moore said. "That's the way we do it. I'm gonna love fucking you up. It's gonna last forever. I'll cut off your balls… for real. Don't think I won't, 'cause I'm not kidding around. I'm going to cut off your balls one at a time. And it's gonna hurt bad, son. You'll pray for death. I know you will."

"Go fuck your hand."

Moore grinned. "Yeah, okay. Go fuck your hand, huh? Yeah, that's funny all right… that's a good one. But I've got a better idea. How about this: how about I step outside for a minute, and when I get back, I cut off your baby-fingers. And after that, I break both your legs. Is that 'go fuck your hand' enough for ya? And I hope you kissed your girl good-bye. I think she's sick." Moore laughed. "Yeah, she looks sick to me. And by the way, just so you know, I had a great time fucking her. She's got nice tits. You know about that, right? About her and I? And Elmer fucked her too. It was the three of us, all together at the same time." Moore watched James squirm. "She really enjoyed having my cock in her ass."

"You're a liar."

"Oh yeah? Look in my eyes. Tell me I'm lying. Tell me I didn't fuck your girl."

James was speechless. Somehow, this tidbit of information hurt more than the rest of it. Did those two bastards really rape her before they played woodshop on her leg? He hoped not.

"Bye-bye," Moore said. He walked down the hall laughing, with the shotgun hanging loose in his hand. He opened the door, waved and was gone.

James was whirling, distressed beyond repair. He glanced at Elmer.

Elmer was looking across the water, listening to the radio. He seemed to be in a completely different headspace, a completely different world.

He looked at Debra. She was lost. The puddle of blood looked huge now, and the edges had grown hard. Her severed leg looked like an island.

He turned his wrists in circles and tried to pull his fingers together. The ropes were loose and had been for a while. With Moore sitting in front of him, talking like a cracked-out thug, James didn't move. But now that Moore was gone and Elmer was on the patio, things changed. He continued working his wrists, and thinking about Debra. Then another thought came: the third guy, the one that re-tied him and left the ropes loose, whose side was he really on?

Was he a friend or an enemy?

As James wondered, he eyed Elmer's handgun. It was sitting on the table.

114

Debra felt the hammer at first, then after a while she didn't feel anything. Her eyes opened and closed while the pain was still burning. All she could see was Elmer and the hammer—Elmer and the hammer—Elmer and the hammer. And Elmer looked insane, truly insane. His eyes were wide and bulging. Spittle hung from his chin. His nose flared. His lips were pulled back. His teeth were exposed and chattering.

The hammer was red with gore.

Deranged, Debra thought, before the hammer dropped the first punishing blow. *This man is truly deranged.*

Then it was pain, splattering blood. After that, it was something else. It was death.

115

Moore walked down the slope of the two hundred and fifty foot driveway, inside one of the two trails that the car tires had created. Both trails were wet and muddy, covered with small rocks. The rocks helped the journey for a while. But when Moore hit the halfway point the rocks disappeared and the trail became mucky. Moore stopped walking and cursed. Not wanting mud up to his eyeballs, he changed his footing. Now he walked on the grass that divided the two trails. Tall trees, covered in bright green leaves, were like giant walls along side of him. And because of the trees, and because Moore walked carefully, watching his step, he didn't realize that seven police cruisers were at the bottom of the slope.

Officer Alice Romero, one of the few female officers on the force, noticed Moore coming. She nudged her partner, drew her gun and said, "Hold it right there, buddy."

Officer Wayne Carey, Alice's partner, looked up. He reached for his weapon.

Without aiming, Moore opened fire.

The first shotgun shell caught Alice Romero in the right leg, breaking bone, destroying her kneecap and tearing off two pounds of muscle. As Romero fell, she fired wildly into the sky. Carey drew his gun. Then Moore fired another shot and scored another hit. This time the slug caught Carey in the chin, obliterating it. When Carey fell back, his feet lifted four inches off the ground. His gun twirled over his shoulder.

Seven police cars, thirteen officers. Two officers had fallen; the other eleven were scrambling.

Moore turned and ran up the driveway; he didn't like being out in the open.

He ran through puddles and long wet grass, with his shoes squishing in the mud. He ran past an overturned canoe and a washed out fire pit that had several logs around it. He leapt over a small, empty flowerbed. Trees and shrubs dripped around him. Crickets chirped.

He shuffled the shotgun from hand to hand; he didn't care much for it. It was a powerful weapon—and so far, he was two for two—but he had no experience with a shotgun and he wasn't sure how many shells it held.

The answer was six; he had four shells left.

The police opened fire.

116

The first rope fell. Quietly, James untied the rest.

He stood up, approached Debra and put his hand on her chest.

She wasn't breathing. She was dead.

Having expected this, James didn't show any emotion. The crying and laughing would have to come later, when he had time. Now was time for killing, time for vengeance, time to chop off her head.

James turned around, looking for the axe. He spotted Elmer through the broken patio door, gazing across the water, lost within his thoughts. James lifted the handgun from the table. The weapon felt cold but good. If he wanted to, he could pop Elmer right then. He hesitated, and felt his nerves cracking.

James wasn't a stone cold killer, and shooting a man in the back seemed wrong. And in most cases, it was wrong. But was it wrong here? Now? Was killing Elmer wrong? Or was killing Elmer the only true option that he had. And what about Debra? Didn't she deserve justice? Didn't she deserve a bullet in the head too?

He considered the situation, thinking murder was the right thing to do. And maybe it was. But James didn't like it; he didn't like it at all. If he were alone with Elmer, it would be one thing. He could detain him, get the police involved and try to gain control over the situation. But Elmer had two thugs with him, and the relationship that James had with the police wasn't too good these days. They probably wouldn't even listen to what he had to say.

Somewhere in the back of his mind, James remembered Switch.

Switch left the ropes loose; he was an unknown variable. Moore and Elmer were not. They were the enemy. But Switch—

He raised the gun, and pointed it towards Elmer's head. His fingers tightened. His eyes widened.

This one's for Debra, he thought. I hope it hurts like hell.

Then he pointed the gun at Debra.

Ah, fuck it, he thought. This one's for me.

117

The poodle-loving asshole tossed a chewed tennis ball from hand to hand, keeping the dog amused. The dog barked twice and jumped up and down excitedly with its clipped tail wagging and its head bobbing. It wasn't a bad dog, as far as its demeanor went, but the haircut that covered its frame suggested that the owner either hated the animal, or simply liked having a dog with a style best suited for a music video from the 1980s.

The dog barked, snapping Elmer from his daze. He shook off the cobwebs, grabbed his beer from the railing and swirled the beer inside the can. Little did he know—James was free. After a drink, Elmer pulled his gun from his waist.

He wanted to shoot the poodle-man.

"You're lucky, fucko," he said, stroking the weapon. "Lucky I don't blast you and that stupid dog."

On the other side of the cottage, the gunfire began.

Elmer panicked and fired three shots. Two bullets went into the sand; one hit the poodle-man in the face. As poodle-man fell, the chewed ball rolled from his fingers. The dog snatched the ball from the sand and ran across the beach, more excited than ever.

Elmer spun around.

A man in a blue baseball hat walked along the shoreline with two women. Both women were in their fifties. One had a bathing suit and sandals, the other, jeans and a bikini top. All three of them stopped walking when Elmer began firing. The man said something and ran; the two women followed close behind.

Elmer fired more bullets.

One bullet hit home, dropping the man to the sand. The two women kept running.

Elmer fired more bullets; he was panicking now. He didn't know what he was doing or why he was doing it. All he knew was this: he had to kill James quickly and get the hell out of dodge.

He stopped firing. Everything seemed quiet. Feeling the coke in his system and the anxiety of the moment, he stepped inside and pointed the gun at James. But James wasn't there; he was gone.

"What the fuck?" Elmer said. "Where is he? Where is everybody?"

Then Moore came through the door on the far side of the cottage like a bear, shouting, "The cops are here! The cops are here!"

"Where's James?"

"Huh?"

"Where is James? Look! He's gone! That little fucker is gone! Where is he?"

Moore was obviously surprised. "I don't know man, but we don't have time for this."

"Where's Switch?"

The door blasted open and two officers came charging inside.

"Freeze!" the first officer said.

Moore turned quickly and pulled the trigger. The shotgun blasted both officers at once. He pulled the chamber and fired again. The two men were still in the same spot, give or take a few inches, and the second blast finished them off. They tumbled backwards, flopping against each other with their bodies destroyed.

Then a third cop appeared behind the two fallen men and fired a pair of shots. The bullets went into the wall. Moore fired again, missing his target for the first time.

He didn't know it, but he had one shell left.

The officer shot another two bullets and tucked out of sight. Both bullets zipped through the air, between Moore's left arm and his ribcage, hitting his clothing but missing him. It was an impossible shot, had the officer tried to make it—one in a million. Moore didn't realize it happened. He thought the bullets went wide.

Then came the shouting.

"Freeze!" Officer Scriber said. He stood at the broken patio door with Officer Markus White. White was a big man with a large mouth. He didn't talk a lot; his mouth was large physically—big lips and a lot of teeth.

Scriber was glad to have White as his side instead of Layton—the asshole. And Scriber liked White, even if White was an out of shape slug that had lost his lust for life. The thing was, Scriber hated Officer Layton so much he couldn't sleep at night, and White was a good shot—a very good shot. He ranked in the top ten percent on the force.

Elmer scrambled behind the kitchen counter, firing two shots wide.

Scriber pulled the trigger five times. The bullets hit everything except his target.

Moore snapped off his final shell, tearing the top half of Scriber's head off, and that was the end of him.

And during this time, while the bullets soared and Scriber died and Elmer hid behind the counter (and rammed his hands against his ears), White—the man with the amazing shot—steadied his hand, aimed, and fired three times.

Moore took the first bullet in the throat, the second bullet in the chin, and the third bullet in the eye. He was dead before he hit the ground.

Two cops stepped over Scriber's body, then came two more. They were inside the common room with guns raised and eyes wide.

"We've got you surrounded," Officer Layton said, leading the pack. He didn't know if the place was surrounded or not, but he liked the way the words sounded when he said them. His meat-hook hands strangled his gun. His legs were in an open stance.

Elmer didn't know how many cops he was up against, but he knew that he was beaten. He tossed his gun where everyone could see and tried to force some tears.

"I'm the hostage," he said. "I'm one of the good guys. I'm sorry I fired at you. I thought you were the man that kidnapped me! I though you were James! Be careful guys… James is around here somewhere!"

118

James tucked himself into a bedroom. As the gunfire increased, he dropped onto his belly and slid under the bed. It was a temporary solution, but it was the best he could do.

And now the battle had ended.

He could hear the officers cuffing Elmer against his wishes. He could hear Elmer complaining, saying that he was innocent, saying that he was the victim, saying anything and everything he could think of to free his neck from the hangman's noose. And although the case was cloaked in confusion, Jennifer McCall—the woman that Elmer had beat up and Debra had brought to the hospital—made a full, detailed report. Elmer may or may not have been the victim of a crime, but as far as the police were concerned he was more than likely guilty of one.

James heard the panicked discussions, the officers calling for back up, calling for medical assistance and helping the wounded. He could hear the cries of pain.

The men were checking bedrooms now—gasping and whining as they discovered the four bodies that were piled on top of each other. It was only a matter of seconds before they would enter the room, find him hiding and slap a set of cuffs on him. And James felt that he had no choice but to allow it to happen. He didn't want to fight these men. They had done nothing wrong. They were the boys in blue, risking their necks to make the world a better place.

Why fight them?

Why continue the battle?

The door opened. He could see their feet.

"I'm here," James said. "I'm under the bed. I surrender. I won't do anything stupid."

Then a voice: "Captain," the voice said. "We've got one!"

119

There was a stampede of footsteps.

"Sir?" The voice sounded tough, professional. "Are you armed?"

"Yes," James said. "I have a handgun, but I will not use it."

The tension mounted.

"Throw the gun where we can see it."

James could hear the sound of weapons clicking and feet shuffling. They were fully prepared to fire upon the bed; fully prepared to kill him.

James slid the gun along the floor, where it spun in a circle before coming to a complete stop. He expected one of the cops to grab it. Nobody did.

"Sir? Do you have another weapon?"

"No."

"Are you positive?"

"Yes. That was my only weapon."

"What is your name?"

"My name is James McGee."

A collective gasp filled through the room. Then came a pause. James wondered what they were doing. He stretched out his neck, attempting to steal a glimpse. He saw nothing but feet, and was about to ask a question when the dialog resumed.

"Sir? We would like to see you hands, one at a time. Do it slowly. No sudden movements."

As James put his first hand where they could see it, someone picked his weapon off the floor. It happened very quickly, as if they expected the floor beneath the gun to be booby-trapped. He shifted his position and slid his other hand out. They grabbed him immediately. Seconds later, James was in cuffs.

120

They stood James up, read him his rights and walked him out of the bedroom. He tried to turn left, towards the door, thinking they'd walk him outside and throw him in the back of a cruiser. They didn't. They walked him into the common room and sat him in a chair.

Across the room, Debra slumped into herself. Her skin was phantom white; much of her blood had drained out of her.

James hated seeing Debra this way, and wished that someone would throw a sheet over her. After punishing himself with her image awhile, he tore his eyes away and spotted Moore lying on his back with a pool of blood around his head. He looked past Moore, to a place where two officers were talking. There was blood on the walls and ceiling around them. Just outside the door, another two officers had fallen. One man was alive and one was dead. James could see neither man, but could hear a third officer talking with the injured man. The conversation wouldn't last long. The wounded man was thirty seconds from dying.

He glanced at the broken patio door. Scriber's feet were inside; the rest of his body was out. James didn't realize that part of the man's head had rolled off of the patio.

Officer Layton stepped out of a bedroom and approached James. He looked fifty percent pissed off and fifty percent ecstatic. He said, "So tough-guy… you proud of yourself?"

James ignored him.

"I asked you a question."

"Why am I sitting here? Why not throw me in a car?"

"Why should I tell you anything?"

"I'm just curious. I don't care much for the view is all."

"I find that hard to believe, considering you're the guy responsible for this fucking nightmare."

"No I'm not."

"Yeah right."

"I didn't do this."

Layton released an exaggerated puff of air. "I've seen guys like you before. I've seen guys like you a million times before. You think you're smart. You think you're tough. But you know what? You're just a gutless piece of shit… you know that? A gutless piece of donkey shit. You know what your problem is?"

"I've got a feeling you're going to tell me. I also have a feeling that you don't know why I'm sitting here. It's not up to you, is it? You're just a little fish, a nobody… the last guy that people want to talk with, isn't that right?"

Layton's face turned red. "We're securing the area, asshole. And asking your buddies some questions you're not allowed to hear."

"And waiting for back up?"

"That's none of your business."

"Well, why not tell me? Jesus."

"I don't have to tell you shit."

"Why are you talking to me this way? Is this really how you small town, half-wit, police force, Rambo wannabes do it? Fuck. Don't you have protocol to follow or something? Can't you see that I'm upset? My girlfriend is dead!"

"And you killed her!"

"No I didn't!"

"Sell it to the judge, asshole. Because nobody here is going to believe you."

"My God man, leave me alone. Get out of my face, you stupid prick."

"Now listen a minute. My partner's dead, in case you didn't know it. And I'm thinking that you killed him. We're all thinking you killed him. This is your fault… you and your buddies. Look at that!" Layton pointed at Moore. "I bet your upset about that one, aren't you? You're friend is dead."

"Are you crazy? That fucker…" The words got caught in his throat and a wave of sickness flashed through his body. "That fucker raped my girl."

"You probably raped that poor girl."

"You're an asshole."

"Yeah right. I don't think so. You're the one going to prison."

The back door opened and a man in suit entered the room.

"Officer Layton," he said flatly.

Layton turned. "Yes sir?"

The man in the suit seemed very professional. His name was Henry Wilson; he just turned fifty. "I want you on the road," he said. "You're going to ride with Dylan… escort this guy here to the station." He nodded in Elmer's direction. "When you get there, file your report. Don't stand around talking about it. Do it. File it first, before anything else. I want to read the report when I get back, you understand?"

"Yes sir."

"Okay. Good. I'm going to have your car. Get lost."

"Sir?"

"Yes Officer Layton?"

"Who do you want me to ride with?"

"Dylan."

"Dylan's dead sir."

Wilson sighed. "Oh. I'm sorry to hear that. I want you to go it alone, then. Take Dylan's car. Neilson has the keys."

"But sir—"

"Don't talk to me about protocol Layton, not on a day like this. You're to go it alone, and call for back up at the station. Someone will assist you with the suspect here, and there. Is that understood?"

"Yes sir."

"Okay. Call it in and prepare for transfer. Get out of my face."

Layton haled Elmer away in cuffs. Two officers followed. Wilson apologized, and said something about the men being upset.

James nodded; he closed his eyes and mumbled, "Don't worry about it."

Wilson grinned an unhappy grin. "Very well."

It was clear that Wilson wasn't impressed with Layton. *Perhaps Layton was a pain in everybody's ass,* James thought. *Oh well. Your problem, not mine. I've got my own things to deal with.*

121

Officer Layton, Elmer, and two other officers walked the slope of the driveway, watching their footing the same careful way that Moore had three minutes and thirty-seven seconds before he took a bullet in the throat and two in the head. When they reached the road, Layton noticed that more police cars had arrived. An ambulance was speeding towards the scene with lights flashing. There was a sheet covering Officer Wayne Carey, the officer that had taken a shotgun shell in the chin.

Officer Alice Romero was crying, half-mad with fear, shock, and pain. She had lost a lot of blood, and was moments away from passing out. At this point, the female officer hung on through determination alone. Her leg would never be the same.

Layton and Elmer approached Officer Neilson, who was standing next to a cruiser. Neilson rolled his eyes. An ambulance drove past; it turned a corner and disappeared into the shadows of the cottage driveway.

Then another cruiser pulled away; Switch was in the back seat. He looked sad. He didn't realize how lucky he was to be leaving.

"Good morning," Layton said with a sick, careless grin. "Nice day for a slaughter, isn't it?"

"Fuck off, Layton." Officer Neilson said.

Elmer was stuffed into the backseat of the cruiser.

"What's you're problem?" Layton asked.

"You're kidding me, right? Do you have a lump of coal where your heart should be?"

Layton shrugged.

"If I have to spell it out, my problem is you. You're impossible. We have four dead policemen and one wounded, plus four civilian bodies that we found in a bedroom, two dead civilians on the beach, and one dead fucking asshole suspect. The body count for this morning is eleven dead and one wounded, in case you hadn't noticed. And you're asking me what my problem is? My problem is you, you insensitive, silver spoon, half-wit ass-licker. Get the fuck away from me. I would rather ride the lightening with my mother sitting on my lap than talk with you."

"I don't care. I've got to bring this guy to the station." Layton pointed at Elmer.

"You're kidding me right?"

"Nope."

"But this is my car."

"Doesn't matter."

"Are you sure?"

"Everything is screwed up today. Half of us will be riding alone, and most of us will be in different cars."

"And who are you riding with? You're not bringing him in by yourself, are you?"

"It's just me."

"Yeah right."

"Honest. Big man Wilson told me to call for back up when I get there."

"So I lose my car?"

"I just lost mine, so it looks that way, yes."

Neilson sighed. He hated losing his car almost as much as he hated Layton. "All right. Fine," he said. "Take my fucking car. See if I care."

PART SIX:
THE END OF IT ALL

122

Officer Layton and Officer Neilson turned towards the sound of somebody screaming.

The screams came from the extra large mouth of Officer White—the cop with the excellent shot. A moment before, without warning—unless you consider ice-cold air a warning—both of Officer White's arms snapped simultaneously, just below the elbow. From what people could tell, there was no possible reason for the occurrence. It just happened. Then his arms snapped again. Then his arms snapped again—and his mouth opened. He embarked on a tremendous mount of screaming, letting it all out. The pain, shock, wonder and amazement—all came pouring out his mouth in a monumental wave of horrified noise. Then at the end of his screaming, his wrists snapped, cracking like two thin strips of dry and brittle balsa wood.

White fell to his knees. The look on his face was one of complete terror. His arms had become something resembling circles.

"Help me," White said. "Help—"

Then both of his legs snapped twice and his neck snapped once.

Officer White fell onto his back, silent and mangled beyond belief, beyond repair. The eight police officers that watched it happen were frozen in shock. What they had witnessed was something from a nightmare. Something unnatural.

Officer Steve Carney—a young man that was new to the force—was the first person to speak after White went down. He said, "I'll go to the cottage, get the medics." But then he didn't move. His feet felt glued into his boots, which seemed to be nailed to the earth with railroad spikes.

Thomas Barnet—he was the first to move.

Barnet was an older man. He had a potbelly and a crown of gray hair. He had a wife and three teenage kids—two boys and a girl. He also had a dog, a line of credit, a mortgage, a new car, and a dentist appointment later that afternoon. He walked slowly towards the coils of White's body, as if

White had become contagious. He thought about the things that were his life and wondered if he was risking it all. His feet moved slowly. His fingers sat firmly around his gun, drenched with sweat.

Elmer watched Barnet from inside the car, wondering if he was brave, or just plain stupid. His eyes were as wide as dinner plates.

Standing outside the car, less than two feet away from Elmer, Layton felt like saying something witty. Instead, he stood up straight and rubbed his hands together.

Steve Carney still hadn't moved. The medical assistance he had promised would have to wait.

Barnet moved closer to the mangled remains of Officer Markus White. He could hear bugs buzzing and peeping as they twittered in the trees. He could smell the fresh morning scent that the storm had awoken. He could see White's body shivering and trembling, looking the way a spider might if you held it under a flame. And he could feel the unnaturally cold air around him that was both unseasonable and wrong. The temperature had dropped below zero where he was standing. His breath hung in the air, along with the aura of an unfamiliar presence.

Something changed inside him. Fear overwhelmed the moment; he wished it were illogical, groundless, or unjustified. But it wasn't. It was justified all right. His head was on the chopping block and the executioner's blade was falling.

Barnet stopped walking.

He turned away from Officer White, biting back the urge to scream.

"Is he dead?" an unknown voice asked in a whisper.

Barnet didn't know. He also didn't want to know. He wanted to resign from this moment of unintentional bravery. He wanted to put his feet in motion and run.

"I can see my breath," he said.

"What?"

"I can—"

Officer Thomas Barnet suddenly folded in half. His legs stayed in place while his upper body was forced backwards, like a human folding-chair. Then he fell onto his side with his mouth propped open. The blood rolled over his teeth and lips. Then someone shouted, someone screamed. People began running, scrambling, covering their eyes and dying where they stood.

Officer Layton watched a man's head snap back and turn in a circle. He watched an officer's spine get pulled through his back. He watched a man lose his eyes and a woman have her jaw ripped off.

One man jumped inside a police car, only to be pulled through the open window with a broken neck. Another had an explosion inside his head. A woman's stomach opened up like a gym bag and her intestines fell in the mud.

And while people ran, and screamed, and tried to hide, Officer Layton slipped inside the police car with Elmer. He slammed the door. The windows were up and the Bakisi didn't catch his scent. And for him, the show continued.

One by one, the people he worked with were being ripped apart, which was fine by him. He didn't like them much anyhow.

123

When the blood began spilling, and bones began breaking, and people began screaming, and running, and hiding, and dying, James knew what was happening. He knew the score.

The Bakisi had finally caught up with him.

He couldn't do anything; he couldn't say anything helpful or explain the situation to the people who were suffering—the cops and the detectives and medical workers. And at this point, he didn't want to try. James was finished fighting, finished running, finished explaining and crying and wishing that things were different. He wanted the Bakisi to do what it was going to do and be done with it.

James had given up.

It took a little more than two minutes for the Bakisi to finish everyone off—for the beast to cut throats and snap necks and do whatever it was doing. And during this time, James closed his eyes. When he finally open them again, he could see it—the Bakisi. It was standing at his feet.

Its black skin was glistening, its huge eyes were gazing. It was filled with hate and rage and seeping with death. Fingers seemed almost broken with curves and bends and far too many knuckles that rested on the floor where it stood. Its feet were like webbed hooves, if such a thing existed. Its teeth draped from its gaping maw, twisted and long—teeth that resembled rusted black nails that had been pulled from an un-giving lumber. Its chest, hairless and thin, seemed to shake and quiver at times, as if the cold air was coming from within.

"Okay," James said, still cuffed and sitting in the chair. "You've got me. I won't run anymore. I'm yours, I'm not sure what you want from me, but I'm yours. I can't run any longer."

The Bakisi seemed to understand this. It stepped away from James and lowered its head, looking meek and somewhat submissive.

James stood up—the only survivor among the carnage of the cottage.

He approached one of the bodies. A set of keys hung from a latch on an officer's belt. He sat on the floor next to the officer and took the keys.

It took James a long time to free himself from the cuffs, almost six minutes. The Bakisi waited patiently. When he finished, he stood up and walked across the room, which looked like the inside of a used blender. Guts and blood and tattered limbs, fingers, intestines and severed flesh, hair and bone and opened torsos, decapitated heads and squashed eyes—it was all here, mixed together like the devil's martini.

James shook his head in disgust; he lifted a gun off the floor. But the gun wasn't for the Bakisi. He finally understood: you can't harm a deity.

"Let's get going," James said. "Let's go someplace new." He walked to the door and then stopped. His eyes flickered. "Wait a minute, will ya?"

The Bakisi gave him some space.

James returned to the center of the room. He set the gun down and picked the axe up.

He said, "I love you," and began chopping Debra's head off. It took three swings. He thought it would make him happy but it didn't. With Debra being dead it just didn't feel the way he thought it would.

Oh well. Such is life.

124

Elmer and Layton sat in the car together, seemingly the last men alive. Layton was in the front and Elmer was caged in the back. But Layton didn't have the keys to the car. Neilson had them, and Neilson was lying outside with his legs torn off. It was dangerous out there.

They talked about the situation, forgetting all police/suspect protocol.

Elmer wanted Layton to go outside, scoot across the road and dig through Neilson's pockets.

Layton didn't. He was thinking something else; he figured, fuck that—Elmer should do it.

Layton took a deep breath, building the courage he needed. If Elmer was getting out of the car, Layton needed to open the door for him. Police cruisers are like that. The back doors don't open from the inside.

He put his hand on the door handle and closed his eyes. On the count of three, he thought. *One*—

Elmer saw James walking down the driveway. "Oh shit," he said. "Look who it is."

Layton opened his eyes and found himself surprised. "That's James McGee, isn't it?"

"That's him. That's the guy responsible, not me. I'm innocent. That's your wanted man, right there."

"What's he doing?"

Elmer seemed puzzled. "I don't know. Doesn't he realize—"

"How can he not realize? Look around you!"

"But he doesn't seem scared."

"He's coming this way," Layton said. It didn't occur to Layton to raise his gun. And he could have; it was in his hand.

James approached the car with his handgun in plain view. He pointed it at Layton and said, "Drop it."

Layton did, feeling like a fool. He should have protected himself, and he wondered why he hadn't.

"Open up," James said.

"No fucking way," Layton replied. Then he put his hands in front of his face like a poor man's shield. "I'm not coming out there."

"Do it. Or I'll blast the window."

"Good luck buddy. It's bullet-resistant."

"Not from this range." James said. Then he pulled the trigger three times.

The first bullet lodged into the glass, causing a spider's web to form around it. The second bullet blasted a hole in the window. The third bullet went through Layton's head, coming out the other side in a rope of blood.

Elmer screamed.

Layton fell back, dead.

James smiled through the broken widow. "Hello Elmer," he said. "Remember me? Do ya? Do ya? Do you remember Debra? Do ya remember what you did to Debra? Remember the hammer? DO YOU REMEMBER THE FUCKING HAMMER?"

Elmer threw his hands in front of his face screaming, "Oh God! Oh God! Oh God please don't kill me!"

"I'VE GOT SOMETHING FOR YOU MAN! I'VE GOT SOMETHING RIGHT HERE!"

Elmer began crying. "Oh God… don't! Don't," he said. "Don't shoot me! Oh man oh man, don't pull the trigger! Oh please God don't shoot me in the fucking head!"

James opened the back door and pointed the gun at Elmer's face, shaking his head back and forth like a rabid dog. He was screaming and yelling and kicking his feet in the mud. Spit hung from his mouth; his fingers squeezed the gun like he was trying to break it. His eyes watered and threatened to pop from his skull.

"TAKE THIS YOU MOTHERFUCKING PSYCHO!"

"No! No! Don't! I'm sorry! I'm sorry! Oh man, I so sorry!"

"BUT I HAVE TO, ELMER! I HAVE TO!" James pulled the gun away. He rammed the barrel into his own mouth, digging the iron into the gums above his upper teeth, screaming, "IF I DON'T PASS IT ON, IT WILL BE WITH ME FOREVER!"

Then, laughing and insane, he pulled the trigger.

The blast was deafening.

125

That first night, while David Timothy Camions (a.k.a. Elmer) sat in his jail cell, cursing and swearing, covered in blood and laced in the cuffs that the police refused to remove, he knew he was not alone.

Something cold was there—watching him, hating him, freezing the air around him.

It took a long time to sleep that night. It was almost morning in fact, before he drifted into the other world. And when he did sleep, when his eyes fell in a frightful, haunting slumber, he saw a boy with a red balloon walking along the edge of a lonely road. And behind the boy, between the trees that seemed to encase the child like impenetrable wooden fingers, he saw the dead. They were crawling from the ditches and the laneways of the cottage. Escaping the bedrooms, the beach and the driveway, sometimes in pieces, sometimes destroyed, whispering in solemn tones and moaning voices.

Elmer wanted the dream to end. But it didn't. It went on and on.

It would go on forever.

He watched them, creeping and crawling with shattered bones, missing limbs and smashed skulls, bloody and broken. The dead parade—that's what they were. The dead parade.

They followed the boy with the red balloon.

And the boy followed someone else, someone he trusted and loved. He followed James.

James, with his vacant eyes and his head destroyed, stumbled along the haunting path with his black tie crusted to his shirt with blood; his mouth smashed and gaping.

He was coming.

James was coming tonight.

THANK YOU...

I have a few people to thank; I'll make this as quick and painless as possible.

First of all, I want to thank Jacob Kier at Swarm Press for rolling the dice on this, my first novel. I can't help wondering, how long would the *The Dead Parade* manuscript remain unpublished, if not for your vision? I also need to thank Kim Paffenroth, a man who has helped me with his insight and his wisdom, and David Dunwoody for writing the foreword. Lonny Knapp is the unfortunate soul that read this book well before it was decipherable. Knowing how rough those first drafts were, I almost feel bad for Lonny. But I don't. I save that feeling for Lisa Yeung, who edited my short stories back when they were no better than dirty limericks scribbled on a bathroom wall. And I do feel bad for her. I really do. Every time I think of her I throw up in my mouth a little.

A couple quick shout-outs: Alan McGee (my oldest and dearest friend), my family, the guys in Human Kind, Luisa Ayala, Mike D., Colin Crawford and Jay Malloy.

I should also mention a few of my writing peers. These guys encouraged me in those (sometimes) small, but helpful ways that turns the wannabe writer into a novelist. Weston Ochse: for not getting to upset when I bug him (all the time). Brian Keene: for being kind enough to send me a box filled with Creepy magazines. Stephen King: for extending me the rights to 'One for the Road'. Sèphera Girón: for making me feel at home during the HWA dinners (even though I wasn't a member). And Bob Booth: for taking the time to make the Canadian Musician guys feel welcome at NECON. I hope to see you there again real soon.

And I guess I better not forget to thank you, the reader. I hope you enjoyed the journey. For me it was five months of writing and two years of editing. But I enjoyed it.

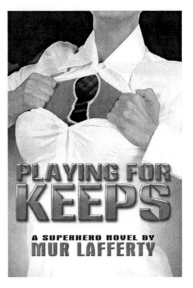

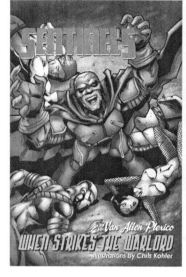

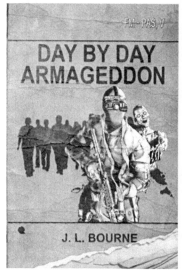
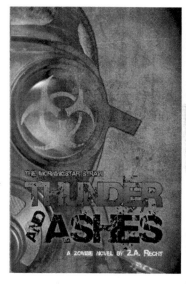

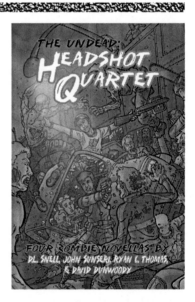

THE UNDEAD
ZOMBIE ANTHOLOGY

ISBN: 978-0-9765559-4-0

"Dark, disturbing and hilarious."
—Dave Dreher, *Creature-Corner.com*

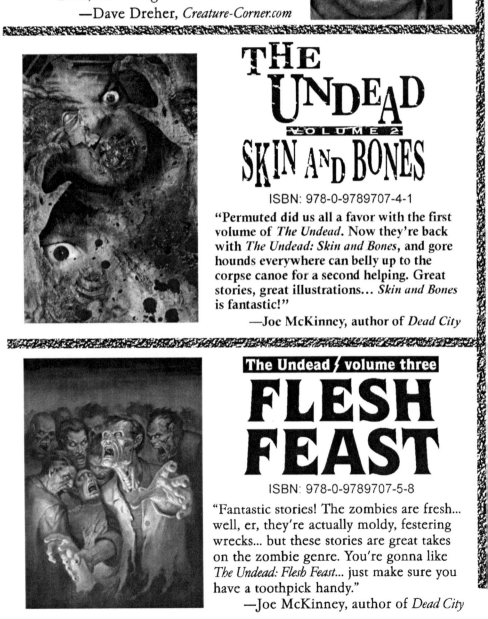

THE UNDEAD
VOLUME 2
SKIN AND BONES

ISBN: 978-0-9789707-4-1

"Permuted did us all a favor with the first volume of *The Undead*. Now they're back with *The Undead: Skin and Bones*, and gore hounds everywhere can belly up to the corpse canoe for a second helping. Great stories, great illustrations... *Skin and Bones* is fantastic!"
—Joe McKinney, author of *Dead City*

The Undead / volume three
FLESH FEAST

ISBN: 978-0-9789707-5-8

"Fantastic stories! The zombies are fresh... well, er, they're actually moldy, festering wrecks... but these stories are great takes on the zombie genre. You're gonna like *The Undead: Flesh Feast*... just make sure you have a toothpick handy."
—Joe McKinney, author of *Dead City*

Printed in the United States
207013BV00002B/118-606/P

9 781934 861103